BUSINESS

BUSINESS
J.P. MEYBOOM
a novel

DUNDURN
PRESS

Publisher and acquiring editor: Scott Fraser | Editor: Russell Smith
Cover designer and illustrator: Sophie Paas-Lang
Printer: Marquis Book Printing Inc.

Library and Archives Canada Cataloguing in Publication

Title: Business : a novel / J.P. Meyboom.
Names: Meyboom, Jan Peter, author.
Identifiers: Canadiana (print) 20200297244 | Canadiana (ebook) 20200297252 | ISBN 9781459747050 (softcover) | ISBN 9781459747067 (PDF) | ISBN 9781459747074 (EPUB)
Classification: LCC PS8626.E923 B87 2021 | DDC C813/.6—dc23

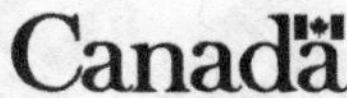

We acknowledge the support of the Canada Council for the Arts and the Ontario Arts Council for our publishing program. We also acknowledge the financial support of the Government of Ontario, through the Ontario Book Publishing Tax Credit and Ontario Creates, and the Government of Canada.

Printed and bound in Canada.

Dundurn Press
1382 Queen Street East
Toronto, Ontario, Canada M4L 1C9
dundurn.com, @dundurnpress

When I was younger, I could remember anything, whether it had happened or not.

— Mark Twain

ONE

Gotta Go

THOSE DAYS MY JOB was at a business that made greeting cards. Social expression products, that's what the marketing hacks called them. I scribbled the intimate messages printed with fake handwriting inside cards of pale watercolour landscapes. "A Very Special Birthday to a Very Special Girl." "Darling, since we have been together, every moment has been so precious." "My heartfelt condolences on this day of sorrow." Et cetera. Et cetera. Et cetera. My writing career.

Our boss, O'Malley, liked us to call him "the Editor." He sported a perpetual five o'clock shadow, his black hair blown back into a helmet. His workday passed in an office with the lights off, the blinds pulled down, face pressed to the surface of a polished empty desk. Fast asleep. Drunk.

A little weasel named Isam owned the business. Given the substandard crap Harmony Greeting Cards produced, he seemed uninterested in profits. It might've been innocent.

He could've been bad at business. Equally, he could've been up to something else altogether. Chained to my station, my thoughts were free to cast him in whatever sinister light I chose. So, I had him money laundering for Hezbollah. Trafficking sex slaves to Bahrain. Importing Lebanese hash for the Hells Angels. Something sleazy and sinful. The others didn't think of him like that, but I'd seen him shout on the phone when he was alone in his red DeVille, his free hand smashing on the dashboard. Mad spittle sprayed the inside of the windshield.

He'd slink through the shop every morning on a cloud of jasmine-scented soap, wring his hands, and grimace more than smile at the staff, his crooked teeth bared like someone had shoved a live electrical wire up his ass. Then, into O'Malley's office for a chat before that idiot was unable to speak. The rest of the day, Isam disappeared into the depths of the Beef Baron, a grotty strip club up near Markham and Castlemore, where he and his other business buddies plotted their next crime wave between lap dances and hot roast beef sandwiches. At least, that's how I figured it.

I was adrift, uninterested in this business or any other. "Business" was an arena of combat, more beak and claw than fair exchange. A slippery shit pile I'd only experienced the bottom of. Exploited and underpaid with no clear way up or out, at Harmony Greeting Cards Co. the deal was hand in your copy and scan the horizon for signs of a channel deep enough to escape these shoals for somewhere better. Beyond the confines of these mouldy walls. Beyond the reach of morons like O'Malley. Head for someplace where your blood pulsed, and your eyes widened. Someplace you could feel free.

Ed Ray caught me with a joint at work one afternoon on the loading docks. A surprise. He wasn't supposed to be there. He didn't work for Harmony Greeting Cards. Ed Ray dated Heather Mann from marketing, which meant a couple of times a week he dropped by in the middle of the day to visit. Half the time Heather was out on sales calls. Ed didn't care. He'd hang around anyway, talk about the Blue Jays and how hot the summer was this year. He'd use the phone on her desk, drink some of the bitter office coffee, and steal off for a smoke out back. That's how he busted me.

"Need some inspiration?"

The rat crept up in the dark, chuckled, and stepped out from behind the rusty yellow forklift they used to move boxes around the warehouse. He paused to light a cigarette between his chapped lips. The flame illuminated his moth-eaten beard before his face fell back into shadow.

"Inspiration?" Dope smoke burned my lungs. "Fuck, no. I need a change of scene."

"What're your prospects?" His eyes watered and didn't blink. "What's your plan?"

Hard to say if he really cared. It didn't matter. High enough to reconfigure the world according to my own compass, I tried to sound like someone with a plan.

"I might go to Dawson. Make some cash. People can do that there. There's still a gold rush going on."

For fifty bucks I couldn't have pinned Dawson on a map. Just read about it somewhere. I only wanted Ed Ray to shut up, leave me alone.

Instead, he said, "Really? Interesting. Don't you need some basic knowledge of geology for that? I'd think so. And you need money, too. For mining equipment and such. You have money?"

We both knew the answer to that.

"You went to art school, right? You might want to consider something you're more familiar with."

A box of mouse poison guarded the door to keep the vermin from the offices. A futile gesture. They were everywhere.

Ed Ray's career advice didn't resonate. The expanse between his ambition and his ability was a harsh swim across an icy lake. Last year he'd written and self-published *The Power of Intuition: A Woman's Secret Path* under the pseudonym Margaret Underhill. He had to have real books, with real pages. Hardcover. No electronic publishing for Ed. Spent all his money on paper and ink. Bad luck for Ed that no one would distribute it because his *Power of Intuition* was terrible. Instead, he'd dumped a thousand copies in the back of the warehouse. Isam and O'Malley never ventured there. The books went unnoticed. Ed sold them piecemeal off his website. His publishing career.

"Something I'm more familiar with? Like what?"

"Like a receptionist," he said, "or doing research. Freelance writing. Organizing things. There're lots of gigs out there."

Ed had no idea how little I cared about anything he'd call a job. From his jacket pocket, he fished a business card.

"There's a guy," Ed said.

With a flick of my finger, the roach trailed into the weedy parking lot. A wrecked car sat on its rims by some dead bushes at the edge of the pavement. I returned to the cool gloom of the warehouse. The card read: *The International Business Consultancy. Finance, Business, Arts, and Sciences since 1998. A.S. Hornsmith, President & CEO. Modern Solutions for Modern Problems.*

"What's he do?" I said, to be polite.

"These guys here would kill me if they thought I was talking to you about him, because they need you here," said

Ed, "and they're afraid of him. Albert Hornsmith is a rainmaker. He sells people ideas. He helps them out of situations. And sometimes those situations become other kinds of situations. Which is what happened here. Which is why they're afraid of him. He always wins."

"What are you talking about? Situations?"

"Complicated situations." Ed pushed my hand away when I started to hand the card back. "Keep it. A gift from me. I like you, and maybe you shouldn't be here. Call him if you want. He might use a kid like you. Just don't tell these guys you got it from me. Which you didn't."

Like most decent people, Ed Ray only wanted to be helpful.

Those days, there was no Plan. The world was a senseless operation hurtling toward inevitable wreckage. A place in this inconsequential cosmic disaster didn't matter. Sometimes there was no reason to get out of bed at all.

At twenty-six, after an expensive, mostly useless education in art history, my brief resume of hopeless temp jobs at slave wages offered a dull read. An aimless year bartending from Amsterdam to Bangkok to Kathmandu had also failed to achieve anything other than a penchant for hash and Scotch. I lived alone. Drank a lot. Smoked a lot. And did nothing slick to move my life along while time leaked away.

Those days, I didn't embrace my story; I endured it like a virus that, at best, might go into remission. I was the only child of people who'd left me on the side of the road like a dog they no longer wanted. Not that they were bad. Just stupid. Too weak to resist the business of the world.

Father: an elected voice of the people who moved to the nation's capital to change the system from within. He ended up a bagman for the Party, betrayed and disappointed, co-opted like every dreamer before him foolish enough to bed down with the ways of man.

Mother: a hippie who moved out to a commune after my seventh birthday. Left a note on the kitchen table: "Love yourself without judgement. Goodbye." The seed of all my future hackneyed emissions.

And so, the grandparents. My mother's folks. Saskatchewan shopkeepers who stepped in when idealism crashed through the door and lured my parents away. The grandparents were serious people who had faith in the world. They worked hard. They believed in the government. They voted as if it mattered. Paid their taxes on time. Answered their phone. Balanced their savings accounts. Idiots. I wouldn't do it. I was out of true. Lived without reason. Worked without purpose. Smiled while it made me sick.

Those days, my goal was to expend little to no energy until a better opportunity presented itself. What shape that took remained to be seen. Sadly, chances were slim. There were no business contacts or prospects to reach out to. The only people I knew were unemployed dope fiends, drunks, hippies, and otherwise marginalized losers. So, I dialed Hornsmith's number. I thought I had nothing to lose.

Hornsmith agreed to meet early one Tuesday morning in August before the heat of the day became unbearable. He waited on an iron bench near Dundas and the Grange. The city already throbbed with streetcars and garbage trucks going about their business. My hopes, unfounded as they were, remained high that he'd have some insight into how someone gets traction in the world.

Despite the summer weather, he came in a brown-tweed outfit. Creased trousers. Jacket. Yellow bow tie. Vest over starched white shirt. Yellow socks peeked out from his pants legs and disappeared into a pair of brown Oxford walking shoes. In his manicured left hand was an unlit calabash pipe made of polished wood, accented by a white porcelain bowl. He stroked his free hand over his cropped beard, seemingly preoccupied. A streetcar rattled by, so loud that at first I only picked up his last snippets.

"… survived death for now. When I got out of the hospital, I didn't have a plan. As unappealing as the idea of going back to work was, I had mouths to feed and bills to pay."

He sucked his unlit pipe.

"Your shoes," he said. "They suit you. Fashionable and modest. Your only pair, I'll wager. Are they comfortable?"

My crepe-soled desert boots had been on sale at The Bay. It was hard to say what they had to do with anything. Hornsmith didn't wait for an answer. His soliloquy proceeded. He stabbed the pipe stem at points he wished to emphasize.

"My brother, Norton Hornsmith, was an evil fucker who got me to quit school to sell bibles when I was fourteen. He was twenty. Already had his first Eldorado convertible. We drove from town to town, selling bibles from the trunk of the car. When he got tired, he'd have me drive. He didn't care I had no licence. In every new place, he'd make me do the first sale. He said it brought us luck."

My ass already felt sore from the iron bench. This was a dead end. Some nut dressed like Sherlock Holmes reminiscing about his teenage bible sales days. Should've stayed in bed. The traffic flowed by, steady. What was it like to have somewhere to go with such purpose?

Hornsmith continued to channel the past.

"We sold bibles for a couple of years," he said. "Lived in the car to save money until eventually we had enough to buy a little printing business. Unfortunately, we didn't have any experience with printing, and so after a year we were back in the car, selling musical instruments. Mostly to high-school bands. That's how I learned the trombone. Self-taught. For years, he had me tied up in his money-making schemes, which were always better for him than for me."

He swivelled his head toward me, startled, like he'd noticed me for the first time. "What person exploits his own flesh and blood like that?"

I shrugged. No idea.

"It's Latour, right?" he said.

"No, it's Wint. Paul Wint."

He blinked in the morning sun, a surprised owl out of its element. "That will never do. You should be Latour. Something like David Latour."

"That's not me."

"Exactly. A new name liberates a man."

A pigeon hopped along the sidewalk beside us. Its head bobbed at some squashed French fries amongst the street trash. Freedom. Bullshit.

Another streetcar clanged by so that only the tail end of his next installment made sense:

"… now that I've had the surgery, I don't have the energy for that. So, Norton stepped in to help. The last thing he did before the aneurysm killed him was buy me a photocopy franchise. Dr. Sure Print. He said it's a money-maker. After all these years, I'm back in the printing business. Good thing I've got other irons in the proverbial fire, Latour."

He stared at the traffic. He seemed despondent. This was a mistake. The way he told it, Hornsmith didn't have much going on.

"I should get to work," he said after some time.

I said, "I should, too."

Hornsmith slipped the pipe into his pocket and smiled, a hairy quivering twitch. "Can I give you a ride?"

In time, Hornsmith revealed that he gave greedily. Turned out, he kept a mental ledger complete with compounded interest for everything he bestowed, with full expectation of a return that exceeded his initial gesture. A return I'd pay until long after he was gone. Nothing would've happened if only I'd declined Hornsmith's offer. But I didn't know much those days.

We drove through the city in his old air-conditioned Buick Regal. Perfect canary yellow. White walls. Blue-tinted windows. Wood grain interior with red velour seats. *The Mikado* blared on the stereo.

"You know who was the most brilliant Koko ever?" he said over the music. "Groucho Marx. I know you were going to say Eric Idle, but for me it's always going to be Groucho. The 1960 Bell Telephone Hour. He's the perfect blend of crazy, evil, and humble. An inspired performance."

"Before my time," I said.

He ignored me and pointed to the ashtray.

"Go on, open it," he said, excited, like some treasure awaited. Inside, there was a lighter built into the ashtray, lit up by a small lamp.

"There," he said, "the lamp. That's what makes this a real salesman's car. Only the best salesmen get that."

"What do you sell?"

"Aspiration by inspiration. I sell people their own dreams. Help them picture possibilities. Enhance their chances. And business is good."

I had no idea what he meant.

"We need to make a stop before I drop you off," he said.

I agreed. Why not? Anything beat public transit.

We drove to one of those downtown glass towers on Bay Street and parked underground. He said to come along, so together we rode a wood-panelled elevator to the twenty-fifth floor. A muted TV monitor displayed the morning's market decline. Up top, we stepped into a vast lobby of quarried limestone, leather couches, and huge red Rorschach-style inkblots framed in chrome.

Hornsmith spoke without moving his mouth. "No matter what happens, don't say a word. Look sharp and stay quiet."

I smoothed out my shirt. Whatever.

He announced our arrival to a stylish receptionist who ushered us through an enormous wooden gate that might have been plundered from an ancient samurai villa into a boardroom with an expansive table and a long wall hung with oil portraits of rich old white guys in suits. Floor-to-ceiling windows overlooked Lake Ontario. A yellow haze hung over the water. Hornsmith settled in one of the leather-padded chairs, his hands folded on the table. Expressionless. Unsure of what to do, I followed suit.

After a few minutes, a door sprung open at the far end of the boardroom. A balding, bespectacled man of about sixty in a tailored blue blazer over a white polo shirt stepped in. The pink marble surface of his clean-shaven face gleamed.

"Gentlemen, gentlemen, my apologies for keeping you waiting. Had I known you were coming I'd have been more prepared." He trotted across the room, hand extended, a waft of cedar cologne in his wake.

"Good morning, Dr. Courtney." Hornsmith rose to shake hands. "I was in the neighbourhood and thought to give you a try. I want to introduce you to David Latour, our new writer. He has the manuscript well in hand. It's been a difficult creative process. And the good news is he's finally got it cracked."

"Yes, yes. I see," said Dr. Courtney. "Good. We were beginning to think you'd disappeared, Mr. Hornsmith. It's almost September. We haven't heard from you all summer." Courtney studied me. "What happened to the other writer? The one I met in June?"

Hornsmith was conjuring some gambit with me as his human prop. His face flickered. He leaned in. He widened his eyes. "Phillip wasn't up to it anymore. Which is not to say that I didn't hire the right person for the assignment, because he was talented." He pursed his lips. He quivered with sincerity. "Sadly, the death of his mother has proven overwhelming. He's wracked with grief and incapable of concentrating on work. I've had to replace him. I trust you understand."

Dr. Courtney frowned like he understood nothing. "We have high expectations here. When might we review something?"

Blank faced, I stared at the grain in the table, grasping to understand what was at hand. The wood reflected back my face, mute, as per Hornsmith's earlier instructions.

"I'm confident we'll have something within the month," Hornsmith said. "Meantime, we feel David needs access to the clinic and your staff, if he's to do a proper job."

He was a lunatic.

To me, Courtney said, "What exactly do you have in mind?"

I'm a stray dog. A hitchhiker lured by a maniac. What I have in mind is to call a taxi.

Before these words blurted out, Hornsmith jumped in: "It would be beneficial if he could interview a few doctors and patients to add anecdotal colour. We've also brought some interesting ideas for illustrations, if you'd care to look?"

With an impresario's flair, he produced a black hand-stitched leather portfolio from his briefcase. He extracted a stack of drawings wrapped in onion skin and laid them out on the table. Courtney approached for a closer look.

Pen-and-ink renderings of sliced human heads spilled across the table. Eyes dissected. Necks in cross-section. Stomachs peeled open. They had a medical quality to them. The oil painting guys stared over the scene. Indifferent.

Courtney scrutinized each drawing one by one. He traced his fingers over the lines and grunted once in a while like a man chewing through a succulent rib-eye. Hornsmith resumed his seat like he didn't care. Pure negative salesmanship. Hornsmith knew how to bring it.

"The attention to detail is exquisite," said Courtney after he'd returned the last drawing to the table. "Easily some of the finest I've ever seen. These lend credibility to the project."

Hornsmith nodded. "Yes, the artist is remarkable. She's a Dutch painter, classically trained in Eindhoven. Her canvases are becoming collectable, and many people in the know see them as a smart investment. You should consider one of her works for your lobby. I could help you with that."

Courtney stacked the illustrations in a neat pile. "I'm not sure a classically trained painter offers the appropriate credentials for our project. We're looking for medical authenticity here."

That was enough for me. It was time to do something. Make Hornsmith see he couldn't play me into some ruse like the fool he took me for.

"We decided that the quality of her work t-t-trumped her credentials, Dr. Courtney." That came out wrong.

Courtney rolled his gaze toward me. Hornsmith winced. I didn't care. I stammered on.

"I may c-c-call you doctor, Doctor?"

"Yes. Yes, of course. I am a doctor."

Hornsmith sensed a gap and plunged back in. "Indeed. And she's not looking for credit. Only payment. It's just business. We can credit anyone we please. We could say you did them yourself. Call it a secret talent or a private hobby of yours. The press will like that."

"We'll have to see," said Courtney. "Meanwhile, I'll speak to Erica about arranging your visit to our facility. I look forward to reading something from you soon, David."

With that, he shook our hands and left through the same door he'd entered from. In the elevator down to the car, Hornsmith hummed under his breath, apparently pleased with what had just happened. Something I had no sense of except that this wasn't my hoped-for opportunity.

"The ride to work still okay?" I said, to salvage something from this waste of time.

"Of course." He broke from his ditty. "That went rather well."

"What was that?" I tried to sound casual, like this sort of thing happened all the time.

"That," he said, unlocking the car, "was the part where you helped me through a little bump in a significant real estate play. Bravo. I particularly liked the stutter. Personally, I find a stammer a hard act to keep up."

"A real estate play?" I said. "Are you kidding me?"

Nonplussed, he settled behind the wheel and started the engine. Unsure whether to get in or not, I stood at his door.

"But next time," he said, "don't use a stutter. It makes clients nervous. Present calm. You're no fool. This business has legs. This could go big."

"For you, maybe. Not for me," I said. "I'm no shill. I shouldn't be here."

Hornsmith flashed his teeth. "Get in. I promised you a ride."

Pissed, I walked around and slumped into the seat next to him. A ride was still better than transit.

"From what you said on the phone," Hornsmith said after letting me sulk a while, "I'll wager you earn about twenty-five thousand before tax writing drivel for third-rate greeting cards. That's not a job for a man. That's purgatory, friend. You have a God-given talent for the Business. Your perfect audition this morning proves it. You're going against the natural order of things if you stay behind a desk working for people who don't respect your true talents."

The silent ebb and flow of the freeway traffic felt part of some other busy universe. One I had no connection to. A tumbler of iced Johnny Walker and a joint would've been good. Hornsmith had it right: the job was a joke. It barely paid bar tabs. Still, Isam and O'Malley didn't trick me into schemes.

They were primitive, transparent exploiters, unlike this lunatic who lied and manipulated without qualms.

"This is insane," I said. "You're insane."

Hornsmith had other ideas. Sell the dream. Close the deal. Resistance would be futile.

"Listen, the plan's good," he said. "I'm going to let you in on it if you swear not to tell a soul. Otherwise, there'll be consequences."

Unbelievable. All preachy schoolteacher going on about consequences.

"Is that a threat?"

"No," he said, "a fact. You swear or not?"

He spit in his palm and stretched out his hand to shake, like a kid who wanted to start a secret club. It was a threat, of course. Which made me curious. After the morning's theatrics, his scheme had to have a motive. Some grand inner logic invisible to mortals. As for me, there was no one to tell — at least, no one who'd care. No one would believe it. I started to laugh at the improbability of it all.

"This is insane," I said and laughed some more.

With his hand still extended, Hornsmith started to laugh, too. Soon we were both in the throes of laughter like a pair of loons. Eyes squeezed shut, tears trickling into his beard, his mouth seemed to cramp open, he laughed so hard. Still the hand remained extended.

Of course, I had to know. So, we shook on his ridiculous oath. Satisfied we were now bonded in spit, Hornsmith laid it out.

"A few months ago," he said, "an ex-girlfriend surfaced. She married a rich old man who owns a hundred acres of industrial land in Washington, five miles from Dulles International

Airport. Fully serviced. Power. Sewers. Roads. Street lights. The works. Recently, she moved the old guy into palliative care after he gave her power of attorney. She plans to sell off his assets. And she's asked for my help."

Around the same time, Hornsmith said, at his club, the New Albion, he'd met our man Courtney from the family that owns one of the foremost cosmetic surgery clinics in the world. Business could hardly be better, but Courtney, the greedy swine, wanted more. A bigger enterprise. Hornsmith pitched an entire marketing plan, social media, the works, to demystify cosmetic surgery, including an independently published book written to drive business to the clinic. Hornsmith represented himself as the one to lead this project. Strangely, Courtney had agreed.

"With the Washington real estate available, I also suggested to Courtney that he build a new cosmetic surgery spa on the property. Open up a new market on a perfect location for international clients. The book, with excerpts published in grocery store magazines and self-help websites, will be part of the engine that drives the business. We'll get on the talk-show circuit. Hire some kids to run social media. Push the clinic big time. I've placed myself in the middle of every financial transaction. I get consulting fees for the book deal, the real estate deal, the construction deals, and the eventual management of the clinic."

Hornsmith also claimed to have secured a multi-book publishing contract with Milne Coberg on the promise that the unwritten book would be volume one in a series of twelve he called "The People's Medical Library." He was now in negotiations with a TV production company to turn the as yet unwritten books into a factual lifestyle series. They were already casting for a host. In addition, he took a retainer from his ex-girlfriend on the promise that he'd coordinate the land sale.

"So far, I've promised a lot, done very little, and collected almost half a million dollars in fees and advances. And there's so much more that can be done before it all ends. I might not have enough time for it all."

In short, his scheme was a masterpiece. Elaborate, detailed, and creative. It sounded so implausible it had to be true.

The car stopped outside Harmony Greeting Cards. In a suburban industrial park surrounded by crabgrass, warehouses, and auto body shops, it was a lone cinder-block building. A couple of windows caked with grime overlooked the parking lot. At the loading dock, men lifted boxes of greeting cards into a truck. I didn't expect O'Malley to notice my late arrival; by now he'd be into his first nap of the morning.

Before he drove off, Hornsmith lowered his window. He leaned out on his elbow.

"How about it?" he said.

"How about what?"

"The Business. Are you in or out?"

I shrugged, unsure what to say.

Hornsmith didn't wait for a reply. "You have talent, kid. Don't wait too long."

With that, he powered up the window and vanished.

The office was an old warehouse once used to store bus engine parts. Five greeting card writers toiled here under white fluorescents set into a water-stained ceiling. The curled linoleum floor, discoloured by years of oily spills and filthy footprints, hadn't been mopped in months. A broken water cooler stood by the entrance, disconnected. Dust-rimmed vents blasted cold air you could almost chew. At the back of the office were two imitation oak doors. One led into a room with the photocopier and the coffee machine, the other into O'Malley's lair.

The rubble across my desk inspired nothing. A mess of coffee-stained scrap paper covered in phrases and doodles and spattered with multicoloured Hawaiian doughnut crumbs. A ripped paperback thesaurus lay next to the cracked plastic in and out tray full of useless memos from O'Malley about statutory holidays and work quotas. My workbench.

Most days, I squeezed out a line or two that reeked sufficiently of sentimentality to pass for an idiot's notion of a heartfelt note marking some weighty occasion or another. "I sincerely hope your birthday is as special as you." "May your best of today be your worst of tomorrow." Like that. On this particular morning, however, things felt different. The groove was missing. The words dried up. Trite epitaphs couldn't be conjured.

Restless and unable to shake the morning's events, I watched my fellow word slaves pass their hours in a patient countdown to five o'clock, when, depleted, they'd eat, sleep, and prepare for their next turn on the wheel. In the meantime, as if unaware this time would never present itself again, they sat scribbling their empty messages for morons even less interesting than themselves.

Like the whores at Gerrard and Church, I'd sunken into a state desperate for just enough money to scrabble by. Stuck in a grind that promised no end. But whoredom only works when your need for money, excitement, or freedom is satisfied. When that fails, when the harness chafes, when you're trading your time for more and more stupidity, you need to move. Or die. And I wasn't ready to die. Hornsmith's invitation looped and swirled in the air. His bold play with Dr. Courtney was almost unbelievable. And, his tactics aside, possibly the antidote to relieve the drudgery that had become my life.

By noon it was clear I had to quit. Tell O'Malley I was out. Conjure up those words and set myself free. Anxious to get on with it, I swung away from the desk, accidently knocking the last of the morning coffee onto the keyboard, and made my way to O'Malley's door. I quit. I quit. My mantra was, I quit. Until I almost tripped over a harried mouse scurrying across my path. Distracted, I opened the wrong door and found myself between the photocopier and the coffee machine. No O'Malley here. Idiot. Save yourself or die. I turned around to try again.

When the darkness of O'Malley's den enveloped me, it reeked of onions, sweat, and stale tobacco. He was in his customary pose, face down on the desk. A stout man. Hairy hands splayed out in front of his head. Cigarette smoke curled from a polished black ashtray, a burnt offering to O'Malley's gods. The door squeaked closed. At the sound, he raised his head and squinted.

"Yes?"

He smacked his cracked lips. His meaty hand reached into the ashtray for the burning cigarette. When he inhaled, its tip glowed in the dark. His sinister little pig eyes sparked red with the flame's reflection.

"Well, what is it?"

A toxic blue vapour leaked from his mouth.

"There was a mouse." I pointed back to the hall.

O'Malley stared and smoked some more. After a while, he stabbed the cigarette into the ashtray with deliberate menace.

In the darkness, the outline of his enormous head nodded like he'd come to some private conclusion. His eyes narrowed as though he were in pain from a toothache.

"So is that it, then? You have something else to tell me?"

He had nothing to do except wait for a reply. That's when I let him have it. I blurted it all out like a prisoner starting to sing before the torturer even gets started.

"I might have a shot at ghostwriting. A medical book," I said. "It's a publishing deal."

"A publishing deal? A medical book? A ghostwriter? You?" His head bounced to the rhythm of his words.

I nodded.

"When?" he said.

I glanced at my watch. "Now. Today. I'd like to leave today."

O'Malley processed. He moved his mouth a couple of times like there was sand on his tongue before a sound came out.

"I had no fuckin' idea you were a doctor." He enunciated every syllable with care. "Or that you could write."

His hand waved through the dark silence between us to chase an invisible fly off his face. With that, his head crashed back onto the wooden surface of his empty desk. O'Malley's benediction.

In the bullpen, the others were frozen at their stations midaction, all colour sucked from their faces. The only sound was the squeak of my crepe soles on the floor. There was no reason to linger. The customary business of cleaning out the desk seemed pointless. It held nothing needed in the next life. And so, without fear of contradiction, I saluted my co-workers.

"Goodbye, you poor bastards. I must go. Moreover, you should consider doing the same yourselves."

No one looked up when the glorious sun burst through the open door. A mighty light filled my eyes and threatened to explode through the top of my head. I was Lazarus, back from the dead. For a moment, it felt grand.

TWO

Marla

OUTSIDE, THE WHITE SUN glowered overhead and killed everything that hoped to grow. At the bus stop, there was no shade, only tufts of bleached grass along the road. Perspiration beaded down my back. Across the road shimmered the hallucination of my former place of employment, where my life had once sold for cheap. Everything was different now. The future was uncertain and happily unimaginable, except for the knowledge that what had come before would never come again.

After almost forty sweltering minutes, a bus floated in on a mirage of silver heat waves. The skeletal driver's greasy hair hung over his collar. Reflective aviator sunglasses made two teardrop holes of light over his eyes. He clutched the wheel in his spidery right hand and grunted when the token hit the cash box. Joyless.

Exhausted from the day, by the time I arrived downtown, a deep-blue tightness clutched my chest. Clammy hands. Dry mouth. At Yonge and Bloor, the cacophony of the city brought on a dizzy spell. A bearded man in a muddy overcoat laughed at his invisible enemies. A stout vendor in a baseball cap passed sloppy hot dogs to a guy in a suit. An old crone with a shopping cart full of rags stumbled over the untied laces of her ripped sneakers. A delivery truck blasted its air horn while two kids kissed by a green light. My new-found freedom took on the stink of anxiety.

There wasn't any dope in my pockets, but there was enough change for a couple of shots, and soon enough, the refuge of a darkened pub offered a place to regroup. One of those phony British establishments with prints of bulldogs and fox hunts. A stern portrait of Queen Victoria stared over the bar. The clock on the wall was stuck at a perpetual 8:15, though by my count it was just after four.

I settled at the bar behind a shot of whisky and a glass of draft beer. The one ignited the other until the world returned to focus.

Manly laughter at the deep end of the bar revealed three business guys at a pool table. They drank beers from bottles and told stories. Off-the-rack striped suits. Clipped hair. No chins. One had a big watch. One was a black guy who kept wiping his mouth between shots. The third had an overbite and brayed as he told his friends some wild story. From their laughter, it all seemed hilarious. Dorks.

Dorks who at least had each other. On the other hand, I was all alone. Unemployed, in a bar in the middle of the afternoon. I did the mind squeeze. Forced out self-pity. Conjured the mists. Offered up Oban. Looked for a sign. The TV above the bar blared baseball and truck commercials. The Jays were up on Detroit. Bottom of the seventh. The commentators tried to sound excited as they propped up the stories of a bunch of millionaires tossing a ball about in the hot sun. God, with his clown nose, laughed. Careful what you wish for, boyo.

After a couple of rounds, a woman materialized out of the back. She made her way to a glass with a chewed-up straw and a lemon rind in melted ice. She might have been in her late twenties. Tall, thin, birdlike. She wore a loose shirt and tight jeans with a silver-studded belt. Her black hair was cropped in a pixie cut. Elegant until she tripped over her heel and stumbled into a table. The pool shooters stopped to ogle. The Watch Guy pointed at her and laughed.

"I'd hit that," he said.

The black guy sucked his beer and nudged his companions. "Fuck, yeah."

The Overbite pretended to unzip his pants. They all laughed some more and pumped their pool sticks with enthusiasm.

At first, she couldn't locate her hecklers in the dim light. She wavered about and tried to focus. It would've been better if she'd sat down. Instead, once she'd pegged them by the pool table, she turned to the bartender.

"Since when you let these cocksuckers in here?" She slurred loud enough for the men to hear. She smiled and waited for the inevitable reaction.

"What the fuck did you say?" one of the drunks said with predictable self-righteous zeal.

She pointed at Big Watch. "He's probably a lousy fuck," she said.

The barkeep held up his palms. A phlegmatic noise gurgled from his throat. "We don't want any trouble here."

"Daddy's going to teach you some manners," Big Watch said as he struggled to get his jacket off over the watch.

The other two cleared a path through the tables and chairs, pool cues in hand. She held her ground.

"You fat fucks think you're hilarious? Making rape jokes? Fucking pigs. All worked up now? Dish it but can't take it? Fucking a-holes. What you want to do about it?"

She kicked over a chair. Fists balled, ready to clobber someone. The dorks didn't seem concerned; three of them against a foul-mouthed drunk pixie seemed pretty good odds to them. They waved their pool cues and jostled each other to surround her.

My default was always to ignore what wasn't my business. But, fresh from my resurrection and fuelled on whisky, the power of the universe throbbed through my veins. They were everything that pissed me off. Confident. Entitled. Co-opted. Soulless. Dorks.

I slipped off my bar stool and landed next to her.

I said, "This isn't right."

"Who the fuck are you?" she said.

The dorks turned on me, too.

"Yeah, who the fuck are you?" said one.

He gave me a shove. Hard. I almost went over.

"Mind your own business, asshole," he said.

With the dorks distracted, she took advantage of the situation to kick one on the shin. He howled in pain. Startled, the others pulled back. In a flash, she had her high heel in her hand and bashed him in the temple hard enough to draw blood. One dork down. Big Watch was the first to react — pool cue raised and ready to strike. I flipped the table for a barrier between us. Glass shattered on the floor. I pushed her toward the door.

"We got to go," I said.

"I don't need rescuing," she said. "I'm just getting warmed up."

"Got to go," I said again. A blow from Big Watch's cue landed on the overturned table. The other dork started to climb over the barricade. She punched him in the eye. He caught her arm anyway.

"Let go," she said. She struggled to twist free.

I grabbed one of his fingers. Peeled it back until something cracked. He let out a terrific gasp. His grip released. His mangled finger stuck up like a little broken wing. Without pause, she tried to claw at his eyes. She fought like she was in an elevator, close and mean. I wasn't wired for this sort of action and began to regret my attempted chivalry. By now she was wielding a chair like a lion tamer. I went behind and pulled her toward the door.

"Let's go, let's go," I said. This time she didn't resist.

We burst onto the street. It was almost dark, the sidewalk crowded with people headed home after work or out for the evening. People dodged our path as we lurched onward for a block until the Dorks gave up the chase. Winded, I rested against a street light. She paced around me, still jacked.

"Where'd you learn to fight like that?" I said once I could breathe again.

"I'm a rock 'n' roller," she said. "I spend a lot of time in bars." She grinned. "I wasn't going to hurt them. I was just looking for a reaction."

"It worked, I'd say."

"Thanks. I've had a shitty day till now." Then, with her nails dug into the back of my head, she gave me a gentle peck on the cheek. She smelled like gin and cigarettes. "I'm starving. Want to get something to eat?"

We went into a McDonald's, where we loaded up on coffees and Big Macs. She said she was a singer in a band called The Raging Socket. While we ate, she produced pink earbuds and plugged them into her phone.

"Listen," she said.

Throbbing guitars and heavy drums filled my head. A human voice screamed incomprehensible lyrics. Cancer Bats meets Korn. After what felt like too long, I pulled the buds out.

"That's you?" I said.

"Yeah, with The Raging Socket. We just got a record deal with some indie label in LA."

"Wow. LA, huh?" I didn't know what else to say. It was hard to imagine anyone wanting to hear them for more than a few moments.

"Except my manager just blew all our money on a new car. Some vintage hot rod thingy. I swear, someday I'll have a hit song and that jerk'll be gone. What do you do?"

"I'm a writer, I guess," I said. "Greeting cards, for now. I also write my own stuff. Not published, though. Besides the greeting cards, that is."

"A writer? Cool." She bit into her burger and talked with her mouth full. A thread of brown juice tickled down her chin. "I write my own stuff, too. Poems. For myself. Songs, too. Not only songs for the band — they're a whole other deal. I write stuff for me. To keep a record of my feelings. Right?"

"Well, I'd like to see your stuff someday," I said.

"Huh, maybe you will someday," she said.

She wiped her mouth. Then she pulled an eyeliner pencil from her jeans, scribbled a number across the soiled napkin, and looked right at me. I noticed her green eyes were slightly crossed.

"This is my number. Call me sometime. My name's Marla. What's yours?"

I almost lied. Call it a knee-jerk reaction. However, she was so serious, I told her.

Rent was due, so a few days into my new found freedom, it was time to track down Hornsmith. See if the job offer held. The address on his card led to a pizza joint on Yonge Street. Not the successful, shiny franchise kind, but the grimy independent kind. Red and yellow hand-painted letters on the frosted window boasted *The Best Piece in Town!* To one side was a battered steel door designated as a sub-address by the letter A next to the street number. A bent-over junkie propped in the door frame scurried off as I approached to ring the bell. After a short wait under the scrutiny of a tiny security camera, the door buzzed open, and a narrow stairway beckoned.

In contrast to the shabby exterior, upstairs was clean and contemporary with stark white walls and blue carpeting as sterile as one of those medical labs where you go for blood tests and sperm samples. Signs on the doors suggested several businesses occupied the floor. *YourTrip.Com. All Bride Films. Dr. Sure Print. Findlay & Sharpe LLB. NL Brokers Inc.* At the end of the hallway, a final open door beckoned.

"Just a bit farther," I heard Hornsmith say. "Come, come in."

Beyond a waiting area with an antique free-standing closet and another room with a kitchen to the side, was his office decorated with an expansive leather couch. A Bang & Olufsen sound system hung over a huge wall-mounted TV muted on

CNN. Persian carpets lay on the maple floor. Floor-to-ceiling filing cabinets covered one entire wall.

Hornsmith sat on a rolling black chair made of metal tubes. His desk was a vast leather-topped writing table trimmed in gold ormolu. He waved to a commodious armchair across from him.

"Latour, have a seat," he said. "I'm so glad you decided to join the enterprise."

I started to correct him, but he silenced me with an upheld hand.

"No, no. Latour will be fine for now. Most of our clients have Anglo family names like Blake and Hardman. Someone exotic in the shop will intrigue them. Give them the sense they're dealing with a sophisticated firm."

Amongst the framed awards and degrees on the walls was a photo of Hornsmith dressed as an angler, waist deep in a raging river. He held a salmon by the gills in one hand, his other arm around the mayor. In another picture, he wore a military helmet and a bulletproof vest and stood on an armoured personnel carrier. Next to him was a famous Thai general who had been on the news recently.

"Friends?"

"Clients," said Hornsmith.

"What do you do for them?"

Hornsmith folded his hands on the desk, his gaze focused on my forehead.

"Here's my proposition: you work for us under some title or another. Let's say, Senior Account Director, or if you don't like that, pick one that suits you. It doesn't matter as long as you do exactly as I say. And do exactly as I do. At first, you won't speak. Speaking will come in time as your skills are honed."

My skills? Ghostwriting didn't seem to be at the top of the agenda anymore. This was some other business, and with all those certificates on the wall, he had to know what he was doing. A plan would be revealed in time. I was almost sure.

"We'll pay you a thousand dollars a month plus expenses. If you're smart, you'll have plenty of expenses. After twelve months, you'll be kicked out unless this arrangement is working, in which case I'll turn over the Business to you. Should that transpire, the purchase price shall be fifty percent of your gross earnings for the next twenty years, or until my death, whichever happens first. If you're good, you'll make a decent living for yourself. After twenty years, it's all yours. Unless, like I said, I should die first. This, Latour, is a great opportunity for you."

"I'm not sure what you're talking about," I said, swept up by his pitch, yet no clearer on what he meant. "Besides, my experience is different."

"Experience we can teach you. Talent is something else. I saw you with Courtney the other day. You have talent. You can do it. As long as you want it. Wanting, in our business, is harder than doing."

He sensed my hesitation and went for the kill. His open hands extended across the embossed gold and leather expanse between us. He smiled like a crocodile in the sun, its mouth open, welcoming.

"Don't you want to be part of a meaningful operation?" he said. "Don't you want something better? Something more? Come into the tent. Isn't that why you're here, Latour?"

I wanted, all right. Wanted to belong. To be part of a meaningful operation. That sounded good. No one had ever seen talent in me before. No one had ever picked me for the team or invited me into the tent. Besides, I'd quit my old job and had rent to pay. I leaned forward, a primed sucker, greedy for success.

"Why not?"

He produced a pen and a typewritten sheet of paper from the drawer of his writing table.

"Let's sign our new agreement," he said.

His confidence was contagious. Overcome by the moment, nothing held me back. He put the pen in my right hand and it was as if the damn thing signed itself. He studied the signature for a moment. He grunted.

"You'll have to come up with something better than that. But never mind for now."

Next, he started to scribble on a notepad. The phone rang. After a while, it stopped.

"Answering service." He nodded at the phone. "The old-fashioned kind with a real person answering. It keeps everyone guessing. Here's your first lesson: be careful with the telephone. It's best to let it ring. If you feel you must answer, act as if you don't have a clue. You're a busy executive who's absently picked up the wrong line. Say you don't know how to transfer the call to reception. Tell them to call back and leave a message."

He paused to make sure this sank in. Then he continued, his finger in the air like a ready weapon to stress the point.

"The same applies if, God forbid, a client ever visits the offices while you're here alone. If that should happen, you say that Mr. Hornsmith and the rest of the senior management team are at an international business convention in London or Barcelona. Don't let them ask a lot of questions. Smile and take a message. Stay aloof. Play up the convention. Business. Suggest that in future they telephone ahead."

"It's a lot to take in," I said. "Contracts. Clients. Conventions in Europe ..."

Hornsmith seemed unconcerned. "Yes, yes," he said, "it's going to take a little time. But you'll get the hang of it. Soon you'll be farting through silk underwear, as they say. Tomorrow we start in earnest." He passed over the sheet he'd been writing on.

"You're going to need some new clothes," he said. "We have an account with this man, Mr. Gupta." I looked over the paper. Handwriting like drunken spider tracks. A Yorkville address. "He's a good tailor. Go see him. These are business expenses. And you'll need to do something about that hair."

I ran a hand over my head. I guess I was due.

"One more thing," Hornsmith said. "Do you have a briefcase?"

"I have a knapsack."

"No. You're going to need a briefcase. Not one of those mean hard-shell jobs with the combination locks. Get something expensive in soft leather that says you're artistic and successful. It gives them a subtle feeling of confidence to see details like that. You'll need it for documents. In meetings, a client will hand me something he thinks we should have, and I'll pass it to you. You'll delicately put it into the briefcase as if this document is the most important piece of paper you've ever handled. Occasionally, as you get the feel for this, you'll say something like, 'Yes, yes, interesting.' Later, you'll file those documents in the filing cabinets here in the office."

He stood up and walked around his table to the wall of filing cabinets. He rolled open one of the drawers and pulled out a handful of glossy issues of what looked like a business magazine. *The International Business Review*. I flipped through a few. They featured articles about business enterprises, new industrial machinery, fast-food franchises, independent car dealerships, private schools, and things like that. Every issue looked identical except for the names of the companies and the colours of the monthly covers. The copy was full of stock phrases. Everything was "modern," using "the latest procedures." All the businesses were built on "long-standing traditions" or "cutting-edge innovations." Tired expressions like "out of the box," "sound business smarts," and "a bold entrepreneurial spirit" jumped out. Sometimes there was a photo of some suited CEO or a little sidebar graph to illustrate a finer point of the company's unique position in the world.

"It's corporate vanity press," Hornsmith said. "Each article is specifically tailored to the nature of the client's business. We also have an online edition which we charge a premium membership fee to access. Sometimes we even place stories in the mainstream media. That's a premium service, too. We also offer other, more discreet services. You'll see."

I handed back the stack of magazines.

"I'm sure there's lots to learn here."

"Latour, the Business is simple. We serve a niche in the industry for those who need to enhance their standing. Improve their public image. We create the semblance of success for our clients in exchange for money. And we're not cheap."

He placed a hand on my shoulder as if aware of my bewilderment.

"I've said a lot, and you have questions. But that's enough for now. Go get yourself cleaned up. Do something about those shoes."

With that, a wedge of cash in a gold money clip came from his pocket. He peeled off ten hundred-dollar bills gangster style and pressed them into my hands.

"Everyone wants to be number one, Latour. Or at least be passed off as number two and climbing. Everyone wants to stake a claim. Hang out a sign. Get that feeling everything's coming up roses. So, we give them what they want. It's expected. Make them number one, even if it's only for the afternoon. That's how we do business."

The plan was to buy new shoes. Instead, I found the McDonald's napkin with Marla's phone number still balled up in my pocket. She was unlike anyone I'd ever met. She seemed to live by her own code. The Marla code. Independent and unafraid. Dangerously so. I liked that. The shoes could wait. I called her as soon as I was out of Hornsmith's.

"I'm going to a gallery opening of a friend of mine tonight. A photographer," she said when I asked what she was up to. "Why don't you come?"

Gallery openings didn't interest me. For the most part, what the posers and hipsters fobbed off as art didn't grab my attention. But I burned to see Marla again.

"I'll see if I can make it." Desperation is so unattractive.

"Good," she said, "there's going to be to be music and lots of wine. I'll see you there."

The photographer called himself Rossini. His pictures were of the faux Polaroid variety. Badly lit, out-of-focus abstracts in bleached maple frames that sold for over a thousand dollars a print. The gallery was packed with girls in black party dresses and guys with pointy shoes and uncombed hair. Rossini held a glass of champagne high above his head in overstated gratitude to the people in attendance. He spoke with a nasal lisp — an affectation, no doubt.

"I want to thank everyone here tonight for supporting these works of madness I've produced from the recesses of my mind," he said to the crowd, who kept their noise down to a reverent tinkle of glasses. "The images you see here represent to me the richness of our sexual nature, the rawness of the laws of attraction, and the sensuality of unfettered animal lust."

His head rolled back. For a moment it seemed he might topple over. As if to steady himself, he swung his left hand deep into the pocket of his trousers. He scratched his balls and leered at a nearby alcohol-flushed groupie completely wrapped up in his act.

"With these pieces," he said, "I am hoping to explore the ambiguous bond between sex and desire in ways that both unite and alienate the viewer. It's a study of my insights while I was in rehab, a period of my life that brought my sexual nature into sharp focus for the first time."

The crowd applauded. Music started to play again. People started to sway. Too cool to dance. Too high to resist. This was no place for me. I made myself exit-ready until I saw her across the room with one arm around that rascal Rossini. She laughed as he whispered something in her ear. Lust and envy clouded my mind. I was uncertain what she could possibly see in his mediocre photos or his tedious speechifying. Unfortunately, my departure was now impossible, because she'd disengaged herself from the pig to make her way over to greet me.

"I wasn't sure you'd come," Marla said when she was next to me. She kissed my cheek, her breasts brushing against my arm.

"I'm not sure if I should be here," I said. "What a crowd."

"Have you seen his work?"

"It's interesting."

"Maybe you don't understand it?"

"I understand it's underexposed and out of focus. Like the 'work' of a child."

"Be nice. He's a real talent." She laughed like she knew a secret in a way that made me uneasy about my outspoken opinion.

"I'll be right back," she said. "Don't leave me here."

She seemed to know everyone in the room, kissing and hugging as she made her way back into the throng, attending to some private agenda. Left on my own, I bravely sniffed around the party's various corners with a vodka and soda in hand. Unwelcome in others' conversations, I soon found myself alone in a back room of the gallery, confronted by three framed nudes.

The model appeared otherworldly, hand-tinted in yellow and green. In one picture, she sat on a wooden chair, legs spread, hands in her crotch, her head thrown back in some small private ecstasy. In another, she was against a plaster wall, wrapped in a stained sheet, as if something horrible had transpired. Her face stared blankly at a spot on the floor. In the third and final print, she was seated on a toilet, her breasts covered by her boney arms as she looked into the lens. It took a moment before I noticed they were all Marla. The realization left me frothy with lust.

"Do I make you nervous, baby?" she crooned in my ear from out of nowhere. She slipped her arm through mine.

"Yes, you do," I said, glad that she was back.

"I did those last year. I needed the money."

"We all do things for money."

"Get me another gin and tonic?"

I complied, and when I found her again in the crowd, she was wrapped around a fashionable guy with a carefully constructed head of blond dreadlocks. A Celtic tattoo ran up his arm, something mystical, no doubt. She saw me with her drink and smiled at me, her neutered pageboy.

She said, "This is Dominic. He's a talented experimental video director from Montreal. Dominic, meet Paul. Paul's a writer."

The director offered his hand.

"She's a beautiful woman who exaggerates my skills," he said in a heavy French Canadian accent as he ran his other hand over her ass.

I pretended to break out in an outrageous cough and poured vodka over his blue-velvet pants. He lurched back. Too late.

"Sorry," I said and staggered off to find the exit before anyone reacted.

Outside, the sweet night air was a welcome relief. I'd hoped to have her to myself and hadn't counted on her social butterfly act. A cab would soon put all this behind me.

"You leaving already, baby?" she said.

And there she was, next to me on the sidewalk.

"Yeah," I said, "it's a great party, but I should go. Work in the morning."

She moved closer. Her breath slow.

"I can't stand it here, either." She pressed a car key into my hand. "I'm trashed. Drive me."

We stumbled in the dark across an empty gravel parking lot. She slipped her arm through mine to steady herself on the loose stones. The touch of her sweaty skin distracted me. A couple of tall cracked oaks swayed in the warm night breeze. Somewhere a dog barked.

At the car, the lock was hard to open in the dark. She watched for a moment before she took back the key. We found ourselves close and awkward against the door until I drew my face into her hot neck. She shuddered, then leaned her ear into my kiss. She squirmed and pulled at my hair. She bit my chest until she chewed right into my heart.

THREE

This New Life

BY THE TIME I showed up the next morning, Hornsmith, dressed in a patched brown-corduroy jacket, worn jeans, and a red plaid shirt, was already at his desk with his feet up, reading the *Globe and Mail*. His pipe smouldered in the ashtray.

"Shoes say a lot about a man," he said from behind his paper. "Yours say you still only own one pair. Comfortable, neutral, and suitable for all occasions. They say you think you can get away with shortcuts. They give you away, Latour. Mine, on the other hand, suggest that while I might look dishevelled, I'm a lively fellow. Someone to be taken seriously. Creative. Innovative. Ready to take my own road. A leader."

He stuck his right foot out to show off a stylish red-leather running shoe.

"Steve Maddens. I don't need to wear anything else when I wear these. People who see me know. Watch and learn."

He pointed to a stack of papers on the floor.

"While you meditate on a man's sartorial choices, we need a new client. Why don't you begin browsing through that for someone suitable?"

Admonished, I retreated with the pile to an empty desk across the room. It was a random collection of business journals, telephone books, newspapers, brochures, and travel magazines.

"What am I looking for?"

"Companies with glossy, slick advertisements are usually a good bet. We like the midsized ones who want to become front-runners. What they do doesn't matter. The Business is sophisticated enough to handle any sort of client."

He pointed to something in the paper.

"Here: the York Hotel. Nine hundred rooms with views of Niagara Falls. Air conditioning and Wi-Fi in every room. Multiple restaurants. A weekend lovers' special, including champagne. That's a prospect. Write these people down, Latour. You can bet these bums don't have nine hundred rooms with Falls views. However, look at the size of the ad. And a toll-free number to convince you how accessible they are. And the photo …"

He held up the page.

"You'd think they were the only hotel in Niagara Falls. I'll wager a view of the Falls involves having to stand on your toes and stick your neck out a little window to peer around a brick wall and over some trees for a glimpse of the water. The swine. And look at that doorman's costume. You can rent those at Malabar. Add them to our potential client list, Latour. Write them down. Write them down."

I dug around the desk for a notepad and pen and wrote *Prospects*, underlined twice, followed by *York Hotel, Niagara Falls*. The place offered no obvious value, since we had no knowledge of the hotel business, and it wasn't even in the city.

"I know what you're thinking, Latour, but don't concern yourself with that," Hornsmith said. "The making of lists needs to be free of censorship. Every idea is valid. Later, we'll review our work. For now, don't hold back. Ideally, we'll end up with twenty prospects: ten in town and ten out of town. All in different industries, for a diversified portfolio."

To me, it wasn't clear what we were doing. It sure didn't look like the ghostwriting business. Hornsmith's plan, if he had one, was elusive. The pile was diversified enough. How it led to business was another matter. Farm equipment. A trucking fleet. A furniture manufacturer. A brochure for a cruise line. A seven-day all-inclusive Caribbean paradise. That sounded good. All-inclusive paradise.

"What about these guys?"

From across the room, Hornsmith squinted over his reading glasses at the glossy sell sheet in my hand. He scoffed.

"Travel? Ha. You know, the word *travel* comes from the French word *travail* — work. They've taken the *travail* out of travel, Latour. You should know this. You're French, aren't you?"

"Says you," I said.

"Well, I can't recall," he said, "but what those people offer is devoid of personal enrichment. It's a staged stimulation sold as excitement to morons trying to mainline the world without taking any risks." He ripped into the word *risks* like a hungry dog on a hunk of meat. "If travel is the metaphor for life's journey, the cruise ship business represents a culture where our lust for life has been replaced by sanitized little doses of sadness disguised as a good time. It's the metamorphosis of Man the Adventurer, Man the Hunter-Gatherer, Man the Survivor into Man the Complacent, Man the Fatted Calf, Man the Hen-Pecked Limp Dick. The journey, the life, becomes the complete antithesis of its intent. Are you listening, Latour?"

The notepad had more doodles than lists. Marla's scent lingered in my nose. My fingers still tingled from her skin. I'd never met anyone like her. She infected me. Defenceless, I yearned for one thing: to crawl back to her.

"It's a metaphor," I said.

"Latour, for a sleepy, callow young man, you manage moments of clarity," Hornsmith said. "That's it exactly. A metaphor. Spiritually, we're all Ulyssians wandering through treacherous landscapes, trying to get back home. In the concrete world, the metaphor degenerates to a hollow experience around a twenty-four-hour buffet at sea. Insight is an inner journey. Not something you get at the salad bar."

He paused to catch his breath. "What the hell, put them on the list. Who else have you got?"

For days, we carried on like this, scanning magazines, talking nonsense, and making lists. Never once did he mention the manuscript owed to Dr. Courtney. Moreover, whenever I raised my concern, he promised we'd get to it soon enough.

"The thing only has value," he said, "if it's late."

In time, brown full brogues replaced my old desert boots. Mr. Gupta the tailor coordinated several stylish outfits, including blue and grey two-button suits. A fresh haircut rounded off my transformation. As autumn started to nip the air, there was enough coke in my apartment to kill a horse and enough cash in my pockets that bar tabs were never out of reach.

Marla said she never liked the movies when I took her to the Bloor Cinema to see *The African Queen* one warm Indian summer evening. She only came along because it was a funky revue theatre and not a mall. She didn't care much for Bogey's act. Too anachronistic, all that he-manliness. Katharine Hepburn, on the other hand, made her laugh. "Could you make a torpedo?" She liked that. Of course she would. She was a torpedo-building kind of person herself. Out on the street afterward, we laughed about the marriage, too. "Proceed with the execution," says the German ship captain right after he pronounces them man and wife. Turned out, that's how she saw things, too. Turned out, Marla had just never seen the right kinds of movies before.

We stopped in a bar for a bottle of wine. Snuck into the toilet and snorted some coke. Laughed. And talked about the movie. When it was time to go, I said I'd walk her home, which was okay by her. Together, we walked along Bloor Street and up Brunswick into the Annex.

"I'm off in the morning," she said. "We're on the road. Up north for two weeks."

She toured with The Raging Socket into the distant territories. Places that people usually came from. Charlottetown. Moncton. Thunder Bay. Brandon. Days on the bus. Nights in beery barf dumps. Her music career.

"It's another world," she said. "The travel is hard, the gigs don't pay much, and my manager is a pain in the ass. Sometimes I let him fuck me just to keep him in line."

"That work for you?" I said, as if this didn't move me.

"It's just business. He's a dope dealer. We launder the money through the band tours. My end of the deal is we get to use part of the money to make our record in LA."

I didn't know what to say. I tried to act casual, like this sort of arrangement was normal to me. Like I was cool and not a hapless lovesick idiot caught in a lusty maze. Lost and confused.

"I don't care what happens to my body," she said. "He can't get to me, though sometimes I don't know who I hate more, the asshole I let into my bed or myself for being so desperate to be humiliated."

"I don't stand a chance, do I?"

"You still have some things to figure out."

I lit a joint as we walked toward her place. She took me on her own terms. She had a life that excluded me. On the dope cloud, I high-zoned through the distance between us. I pretended not to care. To care was weak. Marla despised weak. I was weak.

She laughed at me. "I want a cat in the yard. A swing in a tree. A house with a dining room. A man who loves me. Preferably one who's blind or handicapped. Not crazy or depressed or mean. Someone who relies on me. Someone I can take care of."

Maternal Marla. Hard to picture it.

"That's not going to be me, is it?" I couldn't stop myself.

"No, baby," she said, "it's not."

We walked in silence for a while. Then she pointed to a darkened house. "This is my place, up on the third floor. Want to come up?"

Dope dread made me case the place. I felt something horrible was about to happen. Checked the windows and locks. Lover Man could burst through the door with a smoking .45. Jealous violence. Possession. Cameras. Death threats. Forced to mule dope. Forced to hear them in the next room. Marla keeping Lover Man in line. She watched me, amused.

"Come lie down," she said.

She took my hand. Resistance was futile. Dizzy from the coke and the wine and the pot, I let her lead me to the bedroom, where she wrapped me in a down comforter.

"You're trembling, baby," she said. "You're all jacked up."

"You give me fever," I said, "and it hurts my bones."

The bed felt lumpy. Behind the small of my back was a stuffed brown bear. One ear chewed off. Its beady black eyes reproached me as she took it and cradled it in her arms.

"My mom died when I was little," she said. "Choked on a hot dog at a family picnic. My father lost his mind. They locked him up for a while. He never came back for me. I threw out all my dolls after that. Only kept the bear he gave me."

She pointed to a little lead-framed photo on her dresser. Marla's mom: a girl in a checkered dress standing in a hayfield, squinting into the sun. Cool air seeped through the open window into the room. Outside, a church bell chimed midnight.

"Just twenty-two."

Marla said she'd lived at her aunt's after that. A wild child with no one to watch over her. She lit a smoke and lay down beside me on the bed.

"One day after Mama died, I was sitting at my aunt's vanity playing with her makeup. Uncle Hank found me and slapped me. He reeked of gasoline and cigars. He told me I looked slutty in the lipstick. Then he hit me again, this time with his belt. He was drunk. I was seven."

She looked at the red-hot end of her cigarette.

"By the time I was thirteen, I'd pretty much stopped going to school. No one cared. I followed my granddaddy to the Kaladar Hotel out on Highway 7, where he'd drink with his old army buddies. They wore their medals and berets. They'd get pissed and relive old Nazi battles and talk about friends they'd buried over there. In the corner was a piano where one of them played their songs. He was about eighty. He'd let me sit next to him on the bench so's I could touch the keys and he could touch my hands. I learned the piano like that."

A few years on, the old guys were even older, one or two more were dead, and Marla still pounded the piano in the back, the main entertainment by then. No one thought it strange, a young girl at the piano in the bar. They'd fought the Hun, after all; after that, nothing was strange again.

We lay in the dark for a while, Marla and me. Too tired. Too drugged. Too weak to struggle from her embrace. I drifted downwards into sleep, and a silent black-and-white newsreel played behind my closed eyes. The old guys on a convoy of tanks rolled across misty Belgian farmlands. The enemy was on the run. Grandpa fought the Hun. Marla learned the old songs. My heart was invaded. Occupied. Resisters sent to camps. Grandpa fought the Hun. Marla fronted a dope racket with Lover Man.

Late one September afternoon while Marla was on tour, Bernstein turned up on Yonge Street. In my old life, we sometimes drank together. He was unchanged: a wool cap pulled over his ears in a slavish salute to gangster fashion, his boxer physique draped in a hooded blue NYU sweatshirt. He saw corporate conspiracies. He argued graffiti was art. He wrote poetry and went to law school. He smelled of body odour and self-righteousness, a study in cultivated anger.

"Bernstein," I said, surprised to see him, "how the hell are you?"

He shook his head in disbelief. "Paul Wint," he said. "I didn't recognize you there for a second. Nice suit. Who'd you screw?"

"Life's taken a new turn," I said to keep it loose. "I'm fighting the system from within, as they say."

"Co-opted. That's what they do to you."

He saw life in terms of the Revolution the rest of us knew would never come, tinted by the sanctimonious lens of an unearned moral position and was therefore, to my mind, intellectually corrupt. But always good for a laugh over drinks.

"You were always brighter than you let on," he said. "You're just too lazy for rigorous thinking. Question and meditate. It's the only way. Why does a smart guy like you spend his time doing nothing of interest or importance?"

"You don't know that."

"I know. You got the haircut."

"Fuck you," I said. We both laughed. He couldn't figure me out. Never could. I shrugged. Garlic eater. Should've walked on.

"After you graduated, you had a responsibility to do serious things," he said. "Instead, it seems you're like everyone else who was going to save the world. Nobody did a fucking thing but line their own pockets."

"While you're making the world a better place."

Mistake. Push play: rant on cue.

"Fucking right. I went to the economic summit. Got my voice heard." He jammed his hands into his pockets like he was cold. "I did my part. I set fire to a police car. Got gassed. Got arrested."

"Well, that sounds great, Bernstein. You're a real revolutionary."

He shrugged. "You have twenty bucks?"

"Tell you what," I said, "I scored some coke and was thinking beer and food. I'm buying."

He paused, adjusted his head as if he'd absorbed a punch, and said, "Sure."

We installed ourselves at the first bar we came across. Some place called the Pullman, reminiscent of a nineteenth-century bar car on the Orient Express. Wood panelling. Stuffed red-velour armchairs. Shiny brass foot rails along the bar. Crystal glasses hung from an iron rack. It wasn't my sort of place. Our regular haunts were less precious in decor and generally lacked atmosphere. We didn't care. The Pullman was handy, and it was open.

Inside, a portly bartender in a conductor's uniform tugged on his magnificent curly moustache as he took drinks orders with the seriousness of a man receiving detailed instructions on how to blow up a bridge. Soon, we were set up with double Scotches and beer chasers, which we pursued for several rounds before Bernstein looked around the place with glassy eyes.

"I need to water my snake," he said. For someone with a degree in Italian history and two years of law school, his language often surprised me. "Where's the head?"

The bartender yawned and pointed toward the back at some stairs down to the basement. Bernstein retreated. At the end of the bar, he bumped into a small group, who clutched their drinks to their chests. He mumbled excuses while my hand waved over our empty glasses for another round.

Upon his return, Bernstein said, "Those two women at the end of the bar are talking to a drunk Russian acrobat. He's not making much sense. He's with the Cirque du Soleil in Las Vegas. He's a high-wire act. I think one of them likes me."

"The acrobat or one of the women?" I said.

He gulped his Scotch and chewed the ice. He said, "Stay here, if you want. I'm going to talk to them."

Bernstein lurched back to the end of the bar and into an animated conversation. His new-found audience laughed. It was unheard of. Normally, no one laughed in a conversation with Bernstein. His arguments moved along convoluted philosophical lines beyond the ken of the uninitiated, followed by angry political tirades aimed at the People Who Run the World. After a while, he was back.

"The Russian acrobat wants to do a line," he said. "You're holding, right?"

I nodded. "And the girls?"

He stared down the bar. "Not so much. But they're really into me."

In the basement, the three of us crowded into a cubicle, where I chopped out three lines of coke with my lock knife on the lid of the toilet. Bernstein rolled up a bill that he passed to the Russian acrobat, who pushed his round hairless face onto the toilet lid and hoovered up the lines in one snort. His glossy red lips pulled back into a greedy gap-toothed snarl. A coked up, muscular Elmer Fudd.

"Yuri crawled from mother's pussy soaking wet," he slurred when he was done. "It was disgusting, but never as disgusting as toilet snorting with drunks."

He pushed Bernstein and me hard against the stall with his tough veined hands to clear the doorway. He was strong, but too drunk and too stoned to be effective.

"Get out of my way. Yuri don't like your sad faces," he said. "Yuri wants to see friends. Not you."

He swung his fist at me in a lame attempt to punch my head. Unexplored survival reactions shot up. One hand snapped out to block Yuri's blow. With the other hand still clutching the open knife, I punched his throat. It all happened as if by drunken accident. The cubicle was too small for him to fall to the ground. Instead, he gasped, hands around his throat in pain, and collapsed into Bernstein's arms. As he clung to Bernstein, who gaped at me with disbelief, Yuri's distorted face fell close enough to mine to smell his sour vodka breath. The knife pointed at his nose like I meant to lance him. His eyes goo-goo-rolled back into his head.

Bernstein groped behind his ass and flipped the cubicle handle, which spilled us all out into the graffiti-spattered washroom. The Russian acrobat slipped, hit his forehead on the sink, and tumbled onto the piss-drenched red tiles around the urinals. The scent of mothballs was powerful. We stared at him, unsure what to do next. I folded the knife back into my pocket. Bernstein poked the Russian with his foot.

"Shit, I think you killed him," Bernstein said.

We rolled him over. Yuri moaned. A welt of blood cracked across his forehead. Coke still caked inside his flared nostrils. Urine, blood, and water haloed around his bald head.

"He's going to live," I said. "Fuck him. Let's get out of here."

Upstairs, the girls were oblivious to what had transpired. They stopped us at the bar.

"What did you do with Yuri?" asked one.

Violence was not my world. Electric currents pulsed through my body. My legs trembled. Bernstein said, "We kicked the crap out of him and left him to die on the toilet floor."

They laughed and returned to their business. I steadied myself against the bar while Bernstein talked them up. He was back in his groove. Too drunk to care about what had happened, he laughed with his new companions and ordered drinks for everyone. Alone across the room, I watched in disbelief. My hand quivered. Something tingled over my chest.

To stop my mounting panic, I concentrated on Bernstein's merry companions and noticed, on closer inspection, one of them sported faint five o'clock stubble. The other had a distinct Adam's apple that bobbled up and down, nyuck, nyuck, nyuck, with laughter.

The room swayed. I needed fuel to restore my equilibrium. On my signal, the barkeeper poured a triple, which I dispatched in a single slug. I hoped the alcohol would heal me. The tingle didn't stop. Instead, it moved to my forearm. I was starting to tell Bernstein my suspicions about his new friends when a cockroach climbed out of my sleeve and crawled onto the bar, unseen by anyone but me. The tingle stopped. Everyone laughed at something else Bernstein said. Even the barman joined in the fun.

I placed the shot glass right on top of the cockroach. It crunched and splattered on either side of the heavy crystal base. No one noticed. Downstairs, the toilet door creaked. Russian expletives wormed upstairs.

"Bernstein" — my words rolled like loose bearings around my teeth — "really got to go."

Bernstein ignored me, so I put a handful of crumpled bills on the bar and left him there.

FOUR

The Ellington

COCKROACHES INFESTED the Ellington. In my second-floor apartment, they crawled in and out of the kitchen cupboards, manoeuvred along the ridges of the cracked hallway mirror, emerged out of the bathtub drain, and hiked across the bed at all hours. They licked the paint off the walls, chewed the glue from the book bindings, laid eggs in the sofa, and shit inside the TV. They even lived in the underwear drawer.

There had been a time when the Ellington was more than a roach-infested shell of a building. In the 1920s, it was one of the first apartment buildings to offer three floors of exclusive downtown living. The editor of the *Telegraph* had lived here, as had some famous jazz pianist and a gangster named Mickey Fingers. The building had a uniformed doorman and a servants' entrance around the back. The apartments were lavish in size and rich in detail: polished oak floors, curved lath and plaster walls, arched doorways, and intimate coal-burning fireplaces. Day and night, fancy cars pulled up, depositing women with cigarette holders and bobs on the arms of men in double-breasted suits and fedoras saying "hooey" and "swell" and "bee's knees."

Over the years, the apartments were subdivided into smaller units. The fireplaces were ripped out and the floors covered with cheap broadloom. The doorman disappeared. Hookers gave blow jobs in the servants' entrance. The only cars likely to pull up these days were ambulances and the police.

Even if Yuri, all coked, bloodied, and bruised, found the strength to crawl out of the toilet at the Pullman and seek revenge for my punch to his throat, he couldn't find me. Once inside the squalid embrace of the Ellington, a cloak of invisibility covered all who entered. The building had that effect. The peeling white paint, the cracked, taped windows, and the sagging, rotten soffits suggested the Ellington was abandoned. Sometimes I walked past it myself.

Still, once inside, I locked all three deadbolts. A baseball bat stood ready by the door. The lights stayed off. In the dark, I fumbled for a baggie of pot in a kitchen drawer. I grabbed a glass, checked it for roaches with a finger. Nothing. Under the sink, a bottle of J&B still had some life to it. I pulled a wooden chair over to the window and rolled a joint. There was no ice, but the Scotch washed down the smoke just fine.

There was one good thing in the apartment: the ATN Night Scout Binoculars. They were a work of art. High-resolution 90 mm glass lenses. A light-intensifier tube that amplified light up to thirty-five thousand times. Five times magnification.

Built-in infrared illuminator for no-light conditions. They were a gift from my dope dealer for helping him write a letter to his parole officer about why he'd missed a review meeting.

After a second iceless Scotch, the binoculars came off the nail by the window to scope the darkness outside for signs of Yuri. An old tree on the far edge of the lot groaned as a night breeze rattled its leaves. A waxy burger wrapper curled through the lot from the Mighty Meaty across the street. Two parked cars. A man with a cup of coffee drove off in one. Its lights slashed the night. A garbage truck idled on the street. The driver dozed over his wheel. A big blond-wigged hooker in green hot pants and vinyl boots led some nervous tourist toward the servants' entrance. She laughed. He didn't.

The thing with Yuri still resonated. Occasional adrenalin waves surged through me. I tried to will them away while I remained motionless by the window. Vigilant. My jaws clenched so tight my teeth practically chipped. What happened couldn't be changed. With luck, it wouldn't get worse.

Eventually, the red sun bled through the darkness. To my relief, the Russian acrobat never appeared. He hadn't captured and tortured Bernstein for my address. Most likely, he'd woken up with a bruised throat and no memory of what happened. And Bernstein was possibly in the arms of a cross-dresser, probably not for the first time. It didn't matter. Exhausted, I went to bed fully clothed under the blanket. It may have been an imperfect situation, but this new life still beat the greeting card business.

The phone rang a few times. A fire truck howled by. Seagulls fought for garbage outside the open window. Despite these distractions, I mostly slept through the day. Nothing broke through the surface until well into the evening, when a quiet tap tap drilled through my stupor. Polite. Persistent. Impossible to ignore. Not like when I pounded on the walls with the broom to get Mr. White next door to shut off his wretched alarm clock radio. Or like when Clive the drag queen super came for the rent, which was more of a kick at the door followed by the high-pitched growl of his ridiculous little Jack Russell. This was more like the sound of a timid but relentless mechanical device that had lost its rhythm, as if one cog in the wheel was broken. Ka-chunk. Ka-chunk.

I stumbled off the bed, tripped on the empty whisky bottle, and fell hard on the floor. The noise stopped for a moment, then resumed with greater urgency, this time accompanied by a muffled, sonorous British African voice.

"Paul? Paul?"

"Who's there?" I said through the bolted door.

"Your neighbour across the hall in 211, Mulumba, Akinwole."

My hands fumbled with the deadbolts, the bat nearby in case of a trap.

"Paul, you really must open up to me now."

"Yes, Akinwole, keep your shirt on. I was asleep."

Akinwole blotted out the door frame. His cropped bullet head streamed sweat down around his huge neck into his perfect white singlet, which was tucked into a creased pair of brown trousers. His feet were bare. A few bloodshot threads tore the whites of his eyes. He reviewed my appearance.

"You look like shit, man."

"Thank you. Why are you up?"

"It is the witch upstairs," he said. "There are bad noises coming from her apartment upstairs again. Thumping and dragging noises that have prevented me from sleeping for several days. You must come hear for yourself." He nodded toward his open door and shuffled his feet, impatient, like we needed to get a move on. "I am going mad in there."

I liked Akinwole. He was a good neighbour. We kept an eye on each other's mailboxes and exchanged pleasantries in the hall. Once in a while I'd invite him in to share a drink. Like me, he lived alone and seemed to be adrift in a crazy world, which he faced as best he could.

"Akinwole," I said, "there's no witch. There's no noise besides the usual night sounds. You're stressed and overworked. Try a day off once in a while. I'm going back to sleep."

"Do not be like that, Paul. You are my neighbour and my friend, but you are sometimes an asshole. Come."

He took my arm and led me across the hall into his apartment. It was a mirror layout to mine. We went into the living room. An exposed bulb dangled by a wire from the ceiling. Otherwise, the room was bare except for a leather La-Z-Boy. All was quiet. I groaned and dropped into the armchair. Nauseated.

"Have you got anything to drink? I don't feel good. I'm dizzy."

Akinwole didn't care. "Listen." He pointed to the ceiling. Nothing.

"I need a Scotch and some Advil," I said. "I'm in no mood for this."

Disgusted, he shook his head and retreated to the kitchen. Glass bottles tinkled with the sound of the fridge door being yanked open.

"I am getting you some nice cold water," he said from the other room. "You will find its restorative properties better for you than whatever you have been drinking."

I closed my eyes. Akinwole's voice droned. Water gurgled. Glass clinked some more. Then a distinct low rumble started in the ceiling. Something thumped, deep and ominous.

When I looked up, Akinwole stood over me, swirled ice water in a glass, and passed it over.

"Hear that? How much more of that can I take?" He ran his huge pink palms over his head. "At home we would certainly have sorted her out by now."

"Sorted her out?" The ice water offset my urge to throw up. "You're going to find yourself on a plane back to the Congo, or worse."

Akinwole sighed. "I know you do not feel it, but some sort of response is required."

"Go up there and tell her the noise bothers you. Nicely. That's how we sort it out."

His lower lip trembled. "You think this is foolishness, but I feel danger. You must speak to her for me." He reeked sour and crazy. He rolled his eyes at the ceiling to make sure nothing came through for him at that exact moment. The noise was dull and repetitive.

"I'm not sure I should be talking to a witch on your behalf."

The dope, the whisky, and the lack of food made it near impossible for me to care much longer. Teeth clenched, I fought the urge to pass out. One of these days soon this business needed to stop.

"You people are so cold and rational here. You have no blood in your veins. No souls." He stood over by the curtainless window, a shadow in the shadow. "I wish I'd never left Kinshasa. That place was a shithole, but at least I understood it. Here, I go to work. I come home. Eat processed foods that upset my stomach before I go to bed. I work and I sleep. I make other people rich. I am a slave. I miss the sun and the dust and the smell of food cooked outside. Devils are eating me from the inside."

"Welcome to the land of milk and honey. Not what you expected, Akinwole?" I said. "Was it supposed to be Cadillacs, cocktails, and big mansions? The good life? Streets paved with gold?"

Blue veins as thick as worms bugged out of his head. Maybe, I thought, I should get out of his orbit in case his craziness was contagious. He peered at the late-night traffic outside the Ellington. He raised his arms with an imaginary rifle pointed into the street.

"I have serious reservations about this enterprise," he said.

He bit a knuckle as if to stifle a scream. Concerned, I ventured out of the chair.

"Akinwole," I said, "come sit down."

I led him over to the La-Z-Boy. "Kick your feet up. Feel how great this chair is. I'll go see her right now. Stop talking like that. I'm going to fix it."

He grimaced as he sat down.

"You are a good man, Paul. What you are doing in a place like this?"

"Yes, yes," I said, "I'm the Angel of Mercy come to live amongst you."

He grabbed my wrist. It hurt.

"Do not mock me. Please. Take this seriously. Where I come from, we know about these things. You are so caught up in the material world, you do not know real danger when it comes for you."

I peeled his fingers off and said, "Don't move. Don't shoot anyone. Don't do anything. I'll be back."

Not a chance. At least, not without fortifications. There

was dope back in my apartment to get myself back on balance. That was where I was headed.

At the door, he crept up behind me and pressed something small and hard into my palm. He said, "If you get a chance, leave this in her place."

"What is it?"

"Juju. Protective juju. Don't let her see it."

I studied the thing. An ugly, primitive bit of bent nails wrapped in copper and string. "I see. You're going on the offensive. Where's it come from?"

"I bought it from a man."

"How do you know it's real, then?"

He looked at me like I was an idiot. "Because I believe it."

He waited by the threshold for me to mount the stairs to the third floor. My feet led the way. It seemed like the only way to end this, and with luck, it could be done before another dizzy spell brought me to my knees.

On the next floor directly above Akinwole's apartment, I rested against the wall. Something thump thumped inside. I coughed. Sweat broke across my forehead. I knocked on the door, which soon creaked open, the safety chain still in place. A nest of red hair, blue eyes, and a mud-spattered, freckled face peered up through the crack. This building was full of freaks. She would've been twentysomething, I guess.

"Who's that?" she said.

"Paul Wint, from downstairs in 210. Can I talk to you for a moment?"

"Is something wrong?"

"My friend and neighbour Akinwole Mulumba, who lives directly below you, keeps hearing thumping noises coming from your apartment. He thinks there might be trouble."

"Oh?"

"It's crazy, but he's concerned."

"So, why are you here?"

"He's too shy to come up. But he won't let me sleep until he's reassured."

"I'm fine," she said as she closed the door, "thanks."

I steadied myself against the wall. Blood drained from my head. A cold wind rushed through my body. My knees gave out. My head bounced off the side of the door. My mouth caught the chain on the way down. The amulet rolled from my hand into the darkness of her apartment. Before the shadows overtook me, I tasted rusty blood.

Hands under my armpits dragged me into a tunnel.

Everything smelled of wet earth. A circle of light spun in my eyes. A painful high-pitched electrical whine drilled through my head. She hunched on the floor beside me.

"Hello?"

A firm hand on my face.

"Hello?" My tongue rolled around searching for broken teeth. Speech couldn't come.

She pressed something icy on my mouth. It felt good.

"We'll put your head in the fridge if you stay this way," she said. Or did she?

My head screwed off like an burnt-out old bulb, stuck in the fridge. On a shelf next to an onion. That would have been something new. A lemon-scented wind wafted by. Then darkness. When the world came back, I was stretched out on a carpet with a baggie of ice on my mouth. She soared overhead.

"You're alive."

Checkered curtains fluttered by the window. A large foot-powered potter's wheel stood in the middle of the room.

Fresh clay on the wheel, half formed into a bowl. Pails of water and bags of dry powered clay by the door. A rough wooden table cluttered with jars of paint and other liquids. Brushes in old coffee cans. I made out a kiln in the shadow of her work lamp. The nausea was gone. It felt almost good, except for the tenderness across my mouth.

"You're a potter," I said.

"A ceramic artist."

I stayed on the rug with the ice on my mouth. The pain distant but urgent.

"My friend thinks you're a witch."

"I don't think we've met," she said as she lit up a Camel. The smoke tickled my nose. American blended tobacco always has such pungent character.

"He probably hears your thumping wheel and thinks you're getting ready to eat his soul."

She blew another cloud over me.

"I'm not sure if I should take you seriously or write this off on account of your fall."

"I couldn't make this business up," I said. "You have any dope or something to drink?"

"No," she said, "but you can have a Camel, if you like."

I declined. It was time to get back into a more familiar environment. At the door, I asked her name.

"Rachel," she said. "Take care of that lip, and tell your friend sorry if I've upset him."

FIVE

Hornsmith Was Holding Out

THE MORNING AFTER Akinwole's freak-out about Rachel being a witch and all, I let myself into the office with the key Hornsmith had entrusted to me and tossed the place. Details about the Business made no sense. For instance, the framed awards and diplomas on the wall. Up close: fakes. All of them. Some didn't even have words, only random letters combined to look like words. Hornsmith grinned when he showed them off. "Aren't they good?" he said. That was it. "Aren't they good?" Like they were collectible lithographs he'd discovered at a flea market. He never explained anything else about them.

It didn't bother me that the Business was likely a front for Hornsmith's darker deals. What those deals were was the question, if only because so much effort was going into an enterprise without clear purpose. What did the Business do? Who were its real clients? What was Hornsmith up to? He worked, for sure. Busy all the time. But it all pointed to naught. I had to crack the mystery.

I slipped into the office without leaving a wake. In the darkness, my reflection glinted off the hallway mirror. A small brown stain of snot and blood had soaked through the flesh-toned bandage above my lip from the accident at Rachel's the night before. Burglar behaviour had my nerves on high alert. I monitored the air for shifting molecules. Made sure nothing was out of joint. The place was dim and silent except for the low hum of the fridge. Deep in the earth beneath the building, a subway train rumbled. Outside, the traffic rolled like a steady river. Fried onions wafted up from the pizza joint downstairs. In my mind's eye, the chef stepped into the alley for his morning smoke while a dog pissed against some garbage bags. All clear.

The wall of filing cabinets came first. Jammed between the hundreds of magazine articles and old annual reports, he could've hidden something like bank statements, contracts, or incorporation papers. Anything that might reveal what the Business actually was or did. After twenty fruitless minutes, nothing surfaced. It seemed Hornsmith kept no business records. No invoices. No tax filings. No contracts. Nada. Hornsmith travelled light. Hornsmith glued and pasted his stories together. Hornsmith made it up as required.

Next, I went for the drawer in his writing table. The lock easily popped under my knife. I placed the drawer on the desk. There was a black Moleskine notebook with some folded letters and a thick chequebook. I memorized the arrangement to put everything back together afterward.

The first letter was handwritten on a lined yellow sheet from a legal pad: … *haven't heard from you in a while … Theo never asks for you, but I know he misses you, too* … blah, blah, blah … *I don't mean to impose* … yack, yack, yack … *it's been a tough few months, if you could send us some money to pull us through* … yeah, yeah yeah … *Love, Shirley Rose.*

And, out dropped a photo of an elegant black woman, tall, thin, and defiant, with a bring-it-on-motherfuckers-you-will-never-be-as-strong-as-me kind of smile. She had her arms around a scrawny boy who stared, dipshit blank, into the lens. A mixed kid. Looked to be about seven or eight with a little Afro halo. The envelope showed a Detroit return address.

The second letter, also handwritten, read: *Dear Mr. Hornsmith: The results of your colonoscopy remain inconclusive. In my medical opinion, I recommend we pursue additional testing as soon as you have recovered sufficiently from the previous round of surgery* … blah, blah, blah … *as promised, enclosed are copies of the blood tests, X-rays, and ultrasounds … please be discreet about how you got these, as it's not hospital policy* … blah, blah, blah … *at the risk of sounding alarmist, I trust that you have your affairs in order. While these are still early days, we both know that this could prove to be quite serious … your friend,* et cetera, et cetera.

A woman asking for money. A kid. Maybe a double life. An indiscreet doctor. A terminal illness. Hornsmith was holding out. Finally, some progress.

There wasn't time to see what else could be gleaned from the drawer, because the sound of Hornsmith's voice in the hall talking on the phone tripped alarms in my head. I scrambled to reorganize the papers and slid everything back into the table. By the entranceway, Hornsmith paused at the mirror. He took the phone from his ear to study himself.

"Are you coming in?" he said to his reflection. He tilted his head, sparrow-like, to the mirror and then resumed the conversation: "I have nothing more to say to you at this time. I understand your position. Of course. I must consult with my lawyers before telling you what I plan to do, but rest assured, I will be taking some sort of action, and I will be seeking restitution. Compensation. Yes, if I have to. Goodbye."

He hung his olive safari jacket on the rack. He sighed. His body slumped, shit-kicked.

"Latour, why can't I trust anyone?" he said. When he looked at me, he touched his face as if to ensure it was intact. "What happened to you?"

"Accident. I fell. Hit my neighbour's door." I grinned and tasted blood.

"You're leaking," he said and offered a clean white handkerchief from his pocket. I nodded thanks and dabbed my lip. The handkerchief smelled of lavender. Between dabs, I asked him who he'd been speaking with.

"That swine Courtney," Hornsmith said. "He's having second thoughts."

He dropped himself into the desk chair and rolled his fingertips over the shiny brass trim of the table. "What have you done about the manuscript?"

"You said leave it be. Late doesn't matter, you said."

"I said that? Well, that's usually true. But in this case it would've been better to have something to show we've been working."

"We worked. Only on lists."

"Too bad. Courtney says he no longer wants the book, because if it's traced back to him people may view it as a solicitation for business, which apparently isn't appropriate for a medical professional. He's worried how it looks. He's concerned about his Hippocratic oath, as if he knows what that is. Suddenly, he has a conscience."

"And the spa? If the book goes, does it go, too?"

"He's got second thoughts about all of it. The venture's too costly. His board says it's going to tie up too much capital."

"If you have a contract, you could say he's in breach," I said in hopes that this crisis might tip Hornsmith to reveal where he kept his business records.

He studied the desk drawer for a moment.

"It's not that kind of arrangement," he said.

"What if you showed him the publishing deal? Tell him to buy it out. Lost revenues and such. Make him understand it's a little late to change his mind without having to pay."

"Yes," said Hornsmith as he tested the locked drawer with a gentle pull. "I've been thinking along the same lines, but fear he's not going to be swayed that way. We may need a more compelling argument."

He stretched his arms and studied his nails.

"Let's see what fortune brings us," he said. "In the meantime, last night I met a potential investor at the New Albion. A Vietnamese businessman named Simon Trang. He wants to open a high-end Asian fusion restaurant in our Washington spa. If we let him in, he says he'll also invest in the larger construction enterprise. Maybe he's someone for us."

"The New Albion accepts Asians?"

If our great country was indeed a nation of sheep led by wolves, the New Albion was the wolves' den. It was a private club for rich old white geezers who sat around in leather club chairs, puffed cigars, and lamented the decline of the days when the English Protestants were in charge. Not that Hornsmith fit the profile. He only dressed the part.

"It's true, he's not their usual type," said Hornsmith, "but he seems to be loaded, and he must be connected to get in there. He's also right of centre enough to get past their other requirements. He says he has family money. They made it in trucking on the Ho Chi Minh stock exchange. They want him to help them diversify."

"Aren't they communists over there?"

"Latour, I don't have all the answers, but if a fellow says he wants to invest his family money, I'm pleased to take it."

A couple of office secretaries from a temp agency came in to help with the Trang meeting. Hornsmith sat in his armchair and stared out the window with a cold Heineken while I showed them how to phone each other to keep the lines lively. The prospective client needed to trust we were in demand.

"Stay calm, everyone," Hornsmith said, his voice thin and raspy, his blotchy forehead pulled taut over his skull. "Have some fun and let me do the talking."

The way he stirred suggested he was primed to start his pitch, impatient for the business to begin. The old hound's heart still raged, always ready for the hunt.

"Do you want another beer, Mr. Hornsmith?" one of the temps said. She was gangly with uneven teeth and a husky voice.

I said, "We need him alert."

Hornsmith reeled. "Stop your fretting, Latour. I'll take another beer, young lady. What's your name?"

"Anna."

"Well, Anna, don't concern yourself with Latour. It's his first time. We're going to do fine. You do your part, and it's going to be a sure thing."

"A sure thing?" said Anna. "There's no such thing. How can you be so certain?"

Hornsmith smiled, all teeth and hair. "Because that's what I do. Sure things. You watch and learn. I'll have that beer now."

"Sure thing," she said.

Simon Trang arrived at the appointed hour in time to see Anna on her knees wiping Hornsmith's lap with a paper towel where he'd spilled beer. Trang watched without comment. He was tall for an Asian guy. Greasy grey temples, a bit of a Fu Manchu thing happening on his chin, and a bit of a gut happening over his belt. He removed his blue overcoat and hung it in the closet before shaking hands. When he presented his business card with two hands, Asian style, I thought I saw a flash of a holstered pistol under his suit.

"Thank you for coming," I said.

Anna ushered him into our office. I hung back and checked his card. It sported an embossed red and gold coat of arms. *Detective Sergeant Simon Trang, RCMP*. A toll-free number. No further details. I was unsure what to make of it. He didn't strike me as someone with a membership to the New Albion.

It was too late to warn Hornsmith our guest might be a cop. Hornsmith was already into his act. It probably wouldn't have made any difference. "Policemen have money and families and want new opportunities, too, Latour," I imagined he'd say, and I supposed that was true.

The meeting went well at first. The girls were believable. Occasionally they'd come into the room with papers for Hornsmith to sign, or they'd interrupt with requests for conference calls from overseas that Hornsmith declined with convincing irritability. We spoke in circles for a while about Trang's needs and our alleged credentials, and Hornsmith maintained a credible posture.

"My family wants business in Washington, and I fear disappointing them," Trang said. "I have been charged with helping them create new wealth abroad. This new spa will attract some of the wealthiest people in the world. Famous politicians. Business giants. Movie stars. We would like access to them. What I mean is, we would like to be able to offer them the finest hospitality Asia has to offer. This opportunity would serve as a great honour for us."

Hornsmith grunted an acknowledgement and went to the crux of the matter. "The capital costs of outfitting your restaurant will be entirely yours," he said. "The minimum investment in the overall venture, including the spa and the hospital, is a million dollars, and offers a first recoupment position shared with the other investors, if you come in for more than ten."

Trang listened without apparent concern.

"The operating costs, including security and insurance, run into the thousands every month," Hornsmith continued. "We need assurances that your price point is high enough to absorb these fees while still offering a product that is value for money."

Trang nodded patiently, seeming confident. Hornsmith shone ghostly porcelain. His eyes drooped closed and then fluttered open.

I leaned in to cover. "We can't afford someone who suddenly wants out because his business model isn't working. You'll need to be able to sustain payments regardless of your inflow."

"Payments by my family will not be a problem," said Trang. "We have many interests and assets that can be brought to bear on this situation if needed."

Hornsmith's head rolled to one side. His eyes closed, as if he'd fallen asleep. I stayed calm, curious as to what Trang might do. Trang remained impassive. He was a professional. The family story was good. His real play remained obscure. It wasn't until he noticed the blood leaking down Hornsmith's leg onto the floor that Trang's face twitched, his focus cracked.

"You're bleeding."

Trang pointed to a small puddle pooled around Hornsmith's feet, viscous like dark cherry sauce highlighted by the afternoon sun that streamed through the windows.

Awakened by the alarm in Trang's tone, Hornsmith raised his eyebrows and studied his feet with curious interest, like a man watching an ant with a heavy burden work its way across the floor.

"Yes, I am," he said. "Perhaps we should talk again some other time."

When we were alone, out of Hornsmith's earshot in the hall, Trang's guard came down.

"I don't know what you guys are doing here," he said, "but your Mr. Hornsmith's a sick man. He looks like he's going to die." He sounded concerned. He could almost have been who he said he was, someone who happened to be a cop sent by his family to diversify their investments.

"Yes, I suppose he is. I'm not sure."

Trang shook his head. "You should get him some help."

"I should," I said, "but he's stubborn and secretive. He hasn't told me anything. Intestinal cancer, I'm guessing."

"Shit. That's painful. What's he on?"

"I haven't seen any painkillers or prescriptions," I said. "I don't think he wants into the medical system."

"I understand that," said Trang. "I also accept my mortality. I'd want to die undisturbed."

"Heroin might be good. I don't suppose a man in your position might know anything about getting that for a sick, dying friend?"

Why not ask? I figured a man of diverse interests like Trang had to know something about the narcotics business. Besides, it amused me to say something like this to a cop. Our deal was probably fucked, anyway.

"Careful what you ask for," Trang said with a chuckle over his shoulder on his way down the stairs. "I like you guys, and I want in your business. Get your friend to a doctor. We'll talk more, I'm sure. This is going to be good."

"You can't bullshit your way out of this with me," I said to Hornsmith after Trang was gone. "You need to come clean so I know what we're up against."

He hadn't moved from his chair. "You're witnessing the last days of a man's life," he said. "The last days are the most intense. I feel that every moment in time is crystallized for me to savour."

"I just crystallized you passed out midconversation, dripping blood onto the floor. You scared off our only investor. There's something about your health you haven't told me."

I was about to mention the doctor's letter I'd found in his drawer, but squashed the notion when he teared up.

"I've got what the quacks call an ileal carcinoid tumour. It's complicated by an inherited condition called Meckel's diverticulum, which means I've had painful periodic rectal bleeding since I was a child," he said. "I won't be plugged in and cut up so I'm going to die of small intestine cancer. No one knows. Except a doctor who owes me a favour. And now you."

This could've been one of his acts, motive unknown. He could cry on demand. Practically everyone did that trick. But then he described the bulge in his intestine that was a vestigial remnant of the fetal vitelline duct. He went on to explain the lesions on his feet. Bowel obstructions and polyps. The details were too rich to be invented. Plus, the blood would have been hard to fake.

Bastard. I resented the burden of his secret. But of course, I had no choice. My prying already unearthed it. Now it was confirmed.

His progress down the stairs from our offices that evening was slow. He took each step with his right foot first as he steadied himself on the banister, his fedora pushed back to reveal his reddened forehead. His fashionable tan suit hid any signs of physical deterioration. Only his bloodstained ass gave him away.

SIX

All in the Family

HORNSMITH'S HUSTLE lacked higher purpose. He seemed content with self-preservation. There was no Scotch in his paper cup. No blue in his notes. No regret to his goodbyes. He stood alone in the face of Creation. Shirt pressed, he moved across the stage as required. He talked about the price of gold and the war in the Middle East. He drank Burgundies and single malts. He knew show tunes and operettas. He claimed to like Rembrandt and dislike Byron. He flattered and he smiled and never exposed anything about himself, unless it was meant to seduce. It was all part of his act. He had a family, but it was possible he didn't have friends. He was mute on the subject. His worlds didn't overlap. His boxes didn't leak. He withheld. He ducked. What he thought, who he loved, what he cared about was a mystery.

Except once, early in my apprenticeship, in a rare gesture of intimacy, Hornsmith extended an invitation for Sunday supper at his house. Probably, he'd felt the need to present a picture of his familial status. Sell me on the idea that he was normal. That was how I discovered he had a wife and kid — I met them.

The wife, Katherine, had served beef stroganoff. We ate in silence. The kid, a sullen teenager named Sean with furious red boils on his skinny neck, texted messages to his real life throughout the meal. The click-clack of the little keyboard on his iPhone echoed off the white dining-room walls. Katherine sat straight, her humourless lips taut even while she chewed. Her fingers white-knuckle-wrapped around her knife like she was fixed to keep from violence. Hornsmith slurped egg noodles, expressionless. Paterfamilias.

Afterward, wife and son had attended to the cleanup while we drank Cragganmore in the book-lined living room and listened to Robert Preston belt out "Seventy-Six Trombones" on a vintage turntable. Hornsmith lit his pipe. He gazed through the smoke into the middle distance.

"We don't always understand one another," he said over the din, "but without them I'm certain I'd go off the rails."

Unlikely. He was already off the rails. Presented well. But right off the rails.

"You're a lucky guy," I said for lack of anything better to say.

Supper was never spoken of again.

While Hornsmith never mentioned her, since I knew of Katherine's existence, for about a week I struggled with the temptation to tell her Hornsmith's terrible secret. To vanquish the loneliness of knowing. In the end, I told myself that she must know already. Something like that couldn't stay hidden between a man and his wife. And if she didn't know, it wasn't my obligation to tell her. It was one thing to carry his secret. Something else to bring it into the light. If Hornsmith meant to get exit-ready, he needed to make peace with his world. I'd carry his secret. Not square it for him. So, I remained silent.

The mother-in-law was a whole other deal. Hornsmith liked to talk about her. Grandmother Mathews. She lived on an estate near King City that she never left. Hornsmith said she was loaded. Horses in heated barns. Range Rovers in shady laneways. Mexicans in the garden pruning roses. Trust funds. That kind of loaded. The truth turned out to be different.

He claimed she called his house with daily opinions on family business, like when to buy a new dishwasher, what type of energy-saving bulbs to use, and who to vote for. She phoned in lectures on diet and exercise. She ranted against the pope. She raged about the man on TV who barked the six o'clock news — the one with the hair.

He'd say: "Grandmother Mathews thinks the government should get serious about cap and trade because there's money in it. She's so politically aware." Or "Grandmother Mathews told us we should hold off refinancing our mortgage because interest rates are about to drop again. She's so financially astute."

Disconnected, useless snippets soaked in reverence, undercoated with something like fear. She played large for him, but I never learned what the old goat had over him, because when I finally met her, she'd been dead a couple of days.

We were at the office when the call came. For a change, Hornsmith listened more than he spoke. He said, "Yes, yes," in a tone that diminished as the call went on. By the end, he was slumped low in his chair. All he could say was, "Oh, oh," and finally a single wordless sound sucked from his throat like a pole pulled from a wet mudhole.

Afterward, Hornsmith laid it out: Grandmother Mathews had had a mole on her forehead that, after seventy-two years, she'd wanted removed. Someone had told her that left untreated, it would lead to cancer, which would eat into her brain, which in turn would lead to certain madness, followed finally by a slow, painful death.

Without a word to her family, she'd checked into Dr. Courtney's exclusive clinic in the Caledon Hills where people went for their cosmetic surgery. It had its own helipad so clients could avoid the hour's drive up the 400. Private bedside elevators delivered personal, on-call nutritionists, doctors, and therapists of all stripes to help with the restoration and rejuvenation of the body. At a price.

Distracted by Grandmother Mathews's chatter, the admissions nurse had forgotten to check a box, so no method of payment was secured. It turned out Grandmother Mathews was a roller. It turned out Grandmother Mathews grifted like her son-in-law. It turned out she was broke.

To delay the inevitable presentation of the bill, after the mole procedure, she'd said that she liked the clinic so much she planned to stay. Right there, in the recovery room, she talked Courtney into a complete renovation. Grandmother Mathews was a name-dropper. Grandmother Mathews was a fast talker. Grandmother Mathews mined the Hornsmith connection. As long as she was in the clinic, under the knife, no one questioned her financial status. She knew Hornsmith. Hornsmith knew Courtney. Courtney was in business with Hornsmith. It was all in the family.

The following weeks must've been traumatic for Grandmother Mathews as she became younger and poorer while the knives and acid baths peeled away the characteristic folds and wrinkles that had shaped her over the years. Then, late one night, when Grandmother Mathews had been whittled down to about eighteen years old, she died of septicemia. Even worse, to Hornsmith's distress, she was penniless. There was no estate. No life insurance. No inheritance. No money.

The news was a calamity for Hornsmith because the clinic wouldn't release the body until her bills were paid. Meanwhile, his wife, misinformed at the best of times about the family finances, had started to line up the finest funeral money could buy.

"Do you understand what this means, Latour?" Hornsmith said. "Forehead, neck, face, tits, stomach, the whole thing. At an unfixed price. Plus the funeral. This could cost tens of thousands. We need to get to Courtney. We must work something out."

"I thought we're suing him for breach and loss of business," I said.

Hornsmith almost fell from his chair in his haste to reach for the phone.

"We need a ceasefire to get the bodies off the field. There's no time to lose. Soon the bills will come flying. None of us knew she couldn't pay."

Courtney agreed to meet us at his Caledon Hills clinic with the memory foam beds and fireside leather sofas. Over the phone, Hornsmith said nothing about the money. Said only that he wanted to claim the body and make arrangements. Said he was sick with grief. Courtney expressed condolences. He offered to do whatever he could to make this tragedy easier for the family. Courtney didn't say a word about the money, either.

The afternoon disintegrated into a thunderstorm. Explosions of white lightning filled the sky. Thunder like distant cannon fire underscored the assault of rain hammering the roof of the Buick as we ploughed north along the 400 around slow trucks with red and yellow hazard lights ablaze. Past stopped cars that had lost the nerve to continue through the maelstrom. In places, water flowed axle deep across the highway. I was at the helm, white knuckled; Hornsmith was crumpled in the passenger seat, too distraught to drive. With the silver flask from the glove compartment, he washed down a couple of pills fished from his shirt pocket. Oblivious to the chaos around us, all he seemed to care about was the business with Courtney.

"My body betrays me," he said, "but before my mind goes, I'll make Courtney take this real estate deal."

The real estate deal. He wasn't even thinking about the fix he was in over the old lady, except perhaps how to twist it around to suit his own agenda. The Hornsmith agenda. He slumped back into the seat to savour the dope jolt. Inside the car it was warm and dry. "Come Fly with Me" played on the radio, sweet and low under the relentless rain.

"The swine won't escape," he said so quietly it was almost to himself.

I wasn't so sure. Now that Hornsmith owed him money, Courtney had leverage. If Courtney smelled blood, our whole enterprise would likely go to rat shit. Courtney would kill the book deal for sure. Courtney would weasel out of the spa business. Hornsmith would be snookered.

After a hectic hour of deadly rain-soaked traffic on the highway, the last bit of the drive was a tranquil relief. The storm abated, and a cool, dense mist settled over the world. The clinic lay nestled in a secluded host of ancient pines at the end of a laneway that crossed over a manicured estate of a few hundred acres. Through the fog, we glimpsed meadows, stone fences, and pruned trees.

Security cameras were burrowed in the bushes. At the main building, a sleek limestone bunker designed to blend in with the landscape, a valet dressed in blue scrubs whisked off the car. We were directed toward an elevator that took us one level below the surface, into the mechanical workings of the place. Courtney, we were told, was already downstairs.

In the basement, a breathless porter behind a cart full of medical supplies confirmed we were on the right path. His rubber-gloved finger pointed down the hall. "Keep going to the end," he said with a heavy sigh, as though he'd been lifting weights instead of parking a cart. "You can't miss it. Right next to the loading dock."

We walked on through a long maintenance corridor lined with overhead ducts and pipes stamped *Caution: High Voltage* and *Warning: Steam Under Pressure*, past an industrial kitchen and a laundry room to a solid steel door marked *Visitation Room*. Courtney waited for us under the cold white light of this unfurnished concrete tomb. Beside him was another vault-like door next to a large double-paned window that looked into a smaller, dimmer chamber. Once we were in, Courtney flipped a wall switch, and the adjacent chamber lit up.

"She's here," he said. "You may go in if you like."

Hornsmith heaved open the heavy door to the next room. We followed him in. It was as cold as a meat locker and smelled of solvent. A metal gurney with a draped body stood under pooled lights. Courtney closed the door behind us. Sealed inside, there was no way out. We shivered around the body. Hornsmith pulled back the shroud to reveal Grandmother

Mathews's pale-blue face, serene and smooth. A few fresh scars behind her ears. A slender grin creased her lips.

Hornsmith studied his dead mother-in-law. He brushed a stray hair off her cheek. Traced a finger along a bloody line stitched under her chin. He lifted the covers and peeked at the rest of her naked splendour. Flat stomach. Firm breasts. He nodded, seemingly in appreciation of the handiwork. Our breath hung in the frozen air.

"All right," Hornsmith said, "let's get her to the autopsy." His words rang off the white-tiled walls.

Courtney coughed as though the top of a ballpoint was lodged in his windpipe.

"What are you talking about?" he said when he could breathe again.

"She was a demented old woman who couldn't fend for herself," Hornsmith said. "We need to know what transpired to determine what action to take against the clinic. I want her cut open. Let's find out." So much for the grief-stricken son-in-law. He was all business.

Courtney's hands trembled in the cold. "First, there's the small matter of her expenses," he said.

"Indeed," Hornsmith said, with the shroud poised to cover the body, "the result of aggressive sales tactics on a lonely, incompetent old lady."

They stood on opposite sides of the gurney. Hornsmith leaned over like he might lunge at Courtney who, to his credit, didn't flinch.

"That's outrageous," Courtney said. "Mrs. Mathews came here of her own volition. She was completely of sound mind."

"She should never have been admitted in the first place. And now, under your care, she's dead."

I had no dog in this fight. Grandmother Mathews on the slab meant nothing to me other than the fact that the sooner Hornsmith settled the matter, the sooner we could get back to a warm room and our own business. If Courtney could be swayed.

"Fatal post-op infections are extremely rare, but not unheard of. She signed the waivers. She knew the risk." Courtney's breath erupted in shots of steam as his patience with the matter shortened. "We'll go after her estate for the money and we'll win, even if you don't co-operate." He leaned against the gurney, which rolled into Hornsmith's leg.

Hornsmith pushed it back and said, "We'll produce doctor's evidence of her dementia."

They were practically nose to nose over the body. I tried to move out from between them in case it got to blows. My torso ached from the cold. My feet felt lifeless.

"Gentlemen," I said, "let's go back into the other room and talk this out under warmer conditions."

Hornsmith straightened up, his fists tucked into his armpits for warmth. He stared at Courtney like he planned to eat him.

"I'll get to the point," he said. "You stay in the Washington real estate deal and we'll forget about the book. And the Mathews bill goes away. There's no estate, anyway. She's dead broke."

Courtney tweaked to the proposal. He smiled and shook his head. "Pass. Pay her bill. Forget about our other business and be grateful there'll be no further repercussions."

I was impressed. The weasel had pluck. He seemed to understand that he could maybe get out from under Hornsmith's grip. But Hornsmith, frozen and dope addled as he was, still dealt in petty greed and fear. He leaned on the gurney, his jaw outstretched. Frosty beard bristling.

"Listen, you prick," Hornsmith said through clenched teeth, "when I take this story public, that you killed my demented mother-in-law, you can be sure a plague of lawyers, advocacy groups, media, and other assorted bottom-feeders will be investigating your business for months. Possibly years. Not good for sales. The Department of Health will suspend your licence and the police will wonder who else you've killed."

Courtney looked like he wanted to cry. Lips all pouty. He shivered some more. "We haven't killed anyone."

"Possibly," said Hornsmith, "but by the time that's clear, it won't matter anymore. The damage will be done. Be smart. Do this my way. Do you have a cremator?"

Courtney's arms tensed. His hands gripped the rail. It looked like he might flip over the gurney. The blue veins in his temples throbbed. His eyes went stone-like as he appeared to recalculate his position. After a moment, he nodded.

"The book deal goes away?" Courtney seemed ready to news-proof his world.

"On my word."

"My cousin has a funeral home with a new cremator."

"And a good cremulator?"

Courtney nodded again. "They came as a package."

"Forget the autopsy. She always wanted to be cremated."

Hornsmith held open the door to the observation room and waited for us to move into the warmth. "Just to show you I can be a reasonable fellow," he said, "I'll cancel the TV series deal as well."

We stood around and stamped our feet to get our circulation back. When Courtney looked away, Hornsmith winked at me and gave a big shit-eating grin. His beard was wet with condensation from the icy room. He rubbed his hands and straightened his back.

"This is a win-win," Hornsmith said. "We're all going to get rich. Even you, Dr. Courtney. In spite of your efforts to sabotage yourself. You stick with me. I'll have you farting through silk underwear."

"We'll need a signed agreement," Courtney said, ever practical. "I'll have something for you by Monday at my downtown office."

The poor bastard looked wilted. The few hairs he still had in his comb-over lay across his shiny dome like limp seaweed. His shoulders slumped. His eyes downcast. Silent. When we left the viewing room, he marched off down the corridor without a look back to see whether we'd follow.

Hornsmith chuckled as we watched Courtney's retreat.

"And that's how we do it," he said to no one in particular. "I'm going to miss this business."

SEVEN

Marla's Show

KIRKLAND LAKE, Saturday night: red and blue strobes throbbed. Marla vibed electric. Marla levitated. Marla gyrated on stage with The Raging Socket. She expanded and filled the bar. She threw one hand over her head and brought it down, caressing her body under her clammy T-shirt. With her other hand, she rubbed the microphone between her legs. Sweat flew from her forehead. Her eyes closed in ferocious ecstasy. She twisted and twirled and contorted to the frantic rhythms pounded out by the speed-crazed drummer on his wobbly kit. The skinny guitar player fell to his knees, every sharp note intact.

"It's Saturday night," she shouted, "let's raise some hell!"

The hoarse crowd chanted, "Yeah! Yeah!"

Booze sloshed over the floor. The air was sour with sweat and beer. People danced on tables. People rolled on the wet floor. Bodies dripped against one another in the dark. Bass and drum thumped. Marla, high priestess of the night, transported the locals from their dreary paycheque lives into her mystical circle.

Transfixed, I squeezed against the wall at the back of the bar with the mob. Marla had summoned her fool, and I'd obeyed. Ten hours on the Greyhound, early by a day to surprise her. There I was, excited and filled with desire for her nails in my back. Anxious for her smile and the taste of her salty, smoky mouth on my tongue, I watched her rip up the night. It didn't matter if the warm bottled beer tasted bitter.

She surveyed the crowd and said, "If you never play me, I'll hold you down when it gets rough, I'll protect you from the storm." The microphone amplified her heavy breath. The crowd cheered. "A woman knows a real man can't deny her worth," she shouted over the noise. "You fuck with me, I'll do my worst!"

The noise from the band's amps pushed the air so hard the drapes behind the bar fluttered and the overhead chandeliers swayed. The room howled. Someone threw a bottle at the wall. Glass shards exploded over the room. People screamed. People laughed. She encouraged communal chaos.

When the set finished, the rickety stairway up to the green room strained under a stampede of groupies, roadies, and various hangers-on who all groped through the dark to get upstairs, where the party insiders continued their havoc. Breathless, I followed two steps at a time, eager to find Marla in the crowd. A fat shaven thug in a black T-shirt with some device rammed into his ear guarded the door at end of the gloomy corridor. He put a hand on my chest.

"I'm with the band," I said.

He shrugged, zombified, and patted me down before letting me pass. Inside, the party room was choked with the smell of dope and cigarettes. Beer bottles clanked through the blare of music from unseen speakers. Shouts and shrieks of laughter rose above the din.

Marla was at the back, flopped in the lap of an older guy with short silver hair. He wore round red-tinted glasses in a silver frame and a striped black shirt. Lover Man was my guess. Her legs dangled over the arm of the couch. He stroked her thigh. She laughed. She didn't notice me. A hot shock flashed across my chest. It wasn't supposed to be like this. She'd said he wouldn't be here. I hung back. Reconfigured. Adjusted to the new picture.

I always played her cool. Out of sight, out of mind. That suited her. She banished all who came too close or clung too desperately. We had our own code. A secret understanding. A matter of unspoken passions that no one could come between. I wanted to believe in our little conspiracy. Just Marla and me. I realized now I could've been wrong.

The lights flashed on and off without warning. A bell summoned the crowd. Everyone cheered. The next set was imminent. When I approached the bar with its sombre bartender, his thick hands laced at rest over his belly with the patience of an executioner, the crowd, moving in unison under some invisible command, hoisted Marla on high and carried her out to the stage. I showed my back to the room and signalled for a drink. I didn't want her to catch me. My legs almost buckled under the weight of this new-found calamity. The bar held me up. I reconsidered. I made myself invisible. I should've stayed away.

A few people lingered in the litter-strewn room. Muted voices of a more serious note hung in the air. Lover Man huddled with a long-haired First Nations guy who sported a fistful of silver rings and a black silk bomber jacket with a red and gold crest that read *Eagle Creek First Nations*. They moved over to the bar next to me. Invisible, my ears cocked dog sharp into their business.

"I'm expecting a big shipment," Lover Man said. "We can hide it in the mine shaft for now."

"Sure," said Eagle Creek. He poured himself a glass of Diet Coke from the can served up by the executioner behind the bar. "We'll keep it there till the coffins are ready."

"When's that?" Lover Man lit a smoke with a wooden match. Sulphur filled the air. He looked right through me with his red lenses. My invisibility held.

"A few weeks. We just got the cedar."

Lover Man grinned a row of rusty nails.

"And no more middlemen, right?"

Eagle Creek scanned the room, then sawed a ringed finger across his throat. A silver skull flashed in the light.

"Don't worry," he said, "the mountain keeps its secrets."

They moved away. Snatches of their conversation trailed. Eagle Creek said something incomprehensible, then: "The paper said he was from away, by the clothes. The body was found in the place of sacrifice. Headless. Hands cut off, too. No way to ID."

Lover Man nodded. "That'll give everyone something to think about."

Both men laughed. Their shoulders heaved. Pirate humour. I'd heard enough. It sounded like they were talking murder. Marla's playmates sounded like stone cold killers. Ice crawled across my scalp and down my arms. It was time to go.

In haste, I tripped over my feet and fell down the last three steps into the bar downstairs. From his perch on high, the bored security guy watched me pick myself off the floor. The band was playing onstage, but instead of the adoring throng, hollow-eyed demons jerked to the beat. I elbowed through the crowd to the exit. No one seemed to notice or care about the violence with which I rammed myself through the room. The thump of my heart was the only sound in my ears.

It was Saturday night in Kirkland Lake. A light rain glittered up the street. Marla had said to meet her Sunday morning at the HoJo on the Trans-Canada Highway. I'd arrived early to surprise her. Now I wanted to get away any way I could. Too bad the last bus home had departed hours ago.

I stood outside the bar, looked at the rain, and wondered what to do, when Eagle Creek came out behind me. He lit a cigarette.

"This puts a damper on the night," he said after a while. My invisibility had worn off.

"Yeah, I guess," I said.

"Where you from? You look like you're lost." Eagle Creek flicked his ash at a raindrop.

"Down south."

"Looking for something?" He had a hint of steel in his voice.

"Nothing." I didn't face him in hopes he'd go away. "Waiting for a friend."

"What kind of friend you waiting for?"

"Girlfriend," I said. "I'm going to meet her in the morning. I'm early."

"Women," he said, "they'll get you to do the dumbest things. I had a woman once got me so crazy I actually did time for her."

"Really?" I should've kept quiet. This was dangerous ground. The longer we engaged, the stronger the pull into Marla's other world. Her dark world.

"Yeah, she had me thinking there was another guy. She made me nuts with it. She had me believing like it was this guy who worked at the hardware store. I finally stabbed him through the lung. Almost killed him."

He laughed and produced a long serrated hunting knife from his waistband. The thing looked like a sword. He jabbed at his invisible foe with conviction.

"Turned out she wasn't doing him at all. She was just working me up."

"Shit," I managed.

He laughed some more and stuck the knife/sword back in his pants.

"Don't worry, buddy, I'm just having some fun with you. Where's your car?"

"I came on the Greyhound."

"Man, you travel rough. This chick better be something. Where you staying?"

"The HoJo on the Trans-Canada, I guess."

"Need a little dope? Some smack? Some coke? Some meth?"

"Thanks, I'm fixed," I said.

"Then let me give you a ride. It's too wet and too far and there's no taxi in this town."

"It's okay," I said.

"No, I insist," he said. "It's my civic duty to help strangers get where they're supposed to be without anything happening to them."

There was no choice. He took me by the arm through the rain across the street to a restored black '64 Thunderbird.

White walls. Dual chrome exhausts. White leatherette seats with red trim. A dream catcher dangled from the mirror. Big trunk. Think: body disposal.

The rain spiderwebbed on the window. Eagle Creek drove into the night. We seemed to be headed out of town into the dense treed wilderness. Fear this, my mind said. If he reaches over, jam your fingers into his eyes. I glanced at him to target the spot. My fingers gripped the leatherette.

To fill the silence, I said, "What business are you in?"

"Coffins," said Eagle Creek. "I'm the sales rep for a coffin maker. We make them out of cedar lined with silk or cotton printed with traditional patterns. Cedar purifies. We ship them to the Indigenous People across the country."

"Business good?"

"Oh, yeah. People are dying to get them."

He laughed too loudly at his own joke. He lit a joint from the car lighter and passed it over. Shadow goblins flitted by the roadside. Telephone poles like crucifixes. Something rattled in the back of the car every time we hit a pothole. Metal on metal. Like a shovel or a pick banging the side of the trunk.

After a while, he wheeled the car off the road into a dirt patch by an old trailer. We bumped to a stop. My body tensed like a sprinter at the gate. My hand gripped the door handle, ready to yank it open and flee.

"I gotta get something," Eagle Creek said. "Stay here."

He was out of the car without another word. A yellow light burned through the cracked window of the trailer. Some busted lawn furniture and a rusty barbecue lay tipped over in the rain, monuments to parties past. A huge mutt on a chain exploded from under the trailer. White teeth flashed in the night. Eagle Creek kicked the dog in its ear with enough force that it yelped back to its lair. He entered the trailer without knocking.

Unsure where I was or where to go, I stayed in the car. Took a couple of breaths. Told myself this would be all right. Marla trucked trouble in ways that were becoming clearer, but for now her murderous her pals didn't know who I was. They had no reason to harm me. So I told myself.

After about ten minutes, Eagle Creek returned to the car, slightly winded. No explanations. He sniffed hard, exhaled, and squared his shoulders. Off the glow of the dashboard, his silver rings glinted with blood, which he wiped off on his jeans. It could've been barbecue sauce. Sure. Like he'd stopped in for a quick bite and a kind word with an old friend. Why not? Could've been. Could've been anything. But I'm pretty sure it was blood.

Once the car was back on the road, he said, "If that girl shows up, you'd best go back wherever you came from. You shouldn't be here."

"I guess you're right."

We rode in silence for the rest of the drive with just the windshield wipers scraping over the glass to keep us company. Eventually, a yellow HoJo sign beamed out of the dark: *The Road Ends, Relaxation Begins*. A cheerful beacon of hope that this night might end well after all. We parked under the awning. My hands unclenched. Fingers aching.

"Thanks for the ride," I said, grateful we'd arrived to a place of safety.

"I'm sure I've seen you somewhere before," he said.

"I don't think so."

"Well, I'm going to think about it. I hope it wasn't something bad."

After Eagle Creek peeled away in the Thunderbird, I entered the motel reception area and rang the little counter bell they kept for late-night travellers. The old lady who came out in her housecoat didn't want to give me a room. I had no credit card. No luggage. No car parked outside. At the offer of cash in advance, she relented.

In the room, I slammed in the deadbolt. Moved the TV from the desk to the floor and pushed the desk against the door. Then I piled a chair on top of the desk. Anyone coming in after me would have to work for it. Door secured, I retreated into the bathroom for a hot shower.

Marla was out with Lover Man. Maybe somewhere for dinner. Then who knows what. Probably in this motel. I curled up, naked and wet on the bed. Stifled my rage and my sorrow with a pillow between my teeth. I pictured her across his table. Smiling. Flirting. Listening like she cared. Hiding her loneliness. Seeking something that devil could never give her. Seeking something she didn't even know she wanted. She liked me, sure. But she didn't consider me a good catch. She missed my potential. Thought me too broke. Too naive. Too much soul and not much else. She lacked the imagination to go to the ends of the earth with me. She wanted cash and comfort. She had no use for soul.

Though Eagle Creek scared me, fear I could work around. Fear I could protect myself from. Marla made me sad. No amount of deadbolting or furniture piling could protect me from that. I told myself I didn't care. Outside, cold raindrops the size of grapes spattered the window.

Marla was in a booth with Lover Man and Eagle Creek at the motel restaurant the next morning. I couldn't get out of sight fast enough. Eagle Creek spied me first. He deadpanned it like he didn't notice. Marla pretended to be surprised. She waved me over.

"This is my friend Paul," she said, all smiles. "What are you doing here?"

Lover Man had heard of me. He chewed his breakfast steak and said, "The nutty greeting card guy, right?"

Marla kept it tight. Marla told Lover Man I was her writer friend. That worked. For killers like him, we were a neutered species.

"He's here looking for his girlfriend, boss," Eagle Creek said. He seemed to study the three of us for a moment. Then he said, "I found his sorry ass in the rain outside the bar last night."

Lover Man cut his meat. Eagle Creek stabbed his fried egg and watched the yellow yolk bleed into the home fries.

Marla didn't flinch.

"You had breakfast?" Lover Man said. "Have some coffee. Tell us about this girl."

I'd checked my crazy fear from the night before. Now wasn't the time to lose it. Marla moved in a hard world of violent characters. This could end badly and we'd all end up in cedar coffins. Keep it light. That was the plan. They had no idea. If Marla kept herself together, we'd be fine. I slipped in beside Eagle Creek.

"She makes me crazy," I said, improvising with speed and conviction. "She's not from around here. She travels a lot. She said she'd be here this weekend, so I came up ten hours on the Greyhound to be with her. She said it was going to be all right."

"That's a coincidence," said Lover Man. "You here, us here. Running into each other in this place."

"Coincidence, I guess."

He looked at the others and said, "Do you believe in coincidence?"

Marla poured tea from a small metal pot and said nothing. Eagle Creek shook his head.

"I can't decide," said Lover Man. "This girlfriend who travels a lot, what does she do?"

"She's a tour guide," I said. "She takes old folks on bird-watching bus tours."

"Like owls and osprey and stuff?" Eagle Creek seemed interested.

"Yeah, I guess."

Eagle Creek nodded like that made sense. "We have lots of interesting birds up here."

"She's likely held up somewhere with them," I said while Marla played with a spoon. "Or maybe I got the dates wrong."

"Maybe you did," she said, her eyes on the table. "Lucky you found us. We're heading back to the city this afternoon."

"You can go back with the band if you need a ride," Lover Man said.

"No," I said, "I guess I'll hang around a bit longer. Maybe she'll show."

I wanted out of their orbit at any cost. The longer this continued, the more likely it would lead to some tragedy. Mine. Hers. Ours.

"Love is never tired of waiting," said Eagle Creek.

Lover Man frowned a confused look.

"First Corinthians," Eagle Creek said. "The Fathers drilled this Indian. Some things just stay in your mind."

"Maybe something happened," said Marla. "Wouldn't it be better to come back with us?"

"It's like he says about love and waiting." I struggled out of the booth. "Thanks for the offer. I'm going to hang around a while." I wanted to get away from them as fast as I could. I also wanted her to worry. I wanted her to care. I wanted her to wonder what I'd do and where I'd go and I relished that she couldn't ask. "It was a big surprise seeing you, Marla. Maybe I'll meet you back in the city, then."

Lover Man smiled. For him, matters were settled. He returned to his breakfast with gusto.

Unable to say more, Marla stirred some sugar into her tea. "I guess I'll see you next time," she said.

Eagle Creek followed me to the door. Outside, he grabbed my arm, not roughly, but firm enough that I thought he could probably snap it.

"I remember you now. You were upstairs last night. You stood beside us at the bar and had a beer." There was no emotional content to his tone.

"I think you have me mistaken for someone else."

"That's not a mistake I'd make."

I shook my arm loose. "Well, maybe you just did."

He looked at me and said, "You act like someone rattled your cage. Forget about it. Your love's in vain, brother. She has another plan. Go back where you came from. Forget about this."

I looked back into his flat black eyes, so dark they had no pupils, and found no relief.

EIGHT

The Real Dope

THE GREYHOUND rolled south through the night. Slumped in the back, suspended in a semi-conscious state, my back ached. I felt cold and empty like a sacked tomb. Outside the window, in the black emptiness of the northern woods, Marla floated by in a pointed hat, an iron chain clamped around her throat. Eagle Creek waved his giant serrated knife while flames shot from his mouth. Lover Man laughed and pissed on a headless body. I twitched. My head bumped against the glass. Sleep never came.

After the excruciating bus ride, I arrived back in the city without enough cash for a cab. A hard rain made the dark walk through the abandoned streets homeward all the more miserable. It was after three in the morning when I climbed the stairs to my apartment in the Ellington, soaked. The light in the hall was broken. I tripped on a piece of torn carpet in the dark. An inglorious accent to end a thoroughly depressing weekend. The noise prompted Akinwole's door to creak open from across the way. His lights were off, too.

"Paul, is that you?"

His glasses glinted in the dark.

"Yes," I whispered, "sorry to wake you."

"I have been waiting for you. Someone is in your apartment. He let himself in last night. He said you were expecting him and then he told me to mind my own business."

"Was it Bernstein?" Bernstein had a key and sometimes slept on the couch when his roommate had a girl over or he was too drunk to make it home.

"No," Akinwole said, "I do not know this person."

"I'm not expecting anyone."

For a second, Lover Man loomed. Maybe he'd figured it out about Marla and me and sent Eagle Creek over to crucify the neutered writer. Marla, why was nothing simple with you?

"I will come in with you," Akinwole said. That gave me confidence, since he was a big man.

A thousand cockroaches scuttled for cover when the light flipped on. I groped for the bat behind the door. I jangled with apprehension. The heat from Akinwole's body radiated behind me. He smelled of Vicks VapoRub. Over my shoulder, he gestured toward the next room with a gold-ringed finger. I nodded. We moved on. In the dark living room, I flipped another light. Akinwole gasped: someone was asleep on the sofa, face covered, one arm dangling to the floor. Unsure of what to do, I took a tentative step forward and poked the figure with the bat. A groan. He removed his elbow from his face and blinked into the bright light. Simon Trang.

Before I could stop him, Akinwole stepped around me. He grabbed Trang by the collar.

"Who are you?" Akinwole shook Trang. "Why are you here?" He cocked his fist.

Sleepily, Trang eyed his attacker, then came to his senses. Without warning, a blizzard of hands and arms exploded in fluid kung fu motion. Akinwole flew through the air, crashed into the wall, and slid to the floor. Trang rubbed his face while Akinwole struggled to his feet, fists ready to continue.

"Stop," I said, "you're going to knock down the walls." My arms kept the combatants apart. "This is Simon Trang. He's a client of the Business. Simon Trang, meet Akinwole Mulumba."

"Yes, Mr. Mulumba," Trang said as he resumed his place on the couch, calm and smooth like nothing had happened. "The Nigerian accountant here by way of Kinshasa, Congo. Two wives. Seven children. Permanent resident status. Private asset management consultant. Specialized knowledge of coltan and tungsten. Contract position at Kramer Investments."

"Why does he know me?" Akinwole frowned.

"Your neighbour Mr. Wint is a person of interest to us. By extension, we know a little about you," Trang said. "We like to make connections."

"He's a cop," I said. "Like a secret agent type."

Akinwole processed. His frown grew deeper. In Akinwole's former world, men like Trang were the harbingers of bad news. Extortionists. Torturers. Murderers. Men to stay away from. Akinwole concluded this was not to his liking.

"Your business acquaintances are not for me. If you are in no danger, I will return to my own apartment now." He limped toward the door. The force of Trang's defence still visibly resonated through his body.

Trang watched Akinwole go. I followed him out.

At the threshold, he said, "I do not know what kind of trouble you are in, but you had best be careful."

"Don't concern yourself." I held the door open for him.

"Paul, men like that are like snails. There is always a slimy trail of shit behind them." He raised his index finger as if he meant to release lightning from it.

"Thanks," I said before he could deliver the sermon that would surely follow. "You're a good man to go through a door with."

Akinwole had things on his mind. He was probably right. Still, I nudged him out.

"You've been keeping bad company," Trang said on my return.

"What do you mean? Akinwole's a solid citizen," my confidence shot back. No matter what had brought him here, Trang was still better than who I'd feared.

Trang shook his head. "That's not who I'm talking about. I don't care about him."

He fished two photos out of his shirt pocket and placed them on the cracked coffee table. Mug shots. Lover Man and Eagle Creek. Trang stabbed Lover Man in the forehead with a jade-ringed forefinger.

"That's Leon Porter. He poses as a freelance A&R guy who manages new music acts before selling them on. In fact, he's part of a crew that traffic heroin. They like coffins and airplanes."

"Coffins? Airplanes?" I knew they were dope dealers. I didn't know the details. It wasn't my business.

"That's right," said Trang. "Leon did five years in jail down in Florida for his part in a big Air France haul. Lately, we think they've been moving stuff on military planes from Kandahar."

"Who's the other guy?" I pointed to Eagle Creek, sure Trang had made this up to scare me.

"That's Joseph Mathew Two Feathers. Joey was with the Canadian Special Ops Regiment until he became a nutcase. He came home from Kandahar a few years ago under a cloud. Supposedly, he sawed off a Taliban commander's head and left it on a pole in a village. No one could prove he did it. So, they tried to get him on a dope charge. There was a load lined into the coffin of one of the soldiers shipped home. He spent six months in the brig, but in the end, they couldn't pin anything on him."

"What's this got to do with me?"

"Did you imagine my family would simply invest a million dollars into this business scheme your Mr. Hornsmith has developed? That we'd just write a cheque? No, sir. I'm obliged to discover who you are. Who you know. What you're up to. I have my family's interests to protect. It's my duty. Naturally, I use my professional network. And I find you in unsavoury company."

"I don't know those people," I said. "I'm just following a girl around. Marla. She knows them. She's a singer."

"You were seen getting in a car with Joey Two Feathers on Saturday night in Kirkland Lake. Then, you were seen with him and Leon Porter early the next morning in conversation at a motel diner. That's not chasing a girl."

This was unexpected: framed in Lover Man's racket. Trang wanted answers. Trang worked the case. Trang was onto something. Trang had me pegged to things I had no hand in. He waited like he expected me to say more.

"I don't know what you're getting at," I said. "I thought she'd be alone."

He gave me a hard stare like he wanted to waterboard me. "All right, let's go with that for now," he said after a while. "You're on your own if you're bullshitting me."

Trang scooped up the photos and returned them to his breast pocket. "Your Mr. Hornsmith checks out better," he said, his mood lighter now. "He leads a layered series of lies and loves. But he's essentially harmless. I enjoyed our little meeting."

Trang hadn't figured out Hornsmith's latest blackmail scheme to keep Courtney committed to the Business. Trang hunted another class of criminal. Hornsmith eluded him. Hornsmith was a secretive loon, not a murdering dope dealer.

"Actually, I come in peace," Trang said. "I have a gift for my new business partner."

He produced a small packet wrapped in brown butcher's paper and Cellophane. He slid it across the table toward me.

"I sympathize with a man who doesn't want to get into the medical system," he said.

The package dared me to pick it up. Maybe this was a trick. Trang watched me like a lizard watches a fly.

"I was kind of kidding," I said.

He shrugged. Too late for that now.

"This is what they call a finger of Mortal Combat. From Kabul. Confiscated from one of the best heroin dealers in the country. We couldn't meet in public with this. That's why I came here."

"I really didn't think you'd come up with anything," I said, still not prepared to touch it. "Hornsmith's not ready for this."

"But he will be," Trang said, "and if he's terminal, addiction isn't going to be a worry, I'd say."

He cracked open a small corner of the packet, licked his index finger, and took a taste. My curiosity got the better of me. I'd never seen anything like it. I followed his example and took a taste, too. Bitter.

“Shooting’s hard and technical if you’re not used to it,” Trang said. “Blood squirts about. Takes time and practice. And snorting’s painful. His nose membranes will burn, and snot will run everywhere. Use a pipe. That’s his best bet.”

With that, he presented a small glass pipe.

“I hope he keeps his dignity to the end. We will talk more about the plans for Washington. There are many interesting opportunities to be had inside a facility like that, so close to the world’s political centre.” Trang stood up to straighten his pants. “And if you’re really just chasing a girl, be very careful. She runs with dangerous assholes.”

NINE

The Hustle

ON A BALMY September morning, Hornsmith led the way out of Fran's on College Street. We had mint-flavoured toothpicks in our mouths and western omelettes and hot coffee in our bellies. Trang's finger of heroin filled my front pocket. I hadn't yet decided to surrender it to Hornsmith. Part of me was greedy to keep it. The weight of the packet felt thick, solid, and round. It felt dangerous. It felt good.

Hornsmith wore a rust-coloured herringbone suit and a newsboy cap pulled over his ears. The red and grey hairs of his beard stood at fierce attention. His skin had become translucent over the past weeks. Its thin yellow hue gave him a ghostly quality.

We pushed against the crush of people on the sidewalk. Fed, we were off to see Dr. Courtney. He'd lived up to his end of the deal. During my weekend misadventure with Marla in Kirkland Lake, Hornsmith had attended Grandmother Mathews's cremation. Now, Hornsmith had to sign the waiver agreeing not to sue the clinic for additional claims.

"Before I sign anything," he said, "we're going to stick him with a higher price for the new clinic's land purchase. There's a play to be made. Today's the day."

At a red light, a guy appeared beside us. A green and blue bruise bloomed across his cheek. Broken red capillaries in his eyes spoke of late nights and bad choices. He wore a formless white T-shirt and dusty construction boots. He had a ragged mutt on a chewed yellow rope in tow. They had a hapless air about them.

"Can you help me?" he said. "My truck broke down. I got to find a way back home."

The dog looked up at me, too. He followed his master's cue. *Yeah, yeah, we wanna fix the truck. Fix the truck. I wanna stick my nose out the window, yeah, yeah.*

"Where's home?" I said.

"Truro," he said. "I haven't been home since April. My mom's sick and I need to go home."

"So, where's your truck?" I felt a twinge of pity for them. This city had no sympathy for anyone down on their luck. Truro was a long way off, far away and unappealing. No one cared about that here.

"It's at a garage on Shuter and Parliament. Needs a fan belt. I can't go back till I got money for the repair."

We started across with the green light. The guy and his dog dodged oncoming pedestrians to keep up. Hornsmith didn't care. Hornsmith ploughed on. Hornsmith was preoccupied.

The guy said, "I'm twenty bucks short, and then I can do it."

The dog licked his leathery lips and smiled. *Yeah, yeah, like he says, we gotta go home. We gotta go home to Truro.*

Usually, this kind of thing left me cold, but the dog looked so enthusiastic with his hopeful brown eyes, certain I held the key to turning around their misfortune, that I fell for their act and gave them a twenty. The dog panted, all pink tongue, black gums, and yellow teeth. Grateful eyes rolled up at me. *Yeah, that's it. Now we can go.*

Hornsmith had pulled ahead. He liked to walk fast, despite his faded condition. I jogged a few steps to catch up.

"What did you do that for?" he said when we were back in lockstep.

"The guy was in trouble."

"He was lying."

I said, "His truck needed a new fan belt. He had a dog. Guys with dogs don't bullshit about stuff like that."

"You trusted him because of a dog?"

"The dog had a good disposition. You can tell a lot about a person by his dog. You know, like master, like dog sort of thing."

Hornsmith snorted and rubbed his nose.

"The dog was a bullshitter, too," he said. "They're a team. The guy's already in the liquor store and the dog's tied up to the bike rack outside."

"You're wrong," I said. "Sometimes things are exactly as they seem. He had an honest face."

"Conclusions about another person's state based on the face are naive and improbable," Hornsmith said. "But, if you want to go that way, you failed to see the obvious. He had a bruise on his face because he'd been in a fight. And he'd been in a fight because he's an idiot. So, if like master, like dog, ipso facto, the dog's an idiot, too."

He laughed and shook his head. He slipped his arm through mine as if to drag me on.

"Never mind, young friend," he said. "We have our own business to attend to."

High above the grind of the street, Dr. Courtney waited in his boardroom over Lake Ontario. This time, the oil portraits seemed hostile. The meeting was short on pleasantries.

"Let's get this matter behind us," said Courtney, "and see if we can return to the project at hand without further setbacks."

Courtney was all business. The agreement lay ready on the table for Hornsmith's signature. Hornsmith had other ideas. With deliberate ceremony, he produced reading glasses from his breast pocket and perched them on his nose. He studied the document. He sighed. He removed the glasses. He stood up. He paced along the massive windows overlooking over the water.

"I'm sorry," he said, "I'm distracted. As we left the office a small detail came to light that has me concerned."

He addressed the lake, as if too embarrassed to look Courtney in the eye. This was my favourite part of Hornsmith's act — the inspired improvisation, like a jazz player who's stepped up to the microphone for a trumpet solo. On the first few notes, you always hold your breath and wait for it to sail.

"The real estate lawyer in Washington reminded me there's a fee we've not taken into account."

"Like a, what? A land transfer tax?" Courtney's fingers trembled as if poised over an invisible piano, in search of a note of his own.

"It's more like an administrative fee. It was in their paperwork. We stupidly overlooked it."

"What are you getting at?"

Hornsmith wrung his hands, ever the grovelling supplicant. He said, "Plainly put, the deal's going to be more expensive."

Courtney flushed. His shoulders contracted. "I don't know if I like this."

"No, I understand," said Hornsmith. "There's nothing to like about these sorts of surprises. But, there's good news, too. A private Vietnamese investor wants in."

"How's that good news?" said Courtney.

"It means," Hornsmith said, "your financial burden can be shared."

"What sort of overage are we talking about?"

Hornsmith let him have it between the eyes. "Four hundred and fifty thousand."

"That's a lot of money," said Courtney. He jutted his hairless jaw. "Is that shared or each?"

Hornsmith's mouth twitched like something was stuck in his teeth. For a moment, I feared he might go too far.

"Shared," he said, finally.

"I don't like it," Courtney said. "My lawyer will have to examine the details before I'll agree to this." Courtney squished up his eyes. Courtney scrunched up his fists. Courtney sucked it up and held it in. "Send me the documents."

Hornsmith shook his head as if in disbelief at his own error and then resumed his seat.

"My apologies," he said.

He put the reading glasses back on and returned his attention to the document in hand. After studying the text, he looked up.

"If I understand this properly, once I sign, I waive all rights to any claim against the clinic in relation to the death of my mother-in-law."

"That's what we agreed." Courtney's voice sounded tight, like someone had a foot on his throat. "You sign this. We go ahead with the land deal. And we drop the book."

"Exactly right," Hornsmith said, "but to be fair, I should discuss this with my wife, now that we have a document to review. It was her mother, after all."

Courtney's jugular throbbed. "I see. And when do you hope to do that?"

"Perhaps after you sign the revised real estate deal, with the additional fee."

"Gentlemen, this is most unsettling. I need to consider where this is all leading." Courtney's face had transformed into a mottled purple blotch.

Hornsmith folded the unsigned agreement into his pocket.

"I assure you," he said, "we're as distressed by the sequence of events as you. And you have our word that we'll do everything in our power to ensure this business is concluded honourably."

Even high up in a cloud of dope and booze and cancer pain, Hornsmith could still do the deal. He whirled and he twirled; he twisted and he danced. He put the mojo on. He did the ooga booga. Courtney didn't stand a chance, never saw what hit him. We couldn't gauge then how mad he'd become. That came later.

At the elevator, we shook Courtney's hand.

I said, "I think I speak for all of us when I say we look forward to moving past this to a profitable co-venture."

"A profitable co-venture," Hornsmith said once we were back in the lobby downstairs, "is always only best for one side."

We walked across the marble lobby and into the street.

He took my arm, half for support and half to make sure I listened.

He said, "The Pig and the Chicken decide to get into business together. A co-venture. Chicken suggests the restaurant business. Pig thinks that's great. When he asks what kind of place, the Chicken says it's an all-day breakfast place. Pig likes this because people always want breakfast. And pigs like to eat. Okay, says the Chicken, agreed. I'll provide the eggs and you provide the bacon."

We laughed, giddy with renewed confidence. We were in business. We brought the rain. We had the world by the tail. Hornsmith did the headlock on Courtney. Courtney would pay. Oink, oink.

We flagged a taxi at the curb. Hornsmith gave the driver the address to the Business. When the cab pulled into the traffic, we drove by the guy and his dog, still hustling passersby. Hornsmith got it right: the dog was a bullshitter, too.

When Hornsmith saw them, he pointed over the seat through the front window and ordered the taxi to pull over.

"Stop. Right here. Keep the meter running."

The cab pulled up on the sidewalk to get out of traffic. Pedestrians scattered like jumpy sparrows. Hornsmith bolted from the car before it stopped. He pushed people aside.

"Hey, you," he said to the guy and the dog, "I want to talk to you."

He grabbed the guy by the arm and leaned into him to speak. The dog barked. Hornsmith kicked it hard enough to get its tail between its legs. He pointed to me in the taxi. The guy glanced my way. The guy's shoulders slumped. He reached into his pocket, and I saw him give Hornsmith a twenty-dollar bill. Hornsmith pocketed the money, shoved the guy once more for good measure, and returned to the taxi.

He grinned and sank into the seat, trembling from the effort. A thin film of sweat broke across his forehead. I said nothing. I expected him to crown the moment by returning me my money. He didn't. Instead, he leaned back his head and closed his eyes.

TEN

The Heart of the Matter

HORNSMITH STRUGGLED out of the cab into the street. He didn't speak. Tentative, as if blind, he groped his way over the curb to the foot of the stairs before he stumbled. His eyes snapped wide. Surprised. He doubled over. The briefcase clattered to the ground. His arms clutched his abdomen. Mouth pulled sharp across his teeth. A yowl erupted from his bowels. He fell backwards into my arms, almost weightless. Skeletal and flimsy. I eased him onto the bottom step. A couple of shudders coursed through his arms and legs before he went limp. It was pointless to ask if he was okay. Everything was clearly not okay. Me blubbering in his ear wasn't going to help. I was certain he'd rally, given a moment alone. There was nothing to do but wait. I propped him against the wall and went to pay the cab.

After a while, he came to and sat up under his own strength. He said, "I thought I was at the airport. I wanted to get on a plane, but I had to wait for you."

"I was paying the cab," I said.

"Yes, you still had something to do." He grimaced. "It feels like there's a basketball wanting to burst out of my guts."

I said, "We'll sit here till you feel better. We don't have to go anywhere."

"No, we don't. But I want to lie down. This will pass. It always does. Help me up the stairs."

With his briefcase under one arm and the other arm around his waist, I helped him up, and together we mounted the steep stairs one step at a time. Periodically he paused to gather his strength.

"In the end," he said between gasps, "the body betrays us in such an undignified manner. We feed it. We clothe it. We wash it and protect it from harm. It wears out just the same in a fury of pain and blood and confusion. I'm not afraid of what's coming, Latour. I only wish it didn't hurt so much."

Once inside, I laid him on the couch, wrapped in a Navajo blanket from the closet because he complained he was cold. The shades were drawn. Mozart played a violin concerto on the stereo. I brewed a pot of green tea for his revival. Hornsmith fell asleep before it was ready.

I plunked myself into an armchair across the dim room. I needed to reorganize. The tsunami was still far off, but like an elephant that can sense disaster long before it strikes, my instinct for self-preservation stirred. It whispered: Head for higher ground. Get out while there's still time.

The music ended. In the kitchen, water drops clanked in the metal sink. Hornsmith's gaunt, hairy face had marbled. A small glint of light reflected off his manicured hands crossed over his heart. Motionless, wrapped in the blanket, obscured by shadows, he looked like a medieval stone-sculpted knight. You could practically see the sword by his side and a teary angel at his feet.

A violent spasm rattled through his chest. He gasped and resumed his wheezy sleep. Hornsmith was still in the game. Hornsmith seemed to be mustering his forces for the next round. His will to live was relentless. It was oppressive. It was ridiculous.

Dark thoughts fogged my mind. The urge to smother him with a pillow enveloped me. Do him a favour. End it. How long would it take? How hard would I have to press? I studied his cracked lips for a spot to place the pillow. If it didn't break his skin or bruise anything, they'd say he suffocated in his sleep. It wasn't murder. It was compassionate homicide.

The phone rang twice before the answering service kicked in. Hornsmith's eyes popped open. I hovered nearby, the pillow in my hand, killing on my mind. It was already after six. The hour was late. He cleared his throat.

"My father once told me, when I stole a quarter from his night table, 'You're a naughty little boy. Don't get caught again.'"

"That's an odd thing to say." I pretended to fluff the pillow. "Don't get caught again."

"Yes, it was. But I learned. And I didn't get caught again. You could do worse than to work that into your act. It's a good lesson to learn."

"You feel better now?"

"For the moment. But it's hard to know when it'll return," he said. "It comes in waves. Some more violent than others. One of these days, it's going to carry me off."

"Tomorrow we need to get the papers over to Courtney," I said.

At this cry of the bugle, Hornsmith raised himself up on an elbow, bloodied but undefeated.

"Tomorrow may have something else in store for us, Latour," he said. "We need to get organized now, while we still can. I'm feeling much better after my nap. I'm going to use the toilet, and then we're going through our sample contracts for something to satisfy Dr. Courtney."

He planted his feet on the Persian carpet and chuckled at some private joke as he shuffled across the floor. Moments later, behind the closed bathroom door, came a howl of pain followed by the sound of his body thumping against the wall.

I found him on the floor, his pants around his ankles. Pungent copper urine filled the toilet and spilled across the floor.

"Latour," he said, but couldn't finish the sentence. He motioned his hands over his stomach. His eyes filled with tears.

"We've got to get help," I said. "This is out of control."

"No," he managed, "I'm fine."

He let out another guttural moan and covered both eyes with shaky hands. I helped him onto his feet and led him back to the couch. Trang's heroin was still wedged in my pocket. Now seemed as good a time as any. I pulled the armchair next to where he lay. We were nose to nose.

"I've got something I've been saving for you." I produced the packet from my pocket. "Let's see if this will help."

Hornsmith grinned when he saw it. He seemed to know exactly what was at hand.

"Latour, you are the Angel of Mercy."

"We'll see about that," I said.

I lay the packet on the coffee table, and with a flick of my lock knife, widened the hole previously opened by Trang to sample the wares.

"This is the finest uncut heroin Afghanistan has to offer," I said. "It should be savoured like an old Burgundy."

"How did you get it?"

"A friend gave it to us, to help you through."

"We have such kind friends."

I held up the glass pipe for Hornsmith's inspection.

"We're going to smoke it?" he said.

I nodded. A bit of powder on the tip of the blade filled the pipe's bowl. When Hornsmith saw the pipe was loaded, he clawed into his pocket and produced his butane lighter.

"We need to cook it slowly, without burning it," he said. He reached for the pipe. "It goes like this."

He held the flame under the glass bowl and waved it gently from side to side as the powder boiled up. A thick vapour curled and swirled about, trapped inside the glass. When the bowl was filled with a noxious cloud, he took away the flame and sucked the smoke into his lungs.

"I did that in Thailand once," he said. He exhaled a thick dragon's tail of smoke that coiled around his head. "It's like riding a bike."

He placed the empty pipe on the table and rested his head on the couch. Slow grin. "Oh, yes. Come on in. The water's fine."

Hesitation kicked in for a moment. This was beyond my experience. I usually self-medicated with lighter fare. Briefly, an image of me as a soon-to-be shirtless, bearded junkie came to mind. Vomit. Dragon tattoo. Slavery. Death. My throat tightened. My heart paced up. Uncertain though I was at these crossroads, and though my thoughts of flight remained unresolved, in the end I figured, let's jump in. Just this once. How bad could it be? I heated the bowl the way Hornsmith had.

When it was done, the pipe rested on the table. We sat peacefully, sealed in our dope world. Leaden limbs. There was no need to do anything. This was the best place to be. Me, Hornsmith, the Persian rugs, the chair, and the couch, all wrapped in a single membrane. Safe. Hornsmith floated on the couch while my arms dissolved into the leather of the armchair. I wouldn't kill him after all. Couldn't do it. I felt good about that.

Dusky pinks and sapphires bled together behind my eyes. A new light spilled across my darkness. No rush to alter the course anymore. No urgency to find another way. All that crap from before with O'Malley was over. I'd switched lanes. Changed the rules. Gotten a fresh stamp in my passport. Most days I could breathe. Sure, Hornsmith was a madman. His murky schemes were like muddy water, thick with slippery reeds. His words like so much noise from an ice machine. But I would endure his didactic assaults to trudge alongside him for as long as it suited me, keen to stay out of the grimy lower realm from which I'd emerged of late. This was a new footing. It was time to stake my claim. Carve it out. Shore it up. Mine it. For a while. I felt good about that, too. Funny, feeling safe and good in the offices of the Business. At work. Work had never been like that before, a place of sanctuary instead of indentured drudgery.

Back when, my grandfather had shown me work could be okay. It had never measured up after that. Still, the first time was marvellous. A game. We'd dug two deep pits in the earth ten feet apart. As deep as a man standing with his hands above his head. We built wooden ladders to get down into them.

When Grandfather said the pits were ready, we tunnelled from one over to the other. It took days. We built a wooden frame to keep the tunnel from caving in. My grandmother came out with tuna melt sandwiches and lemonade while we worked.

Grandfather never talked. He dug like his life depended on it. Occasionally, one of his old pale pals came by to marvel at our enterprise. Grandfather, dressed only in his shorts, all covered in dirt, wouldn't get out of the hole. I never understood the purpose of it all but that was the last time I'd felt good about work.

Through the cool morning mist of Grandfather's farm, Hornsmith whispered, "That's it." He grinned at the ceiling.

After a while, I leaked out of my ears beside myself into the room. Pressed my foot. The top of my head popped up like a hinged garbage can. I reached in and extracted a small plastic bag of rubbish, then let the top drop closed.

"I'm going to throw this out," I said.

Hornsmith nodded.

"It's about time," he said. "While you're up, you could do something about the tea we never had."

I said, "I'll make a fresh start."

That sounded good. A fresh start. We should do that. Make a fresh start. Drink tea. Drive to the mountains. Swim in the river deep and wide. Have our spirits cleansed. Milk and honey on the other side. Hallelujah. Never come back to this overheated city with its overheated problems.

In time, the kettle boiled. The kettle. Inside the membrane with us. It could come along and be with us. I flipped the stereo on again. Mozart came back. The boy genius. The performing monkey. He was also part of the membrane. We'd bring him along, too.

"I won't be interfered with," Hornsmith said, his voice slow and low. "No quack's going open me up and write about it in a peer-reviewed medical journal."

I pressed a mug of green tea into his bony hands.

"No, he won't. You can decide it all," I said.

He smiled. We didn't have to talk about it any further. Particles of music sat on the furniture with us. We were all secured together.

Back into the chaired position, my eyes swivelled to the door. Focused. A form took shape. Something was there inside a membrane of its own. Light from the hallway glowed over its shoulders like wings. For how long, it was impossible to say. In time, the creature held up a box.

"Is this the office of *The International Business Review*?" The figure didn't come any closer.

"Yes, I suppose it is," I said, unsure if the words were spoken aloud.

"I have a parcel delivery."

Hornsmith levitated almost back to form and floated toward the figure. "I'll take that, young man."

"Wait," I said, "we're not expecting anything here."

"Latour, someone has sent us a package. A surprise to end our day."

"I don't want a surprise."

"Come, young friend, where's your gratitude for being allowed to swim in the soup of life's primeval mystery?"

Hornsmith took hold of the package as the door clicked closed. We were alone again.

"Bring over that knife of yours. Let's have a look at what the universe has brought to our doorstep."

Together at the kitchen counter, we opened the box. At first, there was only wrinkled newspaper. Then, deeper inside was a white cotton dishcloth. Hornsmith pulled it out and laid it on the counter. It was wet. Blood soaked.

Hornsmith unwrapped the cloth. He sucked in his breath. And there it was, laid bare on the marble counter: a bloody, raw heart. Purple ventricles dripped like it'd been ripped from the chest of a live animal. A bloody bit of paper, neatly folded, was pinned on top.

My first reaction: Too big to be human. Maybe a cow. Hornsmith unfolded the note. He frowned. He wiped at a blood smear with his pinky. He moved his lips with deliberate emphasis as he read. No sound came forth.

Impatient for the news, I snatched it from his fingers and read out loud: "Dr. Courtney changes his mind. Now you have to deal with us."

No signature.

Hornsmith laughed as if in disbelief. He wrapped the heart back in the bloody cloth and returned it to the box. He stayed calm. He washed his hands under the tap. I took my cue from him. I didn't panic as the membrane tore asunder.

"Courtney has lost his mind," he said. "We're dealing with a deranged individual. We must be vigilant. He can summon spirits to do his bidding."

He moved over to the window and pried apart the blinds with his forefinger. He scanned the darkened world. Evening had chased the day into the basement.

"How did that messenger of Satan get into our office, Latour?"

Unsure what he meant with his talk of spirits and messengers of Satan, I played along.

"Someone must've let him up."

"Yes, but who? We have an electronic lock on the door to

the street. Did you buzz him up?" His eyes snapped up into his head like a brief convulsion.

"No, I nodded off."

"As did I." Hornsmith frowned. He sniffed the air. "The scent of brimstone lingers."

I sniffed the air, too, to signal we were on the same side in case he turned on me.

"I don't smell anything," I said.

"I have keenly developed senses for this sort of mischief," said Hornsmith as he paced the office. He rattled door handles and peered into cupboards. "The demon delivered its fiendish package, then disappeared on a cloud of smoke."

"I guess someone left the door open downstairs," I said. "One of the other tenants."

Hornsmith stopped. He said, "Sometimes your powers of observation are remarkably dim. Look around, young friend. We are alone. The Business is the only tenant here."

"But there're signs on every door in the hall."

"Yes, of course," Hornsmith said. "The Business has multiple interests, which are all represented on this floor, and I am the sole proprietor of each. We are the only ones here."

"Even the law firm, Findlay & Sharpe?"

"Especially Findlay & Sharpe. In this business you never know when you'll need your own legal practice."

Indeed, there'd never been another person in the building. We were always alone. We'd hired temps for Trang's visit; otherwise, there'd never been anyone else up here. Ever. It was odd, when I stopped to consider it. I'd ignored it. Shut it out. Played along. It was a side to the Business that needed reconsideration.

"Which gets us back to how did he get in?" Hornsmith glared. Crazy. I thought he wanted to lay it on me.

I said, "Broken lock? Master key?"

"The forces of darkness are creeping in. Demons are coming through the walls," he said to himself as he lay back down on the couch, the Navajo blanket pulled up over his chest.

"I saw you with the pillow," he said. "You were thinking about it."

"About what?"

"Putting it over my face."

My throat constricted. "I don't know what you're talking about."

"First Courtney. Then you. Then the demon with the box. I fear what lies ahead."

"The road ahead is clear," I said, my voice neutral. I listed the known facts. Outlined the plan. "Courtney's a runt. We're going to sort him out once we sleep off the dope, when we regain our equilibrium. And rest assured: there're no demons. The courier got in … somehow. It's not a spirit."

"No spirit?"

"No. There's another explanation."

"And you weren't thinking of putting the pillow over my face?"

By now, he'd vanished under the blanket. His voice distant.

Hornsmith was tuned for this sort of weirdness. It left me, on the other hand, lost. Weightless. Struggling not to float up into the ceiling. Hornsmith couldn't be underestimated. Even in his weakened state, he could be dangerous. The only safe thing was to tell it like it was.

"I thought about it, yes."

Hornsmith didn't respond.

"I wanted to smother you. I did. But I didn't follow through." I said, louder, "It's not in my nature, mercy killing.

Or any kind of killing, for that matter. You're going to have to find some other way to die. I'll have no hand in it."

Hornsmith still didn't respond.

"Hey," I said, "you still alive?"

I moved over to the couch. When he didn't react to my tug at his foot, I pulled the blanket back. He lay curled up. I felt his forehead. His skin was cold. Mouth open. Teeth bared, like one of those scary leathery bog people they dug out of the peat in Drenthe. But breathing. Barely.

"Hornsmith," I said, shaking him, "come back."

"Ah," he managed.

"We need an ambulance," I said.

"Nah." One clawed hand waved in random circles.

"This is too much to take on. You'll get through this if we get help. Stay with me."

It could've been a reaction to the heroin. Equally, he could've moved into another stage of his bowel cancer. Whatever the case, it felt beyond my ability. I called 911.

"Wah," he said.

He pointed to the coffee table with the last of his energy: the smack was where we'd left it hours ago. I licked my finger, rolled it in the powder and stuck it in his mouth to rub his gums. He opened his eyes for a moment, grateful.

I folded the package. We would need this again later. While we waited for the paramedics, I jimmied open his desk drawer once more with my knife to stash the dope in plain sight until a better plan presented itself.

"Keep breathing," I called out to Hornsmith as I worked. "They're going to be here soon. Don't leave me now."

He remained silent under the blanket.

The contents of the drawer shifted. The photo of the

woman and the Dipshit Kid shook loose. Her stare caught me off guard. I'd forgotten about them. Her.

"Don't let him die," she said through the space between us. "Don't let him off that easy."

Hornsmith on the couch channelled bog people. She was right. Change of plan. I grabbed her picture along with the letters and a handful of blank cheques. Rammed it all into my pocket with the heroin, ever watchful of the fading Hornsmith. He remained oblivious.

I told the paramedics we'd smoked heroin. I told the paramedics he had bowel cancer. I told the paramedics someone had sent us a cow's heart in a box. I reasoned that the more they knew, the more options might present themselves. I sure hadn't a clue. They pushed me aside before I'd finished my rambling account. They lashed him to a gurney. They secured an oxygen mask to his face. They shot him up with adrenalin and put him on an IV drip. Outside, on the street, they loaded him into an ambulance with cold professional efficiency.

As the doors swung closed, Hornsmith struggled to raise his head. He clawed the oxygen mask from his face. He looked at me. His eyes bright as ever. He didn't seem sick at all.

"Latour, why have you betrayed me?"

With that, he fell back, unconscious.

Furious, I stood on the curb as the ambulance squealed off into the night and vanished around a corner. Fuck you. This act of grace saved your miserable life. Bought you time to make peace with this world before you move to the next. This wasn't betrayal. It was an act of compassion. I could still do that, though compassion was something Hornsmith had grown unaccustomed to.

The siren faded into the general din of the city. I was alone, as if the whole event had never happened. In the new silence, a sharp waft of sweet cologne and raw onion seeped out of the darkness.

"Did something happen to your friend?"

The voice connected to unshaven jowls under opaque maggot eyes. A heavy guy in a leather car jacket like the kind detectives wear in French movies. Beside him, a thinner, shorter guy with an underbite. Oversized Gucci sunglasses.

"Your Mr. Hornsmith." The Heavy Guy had a Russian accent. "Something happen?"

"How do you know his name?" I said. "Who are you?"

Underbite stuck his face in. Peeled off the Guccis.

"You deal with us now." He sounded Russian, too.

"Dr. Courtney asked us to review your file," said the Heavy Guy.

"Yes," Underbite said, "and on personal note, our cousin Yuri has message for you."

With that, he punched me in the gut and drove his knee into my crotch. Light exploded behind my eyes. A train of vomit hurtled up my throat. I landed in a place of darkness. Heavy Guy threw a blow to the back of my neck with something blunt. Next, the world turned upside down. From the bottom of the curb, I chewed rocks and sodden paper garbage. One of them kicked me in the stomach. Another kick landed in my kidney. They laughed.

Heavy Guy said, "You have one week to settle with Dr. Courtney. If you don't, we come back and we extract your liver through your asshole."

A final kick to my temple fell to the thunderous sound of one of them unzipping his pants. A cascade of warm urine splattered me from a thousand miles above.

ELEVEN

Escape

WET WITH BLOOD and sweat and another man's piss, I wormed onto the steps of a nearby church. I curled up. My eyes ached. My ribs felt shattered. My kidneys were swollen. With every twitch, my spine crunched like broken glass. The plan was to regroup and find my way back into the refuge of the Ellington. Instead, I passed out. It could've been for eternity, and it might've been for a few moments. Hard to know.

I swirled through darkness until something clammy nudged my cheek. Cold. Wet. With the sweet stench of seaweed, garbage, and rotten meat. An animal was sniffing around my head. The cracks between bits of gravel on the concrete steps where I'd passed out came into view. I sucked air and battled back to the surface to discover morning. A harsh white sun already dominated the sky. The city was on the move. A vagrant dog sat beside me. Immortal chestnut eyes. Head cocked. Puzzled. *Why someone bed down here?* he asked. *What's wrong? Get up. Go home.*

The mutt grinned and scratched his tattered ear. Sniffed my arm. Licked my hand. Hesitant. Unsure if it was something he might like to gnaw on. I tried to move away. A wave of rope-thick hurt shot down my back.

Help me, I prayed to him. Make me whole again. Bind mustard poultices to my bruises. Set my broken fingers. Stitch the cuts in my head. Take the stone from my heart.

The dog didn't indulge my self-pity. He assured me I had the fortitude to endure. *You'll find your way through this. You're not seriously harmed. You need a plan. That's all. Make a plan.* With that, the dog curled back his lips and stuck out his rosy tongue like he'd decided he found the scent of human urine off-putting. Disgusted, he lifted his leg over my worn-out body. Why not? Everyone else had.

Despite my tenderness, I rolled to one side and kicked him away before another disaster befell me.

I relived every blow on the painful journey home. One eye was swollen shut. Dried blood caked my hair. My bones and organs blazed. I stumbled over my feet. People turned away in disgust. Others gave me long sympathetic looks as if that would somehow make things better. Some crossed the street to get away from me. The thugs had done their worst. Still, I could move. I felt good about that.

Later that morning, in the claw-footed bathtub of my apartment, I soaked my battered body in steamy water, numbed by a tumbler of Scotch and ice and a handful of Advil. Deep under the skin, purple and green stains over my torso marked where their boots had stomped me. The dog was right, a new plan was needed. Where once the Business was exciting because it operated outside ordinary life, this line of work now held an unacceptable degree of danger. The Business had become a liability.

Hornsmith called from a pay phone in the hospital during my nap. He needed to take measures of his own. His situation required pragmatic and immediate action. He had to escape. Otherwise, he would die sooner than he expected, because the doctors wanted to operate.

He said, "Get the car from the garage and come get me at St. Mike's. I need to get out right away."

"I'm not sure how fast I can move," I said. "I've been hurt by people Courtney sent after you left."

"Courtney did that?"

"Two Russian mob rejects. They kicked the shit out of me."

I didn't mention they were also related to Yuri the Acrobat. I didn't want Hornsmith to suspect that my troubles had leaked out of my boxes into his. The overlap was, for now, a coincidence.

"The swine," Hornsmith said. "We must regroup. There's a set of keys taped inside the rear left wheel well. Hurry, Latour. They loaded barium up my rectum and lowered cameras down my throat. Their radioactive needles and catheters are lined up. They're sharpening knives. They're going to slice me from stem to stern. If they have their way, I'll never get out of here alive."

In the background, a woman's voice chirped his name.

"They've caught me, Latour. I'm the main event. Help me. Hurry. Every second counts."

"Mr. Hornsmith," the woman's voice said, "we're not supposed to wander around."

"I'm taking care of business," I heard him say.

"We're in no condition."

"I'll be the judge of that."

"Yes, of course you will, dear. Say goodbye."

"I'm calling my attorney. You have no right."

"Yes, yes. We are tired now."

There were muffled sounds. Clothes rustled. Hands slapped against bare skin. The receiver fell and banged against the wall of the booth. I heard him grunt. I heard him gasp. Then the line went dead.

St. Mike's Hospital reeked of cooking grease and sharp pine-scented antiseptic. Stiff from the beating, I swayed through the lobby where a Rasta dude with a bucket and mop slopped soapy water across the tiled floor, his oversized earphones blocking out the world. A haggard woman in a pink housecoat rolled an IV stand out of the cafeteria. Her wilted slippers sloshed over the wet floor while a young Indian couple in street clothes waited by the elevators — him on a cane, her with a taped-up suitcase. Without warning, an unshaven old man in a wheelchair almost knocked everyone over in his dash from the elevator to get outside for a smoke.

When the woman at the information counter typed *Hornsmith* into her screen and scanned the results, she shook her head. Her lipless mouth clenched firm. They had him on the tenth floor. Death row. No visitors.

I said I was his nephew — the only living relative. "I must see him. He raised me like his own son."

No Lips softened. "Go up to the tenth floor and speak to someone at the nurse's station. You might be able to see him before they take him into surgery. It's not protocol, mind you."

The tenth floor hummed and beeped, a cacophony of concealed electrical equipment like a field of invisible crickets. There was no one at the nursing station. The phone lines all flashed. The corridor was empty. The middle of a shift change, I guessed.

Somebody had left a clipboard on the counter. An alphabetical list. *Hornsmith — 1014*. I found the room easily enough and slipped in unseen. As the door clicked closed behind me, down the hall a bell announced the arrival of the elevator.

Hornsmith turned his head in my direction when he heard the door. They'd trussed him to the bed so he couldn't escape. They'd clamped an oxygen mask over his mouth. A plastic bag of saline hung above his head with a thin rubber hose plugged into his left forearm. He said something angry and incomprehensible from under the mask. I worked to lift it.

"Latour," he gasped when his mouth was free, "thank goodness you're here. Untie me. We have to go." He twisted and turned, impatient for his release. The rubber straps binding him to the bed held firm. "The quacks are keen to get into my guts and disembowel me. The tumour is advanced, they say. They have only a short time left to operate."

He paused to look at me. "Your face," he said. "You look like shit."

I untied his straps. "Courtney's thugs."

Hornsmith grabbed my hand. "We're going to extract vengeance on these bastards. You'll see."

"Yes, sure." In this debilitated state, he seemed an unlikely instrument of vengeance.

"Help me get dressed, young friend. Let's get out of this abattoir."

"Can you walk?"

"I'm dying, not crippled. Let's go before they sedate me."

I released the final strap across his chest. He sat upright and yanked the IV drip out of his arm. A few droplets of blood sprayed across the white sheets. He gingerly swung his feet over the edge of the bed and lowered himself to the floor. He crossed the room, determined, if not spry.

"It was a flare-up," he said. In the closet mirror he caught a glimpse of himself in pale-yellow hospital pyjamas. A ghostly figure. He paused and caressed the fabric of his jacket on its hanger while he considered his reflection. Then he pulled on his trousers and, as if to reassure himself, said, "It happens once in a while. No cause for alarm until one of these times I don't recover. I will simply die. That won't be today."

Dressed, he inspected his reflection again with a single nod. Better. A nurse entered as he adjusted his tie. He frowned at her in the mirror, concerned. Hornsmith had a nose for blood. Hornsmith always attacked with precision. He turned and pointed at the empty bed.

"What have you done with Mr. Hornsmith?" he said.

The nurse's gaze followed the length of his outstretched arm over to the empty bed. She glanced at her clipboard. She looked at the bed again.

"He was admitted last night," she said. "Who are you?"

"I'm his brother, Norbert Hornsmith," said Hornsmith, his

voice up an octave, "and this is my nephew, Paul Latour. Have you taken Albert to the toilet, or the shower?"

"We haven't taken anyone anywhere, sir. It's a new shift. We haven't gotten to him yet. Besides," the nurse said, her tone bitchier, "visiting hours are this afternoon. You shouldn't be here."

Hornsmith clutched the edges of the dresser. Wobbly. For a moment, I feared he'd fall over.

He said, "Surely, you're familiar with the special circumstances when a family member summons you because death is in the air."

The nurse looked at her clipboard again. "He's not dying. He's due for surgery."

Hornsmith clenched his jaw. "Emergency surgery to remove a tumour the size of a grapefruit. He might not pull through. His insides are aflame. He needs a priest, not a doctor, if you ask me."

I opened the closet. "What have you done with his clothes?"

The nurse's cheeks flushed. She looked around the room once again.

"I assure you," she said, "we've done nothing with Mr. Hornsmith."

"I'll wager he's making a run for it," said Hornsmith. "Taking advantage of the shift change. He always was a slippery fellow. Hated doctors. Afraid to die."

"You should alert security," I said to the nurse.

"Yes, I suppose we should," she said.

"Tell them they're looking for an older bald man who walks with a limp in his right leg. Korean War injury. It's obvious," I said.

The nurse picked up the telephone on the bedside table and started to dial. Hornsmith nudged me out the door.

"We're going to see if we can catch him downstairs in the lobby," he said to the nurse, who acknowledged us with a brief wave.

Hornsmith planned to navigate his own transition into the Beyond. He had a solid grasp of his prognosis thanks to the doctor who had sent him unauthorized evaluations of his condition. I'd seen the letters in Hornsmith's desk. He knew what ailed him, and he planned to manage it himself. Right to the end. My pointless attempt to force him into the medical system had only confirmed where he stood: his death was on schedule.

I manoeuvred the car out of the hospital garage. So far, so good. No pursuers in the rear-view mirror.

"I'm not afraid of what becomes of me," Hornsmith said. "I'm not so committed to this earthly flesh that I can't bear to leave it. I'm at peace with the idea that I'll go where we all go. When the time comes, what that means will be revealed. In the meanwhile, the wretched pain that precedes the departure is taking all the fun out of dying."

"Why not let a doctor help you with that?"

"Because those bastards can't resist poking and cutting. It's their sacred duty. Prolong this business of life at any cost. They will not aid and abet in a dignified end, certainly not if it stands in the way of some viable manner of postponement."

"What about the doctor who sent you those files?"

I concentrated on the road while he fumbled in the glove compartment for his flask. Hornsmith needed fuelling up. Hornsmith needed calming down. He tipped the flask to his lips, looked through the tinted window at the people on the street, swallowed, and sighed.

He said, "That doctor isn't going to be of any more help."

"What if you explained?"

"There's only so far I can push him." He had another pull on the flask. Morose. "I should seek the help of a veterinarian. Say I'm an Alsatian. Vets are hip to the notion of a humane death."

"You could go to Amsterdam. Get the injection."

"I'm not so certain I'd pass the sound mind requirement. No, Latour, I will face this journey alone. Here."

Outside his house, I parked the car. He didn't invite me in. He still needed to explain his circumstances to his wife.

After our goodbyes, Hornsmith held me back by the arm. Flecks of red and blue swirled in his pupils. Beyond them, I saw mountains. Beyond them, an ocean. Beyond that, white light.

"You're a good man, Latour. Thank you for trying to help me through this portal."

I couldn't reply. I didn't have the words. We were in unfamiliar territory. I'd once seen a dog hit by a car on a reserve. It twitched by the side of the road in the grass with a broken back. An Indigenous guy helped it out of its misery with a couple of blows from a two-by-four. That was it for Death and me.

I understood his words, of course. Their gravity eluded me. I dodged them so I wouldn't feel their impact. Death's pall wasn't a weight I wanted to carry around.

"Bring me the rest of the heroin," he said, "so I'm prepared for the next wave."

The deeper I looked into his eyes, the farther I travelled. There were caves and fires. There were turbo trains and desert flowers. I feared he'd take me with him. I feared I'd die, too.

TWELVE

Bobby Fischer Said

THE STENCH OF rotten fruit off the androgynous form wrapped in ripped overcoats, asleep on a stack of newspapers at the back of the Queen streetcar, didn't seem so bad. Normally, the idiot with the studded collar around his throat leading a mastiff on a matching leash would've earned a silent sneer. Today, there was no time for that. Equally, I had no interest in smirking at the besuited sad sack who fiddled with his BlackBerry like he was onto spectacular stock trades every few seconds instead of playing Candy Crush. No, I had other considerations. Had a plan to formulate. I'd escaped the workaday world and now faced a return to that cage if I didn't sort myself out. Soon the Business would fold in on itself, and I'd be on the curb. Soon I'd need a new way to cover bar tabs, dope scores, and rent at the Ellington. When Hornsmith died, the Business would go with him. I had neither the experience nor the inclination to pursue it on my own. That much was certain. The rest was unclear.

Then, I remembered the agreement we'd signed. It said the Business would be mine after twenty years or upon his death. Whichever came first. He'd said that. That was our deal. At the time, it had meant nothing, because Hornsmith had seemed death-proof. I hadn't understood. Back then he was already planning his departure. There was a chance the Business would be useful to me after all. If it had money stashed somewhere. If I could break it loose. If Hornsmith's contract was legal.

A big score could lead to a new start. The farther the Queen car ploughed through the city, the better my chances became. My bags were already packed for a move to Panama or Belize or Madagascar. Or Goa. I'd live in a beach hut. Sand and salt in my hair. Eat mangoes and fried fish. Grow a beard. Find a nice island girl and devote myself to a life of domestic bliss. By the time the Ellington came into view, the plan was clear: give Hornsmith the dope and see him off. Then clean out the Business and go lie low somewhere far away. The details needed work.

The front door of the Ellington flew open. A knobby rubber bicycle wheel bounced off my leg. I was so busy with the plan that I walked right into Rachel with her bike in the dim vestibule.

"You look worse every time I see you," she said. "There seem to be new cuts and bruises on your face." She scrutinized my wounds. "Are you one of those guys who do, like, street fighting? For money?"

"No, I'm one of those guys who get the shit kicked out of them by rejects from the Russian mob."

"Sounds like an exciting story."

"It's not. It ends with me getting pummelled and left for dead."

"I'm not sure I'd like to be around you."

"I don't like it much myself."

"And how's your friend? The one who says I'm a witch?"

"Akinwole? His confidence seems to be back. Are you still with the pots or jugs or whatever it was?"

I was preoccupied with Hornsmith's contract. Should've looked at it closer. What if it wasn't written with real words, but gibberish like the certificates on his wall? I tried to picture it. All I saw was static.

"Ceramics."

"Ceramics. Right. I was teasing. Sorry. And the witchcraft? You after someone new these days?"

"Don't tease me." She didn't seem to mind. "I could be coming for you."

"Be warned," I said, "I'm a danger to those around me. I channel havoc and heartbreak."

"Huh. You look more like the bourgeois kind. Slumming it. Soft and white. What possible threat could you be to a street-smart witch girl like me?"

My hands went clammy. Her bright-orange mane radiated defiance. She had perfect full lips. When she spoke, they blossomed, bold and fearless. Chewable. I felt intimidated and spellbound at the same time. I should've kissed her. Maybe things would've turned out different for me.

"None whatsoever," I said.

I held back. Afraid of the possibilities that lay beyond. What if she protested? What if she accepted? She sensed my discomfort and grinned. With a flick of her wrist, she tossed her hair over her shoulder.

"Don't be so hard on yourself," she said.

She slipped her sunglasses over her eyes and wheeled the bike out into the sun. I wiped my damp palms on the back of my jeans and watched her disappear into the street. She didn't look back.

Upstairs in the dresser drawer, amongst the remains of Trang's heroin and the unpaid bills, seemed the most likely place to look for the contract. I rummaged around the mess and in the process, shook loose the photo of Shirley Rose from Detroit and the Dipshit Kid. Fruit of my impulsive theft of Hornsmith's desk. They stared up at me. Hornsmith's other life.

She nodded. *Look after yourself, because he won't,* she seemed to say. *He forgot about us. Why should he treat you any different?* The Dipshit Kid stared into the mid-distance, oblivious. She was right: I needed protection. The packet of heroin went into the front pocket of my jeans, and on an impulse, the stolen cheques were folded into my wallet. There was no sign of the contract. It could still be in the office.

I pulled up my socks and tied my shoes, preparing to leave the apartment when the phone rang. Marla.

"Baby, I'm so sorry what happened last weekend," she said. "I never meant it to be like that for us. He stayed longer than I expected. I had no way of warning you. Will you ever forgive me?"

Her voice threw me off balance. She made me queasy.

"It wasn't good for me, Marla, that's for sure."

"I know. I've been feeling bad for days."

"You could've called."

"I was afraid you'd reject me."

"I'm not going to reject you, Marla. Sometimes I think I should. I should but I won't. Seems like I'm always getting hurt when you're around."

"The band's playing at the Kool Haus tonight. Come with me. I'll be alone. I promise. I'll make it up. You'll see, lover. Please come. We'll go somewhere after the show."

"I have something to take care of tonight. A sick friend."

"Come after. The show goes late."

"We'll see."

"You're not mad at me?"

"No, Marla, I'm tired." I flashed on her in Lover Man's lap. Then Eagle Creek after the trailer. Blood glistened on his silver rings under the dashboard lights. Marla moved in dangerous circles.

She chortled, harlot-like. "Come see me tonight. I'll show you why God made you a man."

Hornsmith's wife, Katherine, answered the door in a blue yoga outfit. Her salt and pepper hair pinned back in a stark bun. Her naked face exposed. Her eyes red-rimmed, swollen.

"Why you didn't tell me?" she said. Her voice cracked under the weight of what she wrestled with. "I don't think I can forgive you. It's true we hardly know each other, but on this, you should've called."

"It wasn't my place to say anything." I stayed by the open door. "What goes on between you two isn't my business."

She was tight, tense, and terse.

"You're a cold man whose moral compass needs realignment," she said. "I'll let you in because it'll comfort him. Not because I trust you. He did me wrong for so long, I'm worn out by it. Still, I love him. I'd do anything to ease his pain."

I was part of his other world, the world that took him away

from her. The world that made him do the ugly deeds he did. She believed we kept secrets from her. Made plans without her. Never considered her. She was right.

She stepped aside to let me in. "He's in the living room," she indicated with a vague wave of her clenched hand.

Washed and wrapped in a red silk smoking jacket over crisp blue cotton pyjamas and brown leather slippers, Hornsmith sat in a club chair with his pipe. He studied a chessboard on the coffee table in front of him. The wooden bookshelves by the bay windows glowed in the last of the golden afternoon sun. Blue caramel-scented smoke swirled around his head like clouds trapped on a mountaintop.

"Latour, you have arrived in time to help me with a complicated play." He waved the burning pipe over the chessboard. "It seems I'm in a bit of a bind against a most cunning adversary."

"I'm not much of a chess player." I drew in the other armchair to sit across from him.

"We're playing shuffle chess. You can't play with memorized opening moves. You play on talent alone. Bobby Fischer played like that." He looked at me to see if I was with him. "Bobby Fischer famously claimed once you start distrusting your mind, you're done. Finished."

"He went insane."

"Indeed." Hornsmith nodded, pipe in his mouth.

I said, "I've brought what you asked for."

I placed the packet of heroin next to the chessboard and gazed over the battlefield. With the random placement of pieces, it was hard to grasp the situation. Where a mortal saw chaos, he saw a conflict in progress. He gauged his next move.

"That's kind of you," he said. His mind seemed more on the game than on my delivery.

"What're we doing about Courtney?" I said, to get onto practical matters.

"Courtney?" He looked surprised. "Whatever for?"

"Courtney's declared war," I said. "He sent us an animal heart. He had thugs beat me up. We have a week to square it. After that, they're going to hand us our heads."

"Latour, don't concern yourself with this."

I thought, easy for you to say, about to leap into the Great Beyond.

"We do nothing," he said. "Something will happen. Courtney is new to this type of contest. He doesn't know what to do."

I said, "His opening gambit has been shock and awe. I have wounds to prove it."

"Yes, he opened strong," Hornsmith said. "He's made a tactical choice to use violence because he thinks he'll reap the benefits. Remember, it's not his world. He hasn't experienced the hazards of violence. It'll turn against him. You'll see."

He moved a white bishop. He looked at the board for a counter. When there was no apparent fallout, he grunted with satisfaction.

He said, "Courtney's already in disarray. On the actions of the enemy, recall Sun Tzu: when speech is threatening and forward actions are taken, this indicates a retreat."

"Sun Tzu? Retreat? Are you kidding me?"

"Latour, he's out of his depth. His downfall is around the corner. Victory is ours."

"And what will that look like?"

"He will stop trying to get out of the Washington business and start making us rich." Hornsmith stood up. "Excuse me, I'll be right back."

I resisted the urge to knock over his chessboard. Take him by the throat. Bash in his head. He'd become nothing more than a self-absorbed, solipsistic old man who couldn't engage. Who wouldn't acknowledge what a world of shit he'd dragged me into. Instead, he left the room on a trail of scented smoke. It was pointless. Hornsmith was in a different movie.

Outside the window in the garden, a miniature water wheel turned endlessly under a stand of old Japanese maples. The more difficult events became, the more alone I felt. A retreat of my own looked inviting. Find a place to dig in. Hide out. Hole up. Hunker down.

When Hornsmith returned, he'd changed into a black suit over an open starched white shirt with large silver cufflinks. The pipe was gone. When he sat down, he removed a silver cigarette case from his breast pocket and extracted an unfiltered cigarette, which he idly tapped on the case. He studied the chessboard for only a moment before he swept away the white bishop with a black knight. He lit the cigarette.

"The best strategy is to crush their plans." He coughed smoke. His voice was raspier than before. His movements more precise. He picked up the packet.

"Did you bring this?"

"Yes," I said, "we talked about that."

"Indeed?" Hornsmith slipped it in his pocket. He studied me through the smoke and jerked his thumb in the direction he'd gone to change outfits. "You know the fellow who left?"

"I'm not sure I do."

"Well, he's a good chap. Wants to do the right thing. Doesn't always manage it."

"Doing the right thing is tricky business," I said, unsure what Hornsmith meant.

"Yes, he doesn't have enough experience. I have to be patient with him. He has much to learn about the Business."

"He seems to manage all right," I improvised.

Hornsmith looked in my direction, his gaze unfocused.

"I'm trying to get him interested in the Business," he said. "Sometimes I fear he might be out to sabotage our efforts. You need to keep an eye on him."

I felt an urgent call to save myself. I leaned across the table. Touched his arm and looked around. I whispered like I feared there were others in the room listening. Like I had a secret to impart.

"There's something we need to do."

Hornsmith focused. Hornsmith looked around. Hornsmith checked that no one overheard us.

"Yes?" he said.

I fumbled in my pocket for the blank cheques.

"In case something happens, and the Business has to pay some bills when you're away, I need you to sign these."

Hornsmith extinguished his cigarette.

"I see," he said. He put on his reading glasses to examine the blank cheques. "There are no amounts here. And they're not payable to anyone."

"No," I said, "because we don't know what's needed. It's in case you're away when the time comes."

"Planning, then?"

"Exactly."

He stared at them a while before he took out his fountain pen. Poised to sign, he said, "Are you sure?"

"Yes," I said, "this is going to help."

He nodded. Okay.

"I can't say what the balance is," he said. He passed the

signed cheques back. "There's less than a hundred grand. Pretty sure. I suggest you get them starched before passing them on."

"Thanks. And that guy?"

"Yes?"

"Don't worry about him. He'll figure it out."

"He will?"

"Yes, he told me so."

"Good."

He pointed at the chessboard.

"That's set up for shuffle chess," he said.

"You told me that when I came in."

"I did?"

"Play on talent, not on memory. Bobby Fischer said."

"Lost his mind."

"Indeed."

THIRTEEN

Trouble in the Night

AFTER OUR LAST mistimed experience, waiting for Marla in a bar until she was ready to leave appealed less to me than waiting outside the dentist's while someone screamed behind a closed door. Besides, the possibility of running into Courtney's thugs cramped my enthusiasm for being out more than necessary. Marla could wait till another day. By ten at night, the Ellington was the only place I wanted to be.

The lights stayed off to make it look like no one was home. In the dark, a glass of J&B and a victory joint by the window celebrated Hornsmith's signatures on the blank cheques. An inspired play. A plan had started to shape up. Fortune seemed in my favour for a change.

He'd said there was under a hundred grand. This meant possibly eighty or ninety. Even with only thirty, things would be better than they were now. It was exciting to catch a glimpse of hope. The only thing to do now was to get the cash and elude Courtney's thugs long enough to escape town. Soon there'd be a higher grade of Scotch to pour and a more secure sanctuary to hide in. That was the new order of business.

The phone rang while I scanned the parking lot through the night-vision binoculars for enemy movement. At the same time, someone knocked at the door. I ignored the phone. Grabbed the bat. In the hall, Rachel called out my name.

"Who's with you?" I said through the closed door.

"Nobody. I'm alone."

One of those security peepholes would've been useful.

"I'm returning something to you," she said.

Odd. She didn't have anything of mine.

"I'm not missing anything."

"You dropped something the other night."

When the locks popped open, she stuck her hand in under the chain. Akinwole's voodoo amulet. The menacing bent nails glowed blue.

"I found it after you left."

I took the amulet through the chained door. It felt rough and heavy in my hand.

"Seeing you this afternoon reminded me of this thing," she said after I removed the chain to let her in. A lemony breeze followed her. "I don't want it in my apartment."

I checked the empty hall behind her and secured all three locks once more.

"You have all the lights out," she said.

"Lights are out, somebody's home." I flipped the kitchen light on and off like it was a joke. "Would you like some Scotch or some tea?"

"Tea's nice. Do you mind if I smoke?"

"Go nuts."

She lit a cigarette and said, "A lot of people are freaked out by the fact I still smoke."

"I'm not." The kettle rattled over the gas flame. "Lots of people still smoke. French girls smoke. It's part of their allure."

"It is?"

"There's something that turns me on about kissing a girl with smoke on her breath. Something defiant about her."

"Huh." Smoke swirled about the kitchen. "That's kinky, Paul." She sat up on the counter. "Ashtray?"

I passed her a chipped coffee cup. "Use this."

She dabbed her cigarette on the lip of the cup. The kettle whistled.

"Kissing a guy with smoke on his breath is disgusting," she said. "It's like kissing a guy who hasn't shaved."

I poured boiling water over the tea bag while she smoked and talked in her singsong voice.

"Sugar?" I said.

"Three, please." She shifted her weight. "That two-day-growth look looks dirty. Sometimes I see guys and get the urge to shave them."

"And that's not kinky?" I said.

"What? No. It's basic hygiene." She blew into the cup to cool the tea.

"So, you'd shave me now? For hygiene?" I said while I rolled another joint.

"Yeah." She cocked her head sideways to examine my face from a new angle. "You need a shave."

We shared the joint in silence. From time to time Akinwole's amulet glowed on the counter. It reeked of bad luck and ancient curses. That thing was going back into his hands first thing in the morning. No need for that juju majick here.

She jumped off the kitchen counter after we finished smoking the joint.

"Okay, let's do it," she said.

"Are you sure?"

"Sure," she said, "the night's shot anyway."

The phone rang again while we headed into the bathroom.

"Don't touch the lights until we've closed the door," I said. "Russians are looking for me, and they'll see I'm home if the lights go on."

"What an exciting life for a guy who lives in a roach-infested dump." She didn't buy it, I was sure. Still, she left the lights out until we were both in the windowless bathroom with the door closed behind us.

Outside in the apartment, the phone rang again.

"Aren't you going to answer that?" she said.

"No," I said and sat down on the toilet. "It's only bad. These bastards are serious people."

She giggled. "You're insane."

"Doesn't matter," I said, "they're still going to hurt me. The gear's above the sink, if you're keen to give this a try."

She opened the mirrored medicine cabinet. "A straight razor. How quaint."

"I like a close shave."

"Towels?"

"The one on the rack's almost clean."

She held one finger under the tap to check the water temperature.

"Better take your shirt off. Otherwise you'll get soap splashed all over it."

She lit another cigarette. I disrobed.

"You're going to smoke while you shave me?"

"It relaxes me," she said. "When I put a razor to a man's throat I need to be relaxed."

She fumbled with the shaving cream. Not the confident moves of a barber ready to lather up another customer.

I said, "It's best to use the brush to get some hot water on the beard first. Then lather the cream over the face with the hot brush. Start like that."

"You're not the first man I've shaved," she said with the cigarette between her lips.

She ran the razor through the lather over my right cheek. Cautious. She frowned. She was tentative. My jugular was in no danger of being slashed. She lacked the pressure and the authoritative swipe a razor requires to get it done.

She squinted through the smoke at my whiskers. When she leaned toward the sink to rinse the blade, her breasts grazed my nose. Lather from my cheek streaked her black T-shirt.

"Take your time," I said. "Get the feel of it."

"Sure. I shouldn't hurt you," she said. "It would be bad for business."

She held up the razor with one hand, pulling the cigarette from her mouth with the other. She eyed her handiwork. With the razor she tapped my Adam's apple and looked me in the eyes. She said, "You do this hard bit in here."

I put my hands on her hips to draw her in closer. She didn't resist.

"You do it."

Neither of us moved. Outside someone hammered at the front door. I slid off the toilet and turned the lights off.

"Stay here."

In the dark, at the entrance, I pressed an ear to the door. Nothing. With luck, they were already gone. Then a force crashed against the door outside like a steel I-beam jolting through my temple.

"Open up, Paul. You got to be home!"

Marla. Hysterical.

"They're coming for me."

She pounded again like she meant to hammer right through the wood. Trouble. And me shirtless, all lathered up with Rachel in the bathroom.

"Marla, stop it. I'm opening up."

She sobbed when the door swung open. "Why didn't you come tonight? Why didn't you answer when I called?" Her hands clutched a purse across her chest. "You were supposed to come. Nothing would have happened."

I wrapped my arms around her and drew her in from the hall. She heaved and sobbed, unresponsive to my touch.

"I told you, I had to see a sick friend. Come. Whatever it is, Marla, you're okay now," I said. "Nothing will happen to you here."

That earned a faint hug.

"I was afraid to go home," she said. "I called you to come get me. There were two guys hanging around after the show."

"What kind of guys?" I said.

"Dickheads." It seemed to me Marla always attracted dick-heads.

"So, what happened?"

"They kept trying to make me go with them for drinks. The more I said no, the more they pawed me. I tried going out the back of the theatre. They had that covered. One guy grabbed me outside."

"How'd you get away?"

"I bit the fucker's ear off."

"Clean off?"

"I didn't stay to see. There was blood."

I flicked on the kitchen light to check if she showed any signs of a struggle. It was hard to tell. She was in a silky black tank top and skirt, her hair the usual mess. If there was blood, it didn't show. She could've wiped it off.

"I ran for a cab," she said, "and tried calling you again. The fuckers followed me in an Escalade. I couldn't go home."

My pulse picked up speed.

"Were they Russian?"

"Maybe. Yeah. They were assholes. Tattoos. Bling. Shaved heads. Baggy pants. Mouth-breathers. Knuckle-draggers. Cave dwellers. A big guy and a little guy."

Her sobs subsided.

"You're okay now," I said, my arms still around her.

"Except," she sniffed, "they're outside."

A sharp current lit up my spine. My breath grew shallow. She broke from our embrace to look at me.

"You were shaving?"

She touched my soap-smudged cheeks.

"What's going on? Have the Russians landed?" Rachel came into the kitchen with the razor in her hand and a smoke in her mouth. The two eyed each other for a moment. Marla took a stance and crossed her arms. It would've been good to vanish in the ensuing silence. Marla wouldn't see this right. Rachel smiled.

I said, "Rachel, this is Marla. Marla, Rachel."

"Is this your sick friend?" Marla said.

"No, Rachel lives upstairs."

"I was returning something," Rachel said.

Marla looked at me for an explanation that didn't come. She had me off balance. I couldn't manage a sensible word. Instead, I went to the window for a look outside.

There were a few cars in the lot, including a white Escalade with shiny silver rims. Through the night-vision glasses, I saw two guys beside the truck. Like Marla said: silver chains and shaved heads. Jeans fashionably lowered by heavy pistols, or else they'd shat their pants. The truck pumped hip hop. Silver and white disco ball lights flashed inside like a nightclub. The guys smoked. They shuffled their feet. I fiddled with the focus and brought them in. Heavy Guy and Underbite shared a bottle from a brown bag. I called Marla over to the window and passed her the binoculars.

"These your boyfriends?"

She peered through the lenses.

"Yes," she said, "those assholes."

She handed back the binoculars. I took another look. I guessed they'd figured out my relationship to Marla. Followed her here. Now they had to figure out which building she was in. If they'd known that, they'd have been up already. The Ellington was still safe, for now.

The night they'd almost kicked me to death, there hadn't been a chance to get a real look at them. Now I could study my tormentors at leisure. Heavy Guy had the shape of a large animal, like a hairless yeti that had recently learned to walk erect. He turned his coconut-shaped head with jerky moves, his nose to the wind for a scent of his prey. His left ear bloodied.

Underbite didn't look so dangerous. A short, wiry monkey. Past midnight and still in sunglasses. Wanker. They seemed to loiter with purpose. Like they planned to camp here.

My back muscles twitched in memory of my beating. These assholes made me tingle and tense. They made me grind my teeth. They inspired loathing with a purity of heart that seemed impossible. I went back to the kitchen, where both women loomed like a pair of owls. They eyed me. They eyed each other. No one said anything. My hand clasped the cast-iron handle of my eight-pound skillet on the stovetop. That felt good. A weapon.

"Paul?" one of them said.

The time to talk had passed for me. I floated out the door. Shirtless. Barefoot. Stoned. Shaving lather still on my face. A simple plan had formed. I'd become the instrument of justice for Marla. Happy to settle the score with my tormentors. I was off to wreak havoc on my enemies.

Outside on the street, I channelled Hornsmith's words. Conflict was a tactical choice, he'd said. The best strategy was to crush their plans, he said. Conflict. Tactical choice. Crush. I'd slept on the church steps soaked in piss and blood and lived. These animals had no idea who they'd stirred up. These punks were out of their league. Emboldened, I felt bona fide dangerous.

I picked up speed. I walked right at the pair by the white SUV. The skillet stayed close to my side, behind my leg. Their guard was down. My heart was up. The rocks in the parking lot cut into my bare feet. Grounded me for what was to come. The city sounds fell away. My breath stopped.

They leered at me in recognition. The Heavy Guy lowered the booze bag and wiped his maw with the back of his hairy hand.

"We looking to party with your girlfriend." His voice sounded like he was under water. "Now we have you. Better."

"Sure," I said. "Party."

I hit him with the skillet square on his forehead. He dropped the bag. The bottle inside the paper bag popped on impact with the pavement. He sagged to his knees. Another blow slightly higher up on his skull did it. His eyes closed. He arched his back. His arms spread out like he was ready to fly. Then he fell to the ground, face first.

That's how it works. Take down the big guy first. Excited, I swung around and crashed the skillet into one of the truck's halogen headlights. More glass exploded. I pounded on the hood. The skillet was made for this. I walked toward the back of the truck. There was no turning back. This is how people murder one another. This is how it's done. Underbite knew it. He could see the blood lust in my swings. He cowered on the other side of the truck. His face in the side mirror showed open-mouthed panic. Bloodied by the mayhem I'd created, every molecule in me screamed for me to kill him.

"Holy shit," Underbite said under his breath. He scrambled to get into the truck and lock the doors. When he had the engine started, there was a moment of uncertainty. To drive away, he'd have to run over his friend's body.

Blinded by a new set of headlights that swept the parking lot, I paused in my work. My free hand shielded my eyes from the light. It was a taxi. A figure lumbered out of the back seat. Slow. Sure. Steady. The figure sprouted wings of light in the flare of the taxi's headlights. Underbite and I stared at what approached. Intervention. Retribution. Salvation. They were all upon us.

"Whatever is going on here, brothers, two wrongs will never make a right." Backlit, Akinwole's massive body emerged from the shadows.

"Akinwole?"

He grabbed me by the scruff of my neck like a bad dog.

"You," he said to Underbite, "pick up your friend. Put him in your car. Go. And never return."

Underbite wordlessly jumped out of the truck, went over to the Heavy Guy, and helped him off the ground and into the truck. Heavy Guy moaned across the back seat.

"And you" — Akinwole shook me by the neck — "what has come over you?"

The SUV tires crunched on the gravel. We watched the thugs roll away. They didn't linger.

Akinwole put me down.

"Let's go inside before the police show up," he said. "Come. Can you walk?"

I nodded. I trembled. He put his arm around my shoulder. I surrendered. Together we went into the Ellington, which embraced us with its customary cloak of security. Wordlessly, we mounted the stairs to the second floor. Outside our respective apartments, we paused.

"Thanks," I said.

"You are sometimes an asshole," he said. "Still, you are my friend."

"I am. You are," I said.

We both laughed a little.

There were two notes on the kitchen counter. One was from Rachel: *Hope you didn't get hurt any more than you already are. R.* The second was from Marla: *I saw why you didn't answer the phone. I'd be crazy to hope we had any sort of future. Take care. Goodbye. Fuck off. Marla. PS: Thanks for getting rid of those guys.*

I trashed the notes and turned off the kitchen light. In the dark, the amulet glowed on the counter.

FOURTEEN

Fire!

SOMEONE RETCHED IN the parking lot below my window. I was sleepless in bed, with Marla on my mind. Since we'd first met on the last day of my old life, she'd made indifferent efforts to keep us together. It was mostly up to me to go down to the well. Call her. Miss her. Follow her around like a lovesick dog bearing tokens of my affection. Guitar strings. Poems by Pablo Neruda. Silver bracelets. Bottles of wine. She'd reciprocated only once with a miniature Spanish dictionary. Everyone could stand to learn another language, she said. The bedside bottle of J&B had a couple of fingers left. The amber toxin swished around my gums. It burned going down. It offered no relief. She was trouble. I was going to miss her.

Outside, the city stirred in its slumber, restless. A horn. A truck. A siren. Another siren and another. My head buried in the pillow, fire trucks bounced over the potholes in my mind. Their diesel engines raced from one disaster to the next. Radios crackled commands. Air horns sounded. Big brakes hissed. A trace of smoke hung in the air. An alarm clanged in the hall. Voices called out to each other through the night. I rolled out of bed for a look. In the parking lot, firefighters hoisted oxygen tanks onto their backs. Others uncoiled hoses from parked trucks. Red lights flashed. Long shadows of firefighters on the run danced over the side of the building like goblins around a pyre. Two firefighters pointed up at the Ellington somewhere over my head until one pushed the other aside. A flaming timber crashed right where they'd been standing. A hose burst to life. White water pounded into the building. Windows shattered with the impact.

Smoke crept into the apartment through the cracks in the walls and ceiling. I made it to the kitchen half-dressed. Orange flames licked around the door frame. An axe head chopped through the door. Wood splintered in all directions. The door exploded. Sparks shot through the air. The tops of the cupboards caught fire in seconds.

A silhouetted figure wrapped in smoke and crowned with a black firefighter's helmet emerged from the fiery haze. Flames danced around his head. Goggles and a breathing mask obscured his face. He held a long axe, which he pointed at me like a staff. I stood transfixed.

"Get out," his muffled voice ordered. "Go while the stairs are still good."

With that, he vanished into the blaze.

Flames sizzled. The crackling wood snarled louder. The smoke thickened. I buckled up my jeans, grabbed the binoculars, my wallet, and, for good measure, Shirley Rose's photo and letter. By now, the entire wall of the kitchen was afire. In the smoky hall, a couple more firefighters pushed by. They headed upstairs, higher into the inferno. It was time to go.

With my arms over my head, I plunged through the flaming portal that was once the doorway. In the smoke-filled corridor, shadows groped their way to safety. Feet trampled over the smouldering floor. Bodies on the move. In the dark, someone coughed from the smoke. At the stairs, someone cried. Akinwole's door hung off its hinges, busted open. Not on fire. Maybe he was still in bed, asleep, oblivious to the chaos. I moved toward his apartment to check when the circular moulding in the ceiling crashed to the floor. Surrounded by fire, I recoiled from the flames, reconsidered my course, and sought a new path out of this burning hell.

People, planks, and ceiling tiles swirled through the dark. Then the floor flared up. The flames were around my neck. The heat scorched my skin. The stench of singed hair filled my nostrils. Soon, I'd be transformed into an ethereal being, a wisp of smoke. Miraculously, a gust of hot air opened a path through the fire. I sucked up a lung full of smoke and leapt through the flames toward the stairs. I galloped down the steps two at a time, my arms flailing into the bedlam ahead to clear any unseen obstacles hidden in the smoke.

I hit the last step on the stairs into the lobby of the main floor when the ceiling collapsed. The circle of fire above had burned right through the floor. More burning planks flew through the air. Flames encircled me once again. Sparks snapped at my head. The Ellington refused to go down alone.

Smoke swallowed the foyer. It consumed the flames. Hot air blasted through the burning hole in the ceiling. The smoke punched from above like a giant black fist and released a ball of fire that exploded, propelling me through the door onto the sidewalk, into the violent spray of the firehoses. I gasped. Stumbled to the ground. Breathless and relieved.

Two firefighters in long black coats ran from behind their defensive lines, grabbed my arms and dragged me through the puddles on the sidewalk toward safety.

"Backdraft — the building's going to blow," one yelled to the other.

There was a thunderous noise from within. One fireball followed another. The roof of the Ellington lifted from its moorings before the entire structure sagged and collapsed into itself. It was doubtful the roaches survived.

They took me to a makeshift triage tent down the street crammed with a small army of harried emergency workers who'd been kicked out of bed to deal with the anxious Ellington survivors. Someone in a lab coat peered into my eyes with a flashlight. Had me cough. Listened to my lungs through a stethoscope. Hit my knee with a rubber hammer. Someone else with a clipboard gave me fifty bucks and a strip of paper with an address. Arrangements had been made for survivors to go to motels across the city and await further instructions. I signed a form. I moved along.

Around noon, a taxi took me from the processing centre past the smouldering ruins of the Ellington out to Kingston Road. The car was clean and air-conditioned. A cool lime-scented air freshener dangled from the mirror. The posted licence said the driver's name was Jaffar Malouf. The photo didn't look anything like him. It didn't matter. I was safe. Mozart played on the radio. Every time I closed my eyes, the flames enveloped me. The stench of smoke seared my nostrils. The chaos of bodies in the dark lingered. It was good to be alive. The driver gripped the wheel with both hands and drove slow. Other cars whizzed past us. Some honked.

After a while, the man who wasn't Jaffar Malouf said, "You were in the fire this morning, sir?"

I nodded. "Yes."

"Such a terrible thing." He wagged his head in disbelief. "It was all on the news. It's only by the grace of God you are all still alive. Who would do such a terrible thing?"

"What do you mean?" I said.

Outside, strip malls and used car dealerships floated past the window. This was an unknown part of the city to me, a suburban land of drive-through burger joints, nail salons, body shops, and hasty marts. A place you wouldn't go unless you had to — unless life dealt you a shitty card.

"The fire, sir," he said. "On the news they interviewed the fire marshal. He said it looked like arson. There's going to be an investigation."

"They always say that," I said. "It was an old building. In the basement laundry you could see exposed wires. Frayed."

The driver looked at me through the mirror. "That may be correct, sir. Still they're saying that someone was seen around the building before the fire started."

"Someone was seen?"

"Yes, and a suspicious vehicle drove away."

"That's what they're saying?"

"Yes, sir. It's a bloody mystery, to be sure."

"People see shit all the time," I said. "They saw flying saucers and Bigfoot in the woods."

The driver chuckled. "Yes, that's true. But these photos are more convincing."

"Photos?"

"Yes, sir. Security camera from the Mighty Meaty Burgers across the way. The footage is already on the morning news."

"You've seen this?"

"No sir, I've been driving cab."

The car wheeled into a parking lot. Propped up against a piece of cinder block was a hand-painted sign that read: *We buy Gold. Old & Broken*. An arrow pointed toward a small strip mall next door. Much of the lot was taken up by an industrial garbage bin cryptically tagged *Moze On* in huge fluorescent-pink letters. The driver stopped the meter.

"This is your destination, sir."

A kid in high-tops with a steel bolt through his nose wandered by with a cardboard box. The overhead sign read: *Havanap Motel*. The word *Vacancy* was painted next to it in equally big peeling letters. A vending machine promised *Ice old* drinks — the *C* in *Cold* having burned out. Home.

"Fire guy?" the desk clerk said.

He checked my name against a list on his desk. Satisfied, he nodded. *Love* and *Hate* were tattooed across his knuckles.

"You're in 101, the unit at the end. Right by the road." He handed over a key. "There's a laundromat across the street and a convenience store next door, by the pawnshop in the strip mall. We change the sheets and towels once a week. If you need more, you wash it yourself. The insurance company only pays for the room."

"Any of my neighbours here?" Akinwole and Rachel were on my mind.

"I guess," he said. "I got the place filled with people from the fire."

I felt lost. I'd ended up in no man's land with nothing.

"How do I get into the city?"

"There's a bus stop across the street. Takes an hour when there's no traffic. It comes every forty-five minutes. Enjoy your stay."

Outside the office a rainbow-stained puddle of water and gasoline left my sneakers cold and squishy. There were twelve grey rooms, each with a dented aluminum door facing the parking lot. They were set off the street in a semicircle, six on either side of the office. A few of the windows were cracked, held together with faded masking tape.

Four lanes of traffic zipped by directly in front of the motel. Beside my door, Akinwole rocked on a straight-backed metal chair. He drank Coke from a can.

"Paul," he said, "we continue to be neighbours into the next life."

I said, "You made it."

"Yes," he said. "They say everyone got out alive."

"The cab driver told me it was arson."

Akinwole shook his head. "Who would do a thing like that? Besides, the wiring was shit."

"Supposedly, there's security cam footage."

"That sounds outrageous."

"Do our rooms have TV?"

"Oh yes, they are comfortable."

"You have low standards." I struggled with the key.

Akinwole grinned. "Sure, so I am easily pleased."

He leaned back in his chair. He crushed the empty Coke can in his massive hand. "This is the life. Living free in a motel. The Havanap. I like it." From his tone, who knows if he was joking.

At first the lock wouldn't turn. Frustrated, I banged it with the back of my fist a couple of times until it finally swung open.

Inside, the room was sparse and clean. Linoleum floors. Vinyl blinds. A small dresser riddled with cigarette burns. A lamp by the bed. An old rotary phone. I flipped on the TV, peeled off my wet socks, and propped myself up in the lumpy bed.

The barking heads at CP24 News liked these local disaster stories. They ran them in rotation every twenty minutes, all day long, between the live traffic cameras and the weather graphics (rain the next five days). It didn't take long for the story to come up.

The reporter was breathless. Wendy Kirpal, earlier on the scene. In the background, the Ellington burned. Over her shoulder, the firefighters dragged me out moments before the roof exploded. Wendy Kirpal ducked. The Ellington collapsed. They showed it from their helicopter. Eye in the sky news. Smoke swirled up from the scene. Text crawled across the bottom of the screen: *HISTORICAL BUILDING BURNS IN EARLY-MORNING FIRE*. Then back to Wendy Kirpal, now in the safety of the newsroom, with a CP24 exclusive: footage from the security camera across the street.

It was like the cab driver said, except impossible to say who or what was in the image. The Sasquatch films were better. The camera took a frame every ten seconds. Grainy black and white still shots. Wendy Kirpal talked us through it. One shape, she assured us, was a vehicle pulled up to the Ellington. She said it could've been a truck or SUV. It could've been a car. It could've been a yacht, for that matter. Whatever it was, a shadowy figure stepped out. It moved in the direction of the Ellington. Wendy Kirpal noted the figure was back within eight minutes and then the thing moved away. Moments later, the Ellington burst into flames. Wendy Kirpal promised us that in the days ahead, police experts would extract more detailed information from these pictures, and when they did, CP24 would be there with the update on this tragic destruction of a city heritage building. Back to you, Jay.

Anyone could have set fire to the Ellington. The owners themselves had motive. The land was more valuable than the building. The pictures proved nothing. Akinwole was right, the wiring in the basement was shit. Still, the Russians had to be considered. They'd have been pissed off after my attack, and we were almost out of time on the Courtney clock.

I phoned Hornsmith to tell him what had happened and warn him we could be targets. He answered on the first ring like he'd been waiting for my call.

"Latour," he said when he heard my voice, "you're alive."

"I'm alive," I said.

"That's good, because Courtney wants to meet. Lunch. Day after tomorrow. Watch. He's going to settle. Go to the tailor and get some new clothes. We need to look sharp."

Whoever was out to kill us seemed more pressing. I said, "Anyone hanging around your house? Strange cars parked on the street?"

"I wouldn't notice that. Why?"

"Because if it was arson at the Ellington, Courtney's thugs should be high on the suspect list."

Hornsmith laughed. "They're only capable of minor theatrics. Go get some new clothes and stop looking for bogeymen. You're going to make yourself a nervous wreck."

"Courtney's thugs are off their leash. He's lost control," I said. "We should terminate Courtney's relationship with the Business."

"Fire the client?"

"Exactly. Our dealings with him are starting to have negative undertones."

Hornsmith wasn't so sure. "Let's see what he says at lunch."

FIFTEEN

Everyone's Out

THE BUS DOWNTOWN took forty-five minutes, like the tattooed freak at the motel said it would. The plan was to visit Mr. Gupta, a second-generation tailor with an inconspicuous shop on Cumberland Avenue. The same shop that had kitted me out a hundred years ago, during my early days with the Business. Set on one of the most expensive shopping streets in the city, it was a walk-up above a lingerie place.

Inside smelled of sandalwood and suggested luxurious afternoons on the shady deck of a varnished yacht. It was a haven of fabric bolts arranged on floor-to-ceiling teak shelves. Patterns for made-to-measure suits waited on a cutting table. Glass display cases featured linen shirts, cashmere sweaters, and silk pyjamas. Deep leather armchairs and free-standing mirrors were arranged so a person could take the time required to select the proper wardrobe for any occasion. In the back, a chrome-plated Italian espresso machine stood ready to serve high-test caffeine to the weary shopper.

A tall man in his late sixties with a hunchback, Mr. Gupta sported salt and pepper eyebrows the size of a snowy owl's wings. His mouth was twisted into a perpetual smile, the scar of a life catering to the whims of others. The cut of his tailored lightweight woollen suit hid most of his disfigured back in nips and folds of hand-stitched perfection. Mr. Gupta traded in discretion and secrets. Business was by appointment only. He never spoke of his other clients, which gave the impression of exclusivity.

My unwashed sweatshirt and jeans reeked of smoke — an affront to Mr. Gupta's sartorial sensibility.

"With respect, sir," he said, "you're looking like a hobo. You could be living in a Dumpster. Are you on undercover assignment?"

"My apartment burned down, and I'm living in a motel on the edge of town," I said. "I have no possessions."

"The Ellington fire." His giant eyebrows flapped as he nodded. "It was on the television. Unbelievable no one was hurt. Is it true what they say? That it was arson?"

Everyone loves a crime story.

"That's what they're saying," I said. "They have some security video, which doesn't prove anything. The building had faulty wiring."

He clasped his manicured fingers as if in prayer and leaned into his words. "It seems everyone is taking an interest. And not only on the news, I mean. I had my supper at Bella Noce last evening, sitting at my usual spot by the bar, and I overheard some Russian gentlemen talking about it."

The Bella Noce was an expensive restaurant down the street from Mr. Gupta's shop. Known for its high-end prostitutes and international criminals. Suppliers of military equipment, cocaine, slaves, blood diamonds, and so forth. Outside, black-jeaned valets who sported earpieces like they were secret agents on a high security detail instead of punks who parked cars shuffled about a small fleet of Ferraris, Aston Martins, and Escalades. Mr. Gupta trolled the place, no doubt, for newly moneyed clients.

"Perhaps you misunderstood. No one's interested in an old place like that," I said. It had to be a coincidence. Mr. Gupta didn't even understand Russian, as far as I knew.

Mr. Gupta pulled some pants from a drawer and matched them to various shirts. He displayed everything on the cutting table.

"Equally interesting," he said, "another man joined them. They ordered a bottle of champagne and toasted the burning of your building."

"Toasted?"

"Indeed, they were merry. Slapping each other on the back and much pinching of cheeks. Now, take off your dirty trousers and see what I want you to try."

Whatever else he had to say was lost to me. The idea that Courtney's thugs were connected to the fire jumped from suspicion to serious possibility. Or worse. Like some type of bat soup flu shooting from outbreak to pandemic overnight, my panic needle snapped to red. Measures had to be taken. Right away. They were out to kill me.

Mr. Gupta took no notice of my spiralling mood. He talked me into a new suit, some shirts, new jeans, underwear, socks, belts, and a windbreaker because, he noted, autumn would soon be upon us. He apologized that the suit had to be an off-the-rack job because there was no time for a proper tailor-made. I signed the invoice, which would be billed to the Business. Then, with my new wardrobe wrapped in tissue paper and folded into brown bags, I descended the stairs back to the street.

Outside, danger skulked in the reeds. The situation needed a cool head, not panic, which I would've kept had I not been so committed to survival. I zoned out. I pictured Courtney's thugs outside Mr. Gupta's shop hauling me into the back of their Escalade. Bolt cutters on my thumb. There was Courtney with my thumb in a shoebox before he flushed it down the toilet.

Distracted, I started down the street in search of the subway entrance I thought was at hand. Keep moving, I told myself, a moving target is harder to hit. So, I was startled when Marla charged out of the lingerie shop and crashed into me. On impact, she toppled to the ground. A bag of lacy red panties exploded over the sidewalk.

"Hey, fuck you!" she said, wild hair in her face. "Watch where you're going."

Marla was riled. Marla had her street face on. Marla was ready to slug somebody.

"Marla," I said. I stopped my flight to collect her silks.

She blinked. Stunned. When she recognized me, she said, "Didn't I just dump you?"

I said, "I guess so."

We both laughed a little. Awkward.

"I didn't expect to bump into you so soon," she said.

"Weird," I said, "running into you like this."

We laughed some more at our dim wit.

I said, "You all right?"

She straightened her clothes. "No harm done," she said.

I scrunched her girlie underthings into the bag and handed it back. For a moment, a terrible yearning to feel her skin on mine again eclipsed all my fears.

"Sorry about this," I said.

Her face sparkled in the late sun. A long black shawl swept over her shoulders like a slow wave on the open sea. She gave me a once-over.

"You're looking dapper," she said. "Bruises healing. New threads. Handsome, indeed."

"I needed some clothes. Lost everything in the fire the night you left."

"I heard the news," she said. "I didn't set fire to your building."

"No," I said, "but your Russians could've done it. I have a bad feeling about those guys."

"Those two Russians? From that night?"

"They didn't want you. It's me they're after. Hornsmith has us in a fix, and these guys are involved. He's going to die of cancer any day now. Which leaves me their only target." I glanced up and down the street. A sitting duck. "It's a complicated story. For now, I need to get out of sight. Lie low. I wish I could get out of town."

She took my arm. Her eyes batted like some serious little bird.

"I've got it," she said. "Me and the band are going to Los Angeles next week. You could come along."

"Didn't you dump me? How would that work?" Desperation drove me to consider any scheme that promised escape.

"I did," she said, "but if you're in trouble, you can count on me. You're my lover. I won't turn my back on you because I dumped you. That's how this works."

It seemed Lover Man had made good on his promise of a shot at a record deal. He had something set up in LA. The whole band was going for a few months. There were gigs to play and a studio to record in. Unbelievable to me that they'd sound any better in a controlled space.

"He's already there," she said. "The thing is he's got this car that he'd like down there. You could deliver it."

There had to be a hitch. Lover Man was a criminal. A drug-dealing smuggler. A killer and a punk. The car would likely be loaded with dope. Marla could be in on it. Setting me up. The idiot greeting card writer/dope courier. Saying she wasn't mad to fool me but really so pissed that she'd send me on a death ride dope run for Lover Man. Still, it could be better than Courtney's Russian mob rejects.

"Drive his car to LA? And what would I do once I got there?"

"Stay with us till you're bored or it's safe to come back. What do you say?"

An insane plan. To hole up with Marla, Lover Man, and the band hundreds of miles from home. What good could ever come of that?

"Where's the car?" I said.

"Here, in town. I'll get the address and call you," she said. "That is, if the Russians don't get you first." She laughed and touched my cheek.

Sure, she was teasing me. And it could've been a trick. It didn't matter. I wanted to believe what I wanted to believe. I told myself she still cared. Imagined we still had a shot. So what if that idiotic notion was wrong? Even if we didn't have a chance, it made no difference. If Marla was offering a way out based on some lovers' code she felt bound to, I'd take it. It wasn't like there was a better plan afoot.

"My phone burned up in the fire. I'm in a motel called the Havanap, in Scarborough."

Across the street, the entrance to the subway opened up. It'd been there all along. With no sign of bad guys around, I kissed her and made my move.

"I'll find you," she said.

In my view, Courtney became unhappy because of our attempts to blackmail him. The way Hornsmith called it, Courtney was a victim of his own greed; he had a soft spot, which we mined. It was a matter of perspective. The only undeniable fact was that our business with Courtney had run aground. For him and for us. The whole matter needed re-evaluation before Hornsmith died, leaving me holding the bag. A meeting would settle it.

We met at a restaurant on King East. White linen tablecloths. Black-bow-tied penguins. Courtney waited for us at a corner table. He looked like he'd come from a tennis match: a yellow sweater over his shoulder to complement his yellow polo shirt. He played with a black opal embedded in a band of gold around his middle finger. A benign smile creased his face.

Our entrance caused a stir with the staff because Hornsmith arrived in a navy-blue suit with golden epaulets braided over his right shoulder. He was on a cane. That bit was not part of his theatre. Also new since his escape from St. Mike's was his hair. He'd shaved it right to the scalp and combed out his beard to puff it out like a hairy nest. No doubt he believed it made him look like a distinguished admiral. From my days at art school, Van Gogh's crazy postmaster came to mind.

In his haste to show his deference to Admiral Hornsmith, the maître d' stumbled over his own feet and dropped the wine list on the marble floor. The clatter stirred Courtney from his trance.

"Gentlemen." He rose and waved the opal-ringed hand over the table like a magician at the outset of some complicated trick. "Please, make yourselves comfortable."

Hornsmith stood by the table. He offered a slight bow from the waist.

"Dr. Courtney, always a pleasure."

Courtney paused to digest the vision of Hornsmith in this new incarnation while the maître d' pulled out a chair. Courtney resumed his own place. The opal-ringed hand checked the back of his head for a misplaced hair before it swooped over to the bottle of rosé that lay on ice in a silver bucket next to the table.

"Wine?" He pointed the neck at us like a weapon. "It's from Niagara. Palatable."

I extended a glass. Hornsmith declined with a faint wave of his finger. Courtney poured us each a glass and drank. He rolled his tongue over his lips, which returned to their blissful smile.

"Let me get right to the point," he said. "I'm going to be forthright with you, because I'm no longer comfortable with the direction we are going." He shifted in his seat, leaned over the table, and looked us each in the eye. "People from all walks of life come through my clinic. Some of them unpleasant sorts. I keep my contacts up because sometimes you need an unpleasant person for an unpleasant job. You understand. Recently, I hired some people who were supposed to deliver a message to you. A warning. I'd hoped to teach you fellows a lesson for meddling in my business and thinking you could so easily take my money. Regrettably, these characters have overreached their assignment. On their own initiative, they intend to harm you."

It sounded like a long-winded preamble to peace terms. The idea inspired a kink in my neck that I tried to massage out while I listened.

"The fact is, these people I hired to deal with you have approached me with more dangerous and, dare I say, more imaginative plans for your discomfort." He dabbed a glint of sweat from his upper lip with a white napkin. "In time, I fear they'll propose ways to kill you. Of course, I don't entertain these notions myself, nor do I condone them. We're colleagues, for God's sake. Admittedly in difficult times. I've already told them I shall withhold their final payment if they continue in this manner. In the end, I fear I'll be paying them to leave me alone. I'm sure of it. Meanwhile, there's little I can do to discourage their campaign of terror. For whatever reason, they've taken a genuine disliking toward you. I'm sorry."

He'd unleashed the hounds. Now he absolved himself from the whole mess. Claimed this wasn't his fault. Called us colleagues. Said he was sorry.

"I'll have the soup," said Hornsmith after some silence. "Excuse me, I need to wash my hands."

He stood up, offered us another brief bow, and disappeared toward the back of the restaurant.

Courtney eyed me over his glass. He slurped his wine and grunted to suggest it was to his taste. I finished the last of the bottle and said nothing. My indifference prompted him to wave over a waiter. He smiled and ordered another bottle of wine and the lamb. I asked for the steak frites and the carrot ginger soup for Hornsmith.

"I liked you better as the stuttering writer," Courtney said after the waiter departed.

"Fuck you, Courtney," I said. "See how you feel when they kick the crap out of you and burn down your house."

His lips twitched like he had a mouth full of vinegar.

I ached to stick a fork in his shiny forehead. Gouge out his eyes with a soup spoon. Clobber him senseless with his armchair. Only the refined atmosphere of the place curbed my blood lust. Instead, I stared ahead in silence with my best simpleton face.

I reflected on Marla's offer to leave town. What with Courtney's confession that he was no longer in control of his thugs, and Hornsmith's descent into dementia and death, it was time to leave. A gloomy notion, since I had nowhere to go except into murkier waters. The car deal could be a trap. Maybe the only difference between Marla's criminal pals and Courtney's thugs was that Lover Man and Eagle Creek weren't out to kill me. Yet. Frustrated, I felt I needed to hang out with a better class of criminal.

Hornsmith stayed away for ages. By the time he returned from his visit to the toilet, the food had arrived. I detected a trace of white powder in his beard under his reddened nostrils.

"Soup." He pulled at his pearl cufflinks and giggled. "Good."

Courtney bit into the lamb. Blood trickled down his hairless chin. "There is one other thing." His mouth rolled, full of red meat. "I've been approached by the man named Trang. You know each other. He says his family has money in Vietnam. He wants to make a substantial investment in the Washington project."

Hornsmith puffed up. "Trang's our client. We brought him to you."

Courtney swallowed and cleared his throat with a gulp of wine. “You’re a dating service. Trang is looking for a long-term business relationship. That’s me. You’re out.”

The steak was pan-grilled in butter and garlic. A perfect medium rare. Coarse salt and black peppercorns ground over top. Freshly made mayo with the fries. The food was the only good thing about the afternoon so far. If Courtney had it right, Trang had changed sides. Cut us out of our own deal. With Hornsmith on the outs, Trang proved pragmatic in the face of facts.

“He’s police,” I said.

Hornsmith tapped the table for emphasis. He said, “Police with dubious intentions. Probably corrupt and certainly dangerous.”

“Who cares?” Courtney said. “I have a financing partner now. The project that stalled due to your inactivity is back on track because I seized an opportunity. I’ve closed a deal you almost let slip by.”

To me, Trang was indeed a dangerous cat who’d probably lured Courtney into a Faustian pact. Trang’s motives were unclear. So was the real source of his money. He’d allowed us to know only part of the picture. He had an agenda. The Trang Agenda. Courtney swallowed it. Good riddance to them both.

“You need us,” said Hornsmith, “because part of our service is to determine the suitability of the people who come to you. We’re your filters. We protect you. If you’re determined to move ahead with this, we’ll take the high road. Go with God. And if it should come to an undesirable outcome, we warned you.”

“Thank you,” Courtney said. “Lunch is on me today.”

Afterward, we said our goodbyes in the rain on King Street. My new suit was sodden. A crystal raindrop dangled from Hornsmith's nose.

"I told you everything would be all right." He scanned the afternoon rush hour for a westbound cab. "We have the upper hand."

"I'm not sure how," I said. "Courtney's hijacked our only other client, and he's unleashed a pair of criminals he can no longer control. How's that a win?"

"Where you see the leaves, I see the sky in between," Hornsmith said. "You need to take another perspective, Latour, set new priorities. We're free to chart a new course."

The way I understood it, we'd lost everything. I shivered in the rain. For once, I couldn't share Hornsmith's enthusiasm. To me, the future looked bleak.

There was no sky between the leaves. There was no way that was clear. There was only trouble ahead.

The next few days were spent holed up in the Havanap Motel with the blinds closed, living like a fugitive. The TV on. A stack of greasy takeout boxes grew on the floor. I felt brittle and blue. Abandoned by luck. Kicked to the curb. Unwanted. I couldn't go far into the world in case the Russian thugs found me. Besides, there was nowhere to go. Hornsmith hadn't been to the office since the night the ambulance took him away. There was nothing to do there. My only hope was for Marla's call while I dreamt of the warm Pacific surf. Those days, that's how it was.

When the phone finally rang, it wasn't Marla. Instead, it was Katherine, Hornsmith's wife, who'd tracked me down to the Havanap Motel. She said the number was scribbled in his notebook. Turned out I was easily found.

She sounded calm.

"He's tripped," she said. "He's fallen down the stairs. You should come, if you can."

From her tone, I sensed no urgency. I should've splurged for a cab. I didn't. So, by the time I'd dressed, travelled the bus, ridden the subway, and strolled the last bit to his house, Hornsmith was no longer there.

"I'm sorry you missed him," Katherine said at the door. "For a while it looked like he'd stay."

She led the way into the living room, gaunt and pale in her tartan housecoat. I glanced around the familiar room, unsure what she meant. His books were all lined straight on their shelves, the coffee table was oiled and polished. In the corner, his unfinished chess game waited on an end table. I sat down next to her on the sofa. She wrapped her arms around herself and spoke like there was someone in the next room she couldn't disturb.

"He was walking around upstairs in his smoking jacket when he stubbed his toe on the railing and came down the stairs," she said. "I was sitting right here when it happened."

"Came down? Like how?"

"He fell. It sounded like a big watermelon rolling down the stairs." She choked back a sob and pointed to the landing near the front door. "When he landed there at the bottom, he gave a little laugh and said, 'Oh shit.'"

She shook her head in disbelief. I looked to where she pointed. A bit of worn oak floor with a Persian runner. I couldn't picture it. The calm house was silent, except for a cheery little radio playing pop tunes somewhere on another floor. She sat motionless, her arms still wrapped around her torso.

"What shape was he in?" I said.

"He couldn't move. I called 911 before I called you. When they came, they strapped him to a board. He died before they could lift him."

"He died?" This was a misunderstanding. The notion that Hornsmith would exit on an accidental fall down the stairs was inconceivable. I'd expected something more elegant. More theatrical. More in line with the way he'd lived. Not a mishap on the stairs. She must have had it wrong.

She said, "He broke his back in three places."

"Shit. That's terrible."

"Not so bad," she said, "because it's unlikely he felt it."

"Why? Did he go that fast?"

Her eyes teared up. She held her hand to her mouth.

"He was so drugged that it's likely he had no idea where he was."

"Drugged?"

"Yes," she said, "the paramedics said he was high. They said his pupils were dilated and he had some type of crack pipe in his pocket. They showed it to me."

"That doesn't sound like him," I managed without much conviction. "Did they say what he took?"

"They couldn't tell by looking at him. Later, after they left, I found a package of white powder in his dresser," she said. "I don't suppose you know about that?"

"No, I don't."

Her voice wavered. "My husband was no angel, in so many ways. And that speaks volumes about your own character. You might fool other people. You don't fool me. I've been around this business for a long time. You're all cut from the same cloth. You're liars."

I hadn't killed him, even if my hand was in it somewhere. I kept it cool. Lying didn't make sense anymore. Not that the full story had to be told, either. Still, the situation called for a little clarity. A shred of truth to help her get the right picture and to contribute to my own absolution.

"It came from a business connection," I said, "a new client. He's in the restaurant business. He wants to get into the hospital project with us." From the look on her face, I saw she had no idea what that meant. "Anyway, he seems connected. He offered up the dope for when the pain became unbearable."

She stood up and looked down at me.

"I don't care about your schemes," she said. "I have my own problems. I'd like you to close down the business. Take whatever you need to carry on with your life and sell off the rest. I'm done with all of it."

I returned to the bench where we'd first met. Streetcars clanged, loud as ever. Pigeons still picked at trash on the street. People still hustled toward their destinies. Nowhere was there a single sign that he'd passed through. It was impossible to grasp that he'd left. For good. He'd eluded us. Checked out without paying his bill. Made a new plan. Slipped down the stairs.

In life, he could only have been trusted to serve his own crazy agenda. Sometimes, you summon a person like that. Against your better judgement, you let them in because something you need is on offer. That was Hornsmith. He'd revealed what I couldn't figure out for myself. He'd shown me how to break free. By example, he'd demonstrated how to live by the courage of your own convictions. Make up your own rules.

Create your own reality. Hornsmith showed me a person could be free. For that, I loved him, and I would miss him.

Air brakes hissed. Jackhammers pounded. The air tasted of gritty exhaust. Hot dogs and garbage soaked the hot afternoon. I rubbed my eyes with the back of my hand. The traffic grew thicker until the world around me ground to a halt, stopped by a red and yellow taxi making a U-turn to get a passenger on the other side of the street. Horns blared. People shouted.

The honking and shouting all subsided when the cab door slammed shut — an exclamation point at the end of a noisy outburst of furious frustration. Wheels started to turn again. Slowly at first. Then back up to speed, the rupture in the flow resolved. The moment passed. World order restored.

The cab, now back in the stream, rolled past my bench, and the passenger window came down. Inside, a glimpse of someone silhouetted in the back. I'm certain it was Hornsmith in his favourite Sherlock Holmes outfit. He leaned out. His beard rippled in the wind. That famous grin. He pointed his finger at me. I thought I heard his voice faintly over the traffic.

"Your shoes. Get new shoes. Carry on."

Stunned, my breath stopped. Then, he waved. The window rolled up and the taxi vanished into the flow.

SIXTEEN

The Rubber Hits the Road

WE WANDERED around for a while without success until it started to look like Marla had given us the wrong address. Then, Akinwole spotted the rusted red and white sign swinging from a post: *MYERS MIRACLE MOTORS: SPECIALISTS IN EUROPEAN CARS — VOLVO, BMW, MERCEDES, ETC. ALSO DETRIOT [sic] BUILT CARS PRE-1975.* A few weedy sumac trees obscured the building from the street. Iron bars secured the windows. Security cameras pointed down from every corner of the flat roof. We entered through the open garage door. Inside smelled of oil and rubber. Cool chrome-plated wrenches hung in orderly rows along the wall. A sleepy pug eyed us from a blanket under the workbench.

There were two cars in the place, one outlined under a tarp. That was likely the one we'd come for, because the other was a mangled BMW. The mechanic on the Bimmer was a short, muscular black guy in orange coveralls. He sucked his upper lip where his front teeth used to be. He thumped out dents in the car door with a rubber mallet. He paid no attention to us.

Two guys owned the place. Twins. They sat behind the counter in the office off to the side of the garage. Built like sumo wrestlers with tiny brown eyes like chocolate raisins set deep into fleshy close-cropped heads. They both sported lightning bolts shaved into their temples. They wore white T-shirts with the sleeves rolled up. Red suspenders held up grey trousers. You couldn't tell them apart, except one had *Barry* embroidered in red letters over his heart, the other *Ben*.

After introductions, Ben asked about my connection to Lover Man.

"I'm a friend of a friend," I said, reluctant to say more about my relationship with Marla.

Barry pointed to Akinwole. "What the fuck does that make him? The friend of the friend of a friend, I suppose?"

I shrugged. "I suppose."

Akinwole stared into the overhead security camera. Expressionless. He flared his nose. Ben and Barry ignored his chill and continued.

"Did anyone tell you what the deal is?" Ben eyed me like he was sizing up a new wreck.

"It needs to be delivered to Los Angeles in one piece. It's his favourite car."

"His favourite car?"

In unison, Barry and Ben let out wet gasps, and for a moment it seemed they might be choking, until I grasped that this passed for laughter. Barry unclogged first.

He said, "This isn't any fucking car we're talking about. This is a rare eighty-five-thousand-dollar 1968 Firebird 400 HO."

After Ben throttled down his own phlegmatic eruption, he said, "The Ram Air II model. First generation, coke-bottle design. V8. Four hundred horsepower. That's a monster car for 1968."

"That's a monster car for any time," Barry said. "Can you drive a stick, son? Because this car has the four-speed floor shifter."

"Yes, I can," I said. Farm vehicles surely counted. Old pickups and tractors. No hot rods. Same vintage, though. It couldn't be that different. Clutch. Stick. One. Two. Three. Four. How hard could it be?

"Well, let's see some ID. We're sure as shit not turning this thing over without knowing who the fuck you are."

I handed Ben my driver's licence. Barry dialed the phone while Ben waddled my licence over to an ancient Xerox machine. It rattled, hummed, and flashed. Duplication of my identity achieved by clunky electronic alchemy. Over the din, Barry shouted on the phone.

"Yeah, boss. He's got some African fella with him. Doesn't say much. In fact, he hasn't said anything. It's possible he don't speak English. Okay."

After he cradled the receiver, he pointed a sausage finger at Akinwole.

"Boss says to get his ID."

Akinwole cleared his throat. "If you care to see my identification, you will not be happy."

Barry and Ben raised their eyebrows in unison.

"If I had it with me, which I do not, I would see no reason to share it with you."

"How about because we don't know a rat's ass about you?" Ben flexed his arms.

Akinwole blinked fast a couple of times like there was dust in his eyes. Then he said, "Something is unusual about your request. I am not a person who needs to show my papers to people who operate a garage because their boss says so. Unless something is going on here that is not apparent."

His quiet tone had them all fired up, blubbering protest noises. Akinwole raised his hands before their clamour could form into words.

"Your business is not with me," he said, "and I have no business with you. File an official request with Immigration if you wish to see my documents."

"Listen, buddy," said Barry, "these are the rules. It's that or the car stays here."

"This does not interest me," Akinwole said. "It is none of your concern who I am. Where I come from, only police ask people for identification. You are not police, are you?"

Barry's knuckles were white from gripping the counter. Ben tripped over a garbage pail on his way back from the Xerox machine. Dirty paper coffee cups and balls of wadded paper spilled across the floor.

"Look," I said, "my friend isn't part of this. He's not coming with me. There's no reason to harass him. It's still a free country. Leave him alone."

"He's not driving?" said Barry.

"He's not going?" said Ben.

"No," I said. "He's keeping me company today. Can we get on with this?"

Ben and Barry exchanged a glance and shrugged. Ben handed back my driver's licence. He said, "If this brother stays home, we can get on with business."

That resolved it. Calm was restored faster than it had been disturbed. Barry lifted a hinged section of the counter and squeezed himself through the opening, his fatty rolls overflowing the banks of Formica.

"Follow me," he said. "I got something to show you."

Inside the garage, Akinwole held me back.

"These men," he said, "something is not correct about them. I have a bad feeling."

In a whisper I said, "The last time you had a bad feeling was about the witch upstairs who turned out to be a cute girl making pottery."

He started to protest when Barry called us over.

"Look at this baby. You've never seen anything like this."

Barry and the toothless guy in the orange coveralls pulled off the tarp. In the shadowy garage, the car sparkled, a shiny black wonder. It was a convertible with two menacing air scoops and a tach mounted into the hood. Red go-fast stripes trailed along both sides. Matching fat red-walled low-profile tires on silver rims. Dual chrome-tipped exhausts poked out the back.

"Not a lot of these babies ever hit the market," said Ben, who'd shuffled up behind us. "We spent months rebuilding the motor. All the original serial numbers still match."

"The only non-stock upgrades are the Fiero front seats," Barry said. "Custom red leather."

I circled the car. It was more like a sculpture than an actual automobile. Lover Man wouldn't use a car like this to move dope. Stealth wasn't part of its profile. It wanted to be seen, touched, and examined. Better to trick out some old Mazda sedan or an ordinary-looking panel van for a dope run. Something to blend in with the traffic. Only an idiot would trap a car like this. And I didn't take Lover Man for an idiot. My doubts diminished. My fears were allayed. This ride seemed to be all Marla said it was.

Akinwole, however, had reservations. He squinted and shook his head.

"If it is such a great car," he said, "why does your boss not truck it to California? That would be safer."

"We're going to break in the rebuilt engine," Barry said, "so by the time he gets it, it's ready to drive."

"Is that difficult?" I said. Farm equipment, beaters, and rental cars never required special treatment.

Ben stroked the trunk. "It's a breeze. Run it five hundred miles under twenty-five hundred RPMs. Then run it hard for a couple hundred more. Like at six or seven thousand RPMs. After, change the oil. Synthetic. And use only high-test fuel with a lead additive. Keeps the valves coated and stops them from burning."

I laughed, nervous. "I'm never going to get this."

"You don't have to," said Barry. "We're monitoring the car from here." He tossed me a cellphone. "We're going to be calling you with specific instructions. If you fuck this up, you'll be into us for eighty-five large."

"And," said Ben, now beside his twin brother, "if you disappear, we'll find you. There's a GPS tracking unit built in. If you steal it, the boss'll send people to find you and kill you. You can be sure."

They looked at me and waited like they wanted a pledge from me. Akinwole snorted. I struggled to find something to say.

"All right," Barry said, "enough talk. We're fucking with you, kid. About the killing. Don't sweat it. You get the picture. Don't screw this up. Let's have a look at the car."

Ben squeezed behind the wheel and fired up the engine. Deafening thunder exploded from the exhaust pipes. The pug under the bench yawned. Ben waved me over.

"There's no trick to this thing," he shouted over the engine. "Use high-octane fuel. You have a week to get it to California."

Hornsmith had figured there was under a hundred thousand dollars in the Business's account. So, I wrote a cheque to cash for ninety thousand. It bounced. There were two signed blanks left. I tried one for fifty thousand and one for twenty. I certified them at the bank. They both cleared. The Persian rugs, the leather couches, the armchairs, and the fancy desk went for another seven thousand dollars. The rest of the office went to the dump. I was free of the Business with seventy-seven thousand dollars. My plan was on track. For now.

Something else became clear. Shirley Rose in Detroit and her Dipshit Kid haunted me. Someone had to tell her he wouldn't be back. I toyed with her picture. I reread her letter. On the back of the envelope, there was a Detroit return address and a name: Shirley Rose Holbert. How had she ended up on the far end of his story? I guessed she liked it like that. Her and the Dipshit Kid in Detroit. Hornsmith far enough away not to be a permanent deal. It sounded complicated. One thing was for sure: the arrangements people live with only make sense from the inside.

I'd fed Hornsmith the dope. I'd taken the money. To square myself with him, as my final farewell, I decided to stop in Detroit. Look up Shirley Rose and the Dipshit Kid. See how they were doing. Break the bad news and leave her with some cash. Twenty-five thousand dollars. I'd already mailed Hornsmith's wife a cheque for twenty-five thousand. The cash had been for the taking. I'd taken it. To appease my conscience, I'd tempered my greed and decided to split it with the women. They had earned it. They were his partners, too, after all.

The rest of the money was my stake. Something to set myself up with once Lover Man's Firebird was delivered. A down payment on a food truck or a couple of vending machines. Something that would pay for itself. A cash drip. Cash. Drip. That sounded good.

The balmy summer weather lingered throughout September. The stale room in the Havanap sweltered. The air conditioner didn't work. Sweat dripped down my back. For relief, I propped open the aluminum door with a chair. The map of America, land of the free, home of the brave, sprawled across my bed: Amarillo, Memphis, Chattanooga, Nashville, Indiana, Flagstaff, Albuquerque, Mesa, Houston, Charleston, Colorado Springs, LA. The names rolled through my head. Exhilarating. Exotic.

Highways were in my blood. My grandparents had lived in the middle of nowhere between Saskatchewan and Alberta along the Trans-Canada Highway, one of the longest, loneliest roads in the world. When I was a boy, the seductive hum of rubber and engine, like the steady siren song of a river, had lured me away. At sixteen, I'd stood on the side of that road, stuck out my thumb, and never looked back. Now, like then, here was played out.

I poured a drink. I lit a joint. Counted down the hours to takeoff.

"Look at you, lounging about in bed in the middle of the afternoon in your shorts with nothing to do."

At the open door: Rachel. Hands on her hips.

"Witch girl," I said, "where've you been? No one's seen you since the fire."

"Oh? Who's watching for me?" she said.

I passed her the joint.

"We displaced persons watch for each other."

She glanced at the map on the bed.

"You're planning an escape?"

"I'm going away in the morning," I said. "Driving. Across America."

"So much for watching out for each other, then."

"It's like a job," I said.

"A job? Like your other jobs?"

"It's simpler. I have to deliver a car."

She looked at the map again.

"Well, I'm sure you'll find a way to make it exciting." She pointed at the map. "What's your route?"

"I start in Detroit."

"Motown."

"Drop a package for someone who's not expecting it."

"Sounds like you're up to your usual bullshit, only in different places."

She handed back the joint. Our fingertips burned on the roach when they touched.

"Supposedly everyone got out from the fire," I said. "Still, I worried about you. The front desk won't reveal guests' names."

"I had stuff to do." She smiled a smile that revealed nothing.

Stuff. Like what? Where and with whom and for how long? I was insane to hold back. She had a pure heart and a clear mind. Cowardice held me in check.

"I like jazz," she said. "Let's go catch some jazz on your last night in town."

I said, "I have to pack and get some sleep. It's an early start."

She rolled a strand of hair around her finger.

"That sounds practical."

I shrugged. Here was played out, I reminded myself.

"When will you be back?"

I said, "I'll see what happens."

"Well, you had your chance, boy," she said. "Happy trails. Goodbye, then."

"I don't like to say goodbye," I said.

"People do it all the time," she said. "It's customary when people go their separate ways."

"Is that what we're doing? Going our separate ways?"

"You are, it seems to me."

Curry wafted through the air. Somebody was cooking in one of the rooms.

"I don't like to go out because I'm afraid the Russians will find me," I said.

It sounded weak. It revealed my cowardly nature. It was the truth. I wished I could take it back.

"They'd have found you if they wanted to," she said. "Nobody cares anymore."

She could've been right. With Hornsmith dead, the whole thing might've faded away. It was hard to tell without testing the situation. But with escape so close, it didn't seem worth the risk. Play it safe. Get out of town. Stick to the plan.

I said, "I'm going to miss you."

"I'll be the one who got away," she said.

"I'll send you a postcard from the desert."

She smiled, like she felt sorry for me.

"No, you won't."

The alarm on the clock radio chimed four thirty. The time when the bullshit of the night has finally ended and the bullshit of another day has mercifully not yet begun. A night bus roared past the open window. In the cool predawn mist, the street lights cast an ominous orange fog over the parking lot of the Havanap Motel. A light drizzle of rain beaded on the Firebird's hood.

I tossed a couple of plastic bags full of clothes into the back and settled into the cold leather driver's seat. The engine growled and spat plumes of blue exhaust, then settled into deep idle grunts. With the clutch engaged and the shift rammed into first, it was a clean getaway.

Then, out of the darkness, someone rapped on the window next to my head. I made out Akinwole's silhouette, all shattered apart like a mosaic by the raindrops on the glass. I cranked down the window.

"Take me with you," Akinwole said.

He was zipped into a grey overcoat with a small blue canvas knapsack in his hand. No hat.

"What are you talking about?" I said.

"I must leave here," he said.

"Don't you have a job? You can't walk away."

"I have not gone to work in two weeks," he said. "I am at the end of my rope. Nothing is going my way."

"You quit your job?"

"No. The market has been unkind to my business. They called it a career change opportunity."

He shivered in the rain. It seemed wrong to leave him. My foot pushed on the gas. The engine howled to be set free.

"Got a passport?"

He nodded. Raindrops rolled off his cheeks.

"Yes. British. Got the US visa months ago on a wish."

"Well, let's go, I guess."

He came around to the passenger side of the Firebird and opened the door. The little knapsack was tossed into the back seat with my plastic bags. He slumped down beside me.

He rubbed his face and said, "I have never been to America."

"Fasten your seat belt," I said.

My foot eased off the clutch in search of the action point. The Firebird lunged forward. Akinwole was thrown back. His eyes widened. His mouth opened. No sound came out. His fingers dug into the dash. The tires squealed across the slick pavement. A haze of rocks and dirt sprayed everywhere. The car spun around. My head bounced from side to side. I fought the wheel before the beast could climb over the curb and tear apart the motel office. A metal garbage can flew into the air, clanged through the parking lot, and crashed into the bus stop by the street. So much for the paint job.

"Don't you know how to drive?" Akinwole shouted over the racket.

"No problem," I said and steered the car into the road.

We fishtailed a bit more before the Firebird settled down. Second gear slipped smoothly into third and up into fourth, the clutch now more familiar. Soon, the engine stopped wailing. Akinwole released his grip on the dash to clip in his seat belt. He blew out a long breath like a steam train at a full stop.

All that restoration time at Myers Motors had paid off; the Firebird chewed up the highway with ease. Everything hummed and clicked with mechanical precision. We were on our way.

After an hour of silence, Akinwole said, "If you get tired, I can drive. In my country we all drive shift."

"Okay," I said. "For now, navigate."

I handed him Shirley Rose's envelope and tapped the return address.

"Our first stop is Detroit. There's a map in the glove compartment. See if you can get us to this place. Assuming you get across the border."

"The only thing my parents did right was put me up for adoption. When I was thirteen, I went to live with a family in England and acquired a British passport. America loves the Brits."

I laughed. "Well, in case they say you're on some African terrorist list, I'm going to say you're a hitchhiker."

"And when it turns out you are on some asshole list, I will say I was abducted."

He studied the address on the letter.

"Why are we going here? Who is Shirley Rose Holbert from Detroit?"

"A friend of a friend. Don't worry about it. I just need to drop something off. It won't take long," I said.

Ben and Barry's cellphone started. A custom ring tone that barked like an angry dog. It took a moment to comprehend the sound until Akinwole pointed to the phone on the dash.

"How's the car?" said Barry or Ben.

"Good," I said. "Lively."

"You're keeping the RPMs down, right?"

"Yes, it's all under control."

"What's the odometer reading now?"

I read it out.

"We'll call you later to get the oil changed. And you don't have that African fella with you, right?"

"Nope."

"Good. When you get to the border, the car's papers are in an envelope under your seat, like we told you before. People deliver cars across the border all the time, so you should have no problem. Don't fuck this up."

The line disconnected.

I looked at Akinwole, who was going through the glove compartment for the map.

"Seems those guys really can read the tracking device."

"If I knew where they put it, I would remove it," he said. "Something is not right about them."

"Well, they don't like you either, brother. They made a point of asking if I left you behind."

"I am grateful you agreed to take me. I was ready to snap," Akinwole said. "Though they sacked me, I was up every morning, dressed in my suit like I still had a job. I went to the food court by the College Park subway and sat there all day, reading newspapers people left behind."

"Sounds insane," I said.

"Yes, it was."

He fell silent and watched the road unroll until his eyes drooped closed. His mouth hung open. Akinwole was out.

I tuned the radio to some classical music and let him sleep. My life looked better all the time.

SEVENTEEN

America

WHEN WE STARTED over the Ambassador Bridge, I nudged Akinwole from his slumber. The armed border guards tending to their heroic duty to protect the free world from terrorists, smugglers, and criminals wouldn't tolerate anything less than our full attention. The Maple Leaf and the Stars and Stripes flapped together in the wind on the bridge's railing to mark where the border stood. Akinwole rubbed his eyes and looked out over the Detroit River, slippery and grey.

"America," he said.

This wet morning, there was almost no traffic. Drizzle chilled the air. We drove through a web of electronics and cameras that probed the car. We surrendered our papers to a customs officer who waved us into a well-lit covered parking area, where more closed-circuit cameras watched us walk into the main building. Inside, we took a number in a grey waiting room with yellow plastic chairs bolted to the floor. A couple of young skinheads in track suits sulked in a corner. A Chinese woman whispered with two old men in another. A portrait of the president beamed down on us. He looked happy to have us come to America.

When our number was called, a uniformed haircut behind bulletproof glass examined the car's papers. He flipped through our passports. He looked us over.

"Wait here," he said and stepped away from his post through a door.

"What is wrong?" Akinwole whispered.

"Why's anything wrong?" I whispered back.

"First they flag us over. Then the man goes into a room. How can that be good?"

"They're checking the car's papers."

Akinwole shook his head. "They've lost their way, these people. The gestapo has taken over."

"Cool it," I said, in hopes he'd stop.

"They suffer from grassy knollism and love military drama," he said, "like those crazy people in Myanmar or North Korea, only without the funny uniforms and much more money."

"Shut up," I said. "These people take this seriously."

I'd agreed to take him along because I'd felt sorry for his miserable state. Now it was plain that Akinwole could also be a real ornery character, liable to get us into deeper trouble than I was prepared for.

The Haircut returned. He passed back Akinwole's passport under the glass.

"You're good to go. Welcome to America, sir," he said.

For a moment, Akinwole looked disappointed. He'd expected a fight. Instead, they'd tossed out the welcome mat. Now he couldn't say I told you so. He slipped the passport into his pocket.

"America loves the Brits," he said.

The Haircut pointed at me. "We need to talk to you. Come around the counter and follow me, please."

Akinwole said, "If you are not out in an hour, I will find you a lawyer."

The Haircut led the way into a small, windowless room with white cinder-block walls. A metal table and chair were pushed up into a corner. Bright fluorescent tubes glowed overhead. The process was unfamiliar. I assumed this was how the business with cars and borders was conducted.

"Someone will be with you shortly," he said.

I tried the door after he left. Locked.

In my pocket, the phone barked. Barry or Ben.

"What the fuck's happening? You've been at the border for two hours. What's going on?"

"Routine," I said. "Checking the paperwork."

"Are you out now?"

"No, I'm waiting to get the papers back."

"Shit. Where's the car?"

"Outside, in the customs parking lot."

"Did they search it? Did they put the dope dogs in it? Did they wreck the upholstery?"

"No. I'm sure it's routine."

"So, you haven't done anything? They haven't done anything?"

"No." Micromanaging meddlers. Their anxiety annoyed me. "It's all fine. They're just taking their time."

"Listen, sonny. That's an expensive and extremely rare car our boss is devoted to. So, don't give us any shit. If this goes wrong because of some fuck-up that you're responsible for ..."

Two suits came into the room. One was an older guy with trim white hair and blue eyes. The other was Simon Trang.

"Got to go," I said to Ben or Barry.

"Hello, Paul," Trang said.

This wasn't simple car business anymore.

Blue Eyes said, "This your man?"

Trang nodded. "I'll take it from here."

Blue Eyes started to say something else. Trang interrupted him with a wave of his hand.

"We'll be fine. We're business associates."

Blue Eyes adjusted his pants. He rolled his head from side to side like a punch-drunk fighter.

"All right," he said. "If he gives you any trouble, push the bell." He nodded toward a red button by the door.

When we were alone, Trang perched on the table and pointed to the chair against the wall like he wanted me to sit.

I remained on my feet.

"We know what you're doing," he said.

"I'm not doing anything," I said. "What're you doing? What's your jurisdiction?"

"I'm with the Integrated Cross-Border Enforcement Ops. A special task force. RCMP joint venture with the FBI. Top secret. Nobody knows us. We hunt bad guys who work both sides, so we work both sides," he said. "We have a wide mandate."

"I thought you were a simple detective with family money and aspirations," I said.

"I want what everyone wants: cellphones, cars, and holidays. How I get there is none of your business," he said.

"Sometimes my worlds overlap. That's how I know you work for that criminal Leon Porter. Someone I want very much."

"You already told me that when you broke into my apartment."

"Any idea where he's at?"

"I don't work for him," I said. "It's about the girl. Marla. She's a singer."

Trang sighed. "Let's cut the crap. Since you're on your way to meet Leon in his fancy car, we're keeping tabs on you. You're going to take us to him. With a little luck, when we find him, we'll discover his car is loaded and we'll finally bust him."

"Loaded?" I said.

"Don't be naive," Trang said. "Leon's a dope dealer. Any chance he gets to move something across a border, he'll take it."

"There's dope in the car?"

In my desperation to get out of town, I'd ruled out the possibility. Marla wouldn't have set me up. She'd surely never considered it. But Lover Man would. Of course, he would. The sound of metal doors clanged in my ears. Orange prison suits. Tin bowls of gruel. Lover Man and Eagle Creek laughing at the bar.

"Who cares?" Trang shrugged. "Why bother searching the car? When we bust him, there'll be dope. We have that end covered. That's a sure thing."

"It would be better for my health to tell them what you're up to," I said. "There's no upside for me to help you. These guys'll kill me."

Trang rolled his fingertips over his knuckles. His voice was so low it almost didn't register over the gentle whir of the air conditioning.

"We'll say we found meth in the car today. We'll say you had maps of New York State with all the power stations highlighted in yellow marker. We'll say we found weapons. We'll say you stole the car. We'll say you trained with Al Qaeda and ISIS. We'll produce photos, witnesses, and DNA evidence. We'll have you in so much shit you'll be fighting for a hundred years before you see daylight. And in the meantime, you'll be locked up and traded around by bikers for cigarettes. How's that sound?"

It sounded bad.

"I could be helpful," I said, uncertain of my footing.

"You have my gratitude. You won't even know we're there."

Trang offered his hand, which I accepted, perhaps too quickly, while my breath slowed down and the urge to throw up passed. Trang wasn't going to frame me for being Lover Man's dope mule after all.

Emboldened, I said, "Like your gratitude for our introduction to Dr. Courtney?"

Trang said, "We did what had to be done. The deal's important to us. We weren't sure our business would be concluded in our best interests through an intermediary."

"Family business? Or is it narc business?" I said.

Trang's eyes widened ever so slightly like a tiger about to kill something. "What difference does that make to you?"

The longer I stayed in his orbit, the more dangerous he seemed. That sick anxiety in my gut was up again. I wanted air. I felt weak. He preyed on weakness. I wanted to run screaming. Instead, I didn't let it leak. Didn't let him know.

"I guess it makes no difference now."

"I'm sorry about Mr. Hornsmith." Trang scratched his nose with a manicured nail. "I trust our little secret stays that way."

"You supplied the dope," I said. "You didn't kill him, did you?"

"No, we didn't."

He looked momentarily distracted. Though I couldn't read him, I imagined briefly that he might feel guilty for his hand in it. But soon enough, he glossed over Hornsmith's death back to his current agenda.

"We're watching you. If you see us, don't do anything stupid like tell him we're there. And call me first if you need to be busted out of somewhere bad."

Trang was back to business. Guessing correctly that I'd lost the first one, he passed me another of his cards. I accepted it only to get out of there. I had no intention of following up. It was hard to imagine how bad things would have to get to call Trang to bust me out of anywhere. And when things did eventually get that bad, I'd already forgotten about his card wedged in my wallet between a Canadian Tire bill and a fiver.

Akinwole waited by the locked car. His arms were wrapped around his chest to ward off the cold. His eyes darted about. On the lookout. Akinwole, the fugitive. Man on the run.

"I saw an unsettling sight." He shuffled from one foot to the other to stay warm. "I saw that policeman who broke into your apartment. He came out of a doorway."

"You saw Trang?"

"Yes. It was him."

"Did he see you?"

"No, I stood behind a pillar," Akinwole said. "I watched him get into a car and leave."

"If it was him — which I doubt, because what would he be doing here? — it's nothing. It's a coincidence."

Akinwole needed to be kept out of the whole Trang/Lover Man story. The shape of that threat was uncertain. The implications weren't clear. Besides, I wasn't up for Akinwole's reprimands. The less he knew, the better.

"It was him. I never forget a face," he said. "Besides, there are no coincidences. An invisible thread connects everything that happens. A membrane holds it all together. Everything has a reason."

"Sometimes shit happens."

"No," he said, "nothing happens without a reason. Everything comes from somewhere. Events happen because they are connected. They happen because they need to happen."

"To grow the ever-expanding universe?"

"Exactly."

"Except that sometimes it's a coincidence. There's no reason."

"You are an asshole, insensitive to the mysterious ways of the universe," Akinwole said.

By now, we were back in traffic on the interstate into Detroit. I glared down the highway. His New Age, no-coincidences, all-connected crap made me edgy.

"Where do I turn?" I said.

"You turn to your heart," Akinwole said. "Let your heart guide you."

I pointed to the map on his lap. "Fuck my heart. Look at this."

He moved his finger along a line and frowned.

"I am not sure where we are anymore," he said. "Get off somewhere. We will ask a local."

The Firebird roared through a tangle of colourful graffiti-sprayed overpasses and underpasses. *Gas Man. Lurk Lurk.*

Dems Reft. Grass grew up through the pavement. Signs flashed by with names that meant nothing to us. There was almost no traffic. No one walked the streets. We passed a burnt-out fire station with a tree growing through its roof. A factory longer than two city blocks stood abandoned; its burnt timber frame sagged over its red brick foundations. There were boarded-up houses with overgrown lawns and signs nailed across their doors that read *This Building Is Being Watched* and *For Sale*.

After a couple of turns we found ourselves on a quiet street by a church with a huge faded yellow cross that read *Great King Solomon* in equally faded black and red letters. God's work being done where it was most needed. Across the street stood a peeling white and green corner store with steel bars on the windows. A sign on its roof offered *Liquor*. All around were weeds and abandoned buildings. A couple of old black guys lounged on lawn chairs in the sun.

"Americans." Akinwole pointed like we'd spotted our first elephants on safari.

I shut off the engine and rolled down the window. The old guys' voices rose above the ping of hot metal under the hood.

I heard one say, "You can't see it if it's got hair all over it."

The other eyed his companion. Dead serious. "Yeah, sure. That's what we keep it trim for."

"Huh. So, you on some health thing now? Eating right. Dressing good. Working out. Look at you."

"Ha," said the other guy, "next thing, you're telling me what hat to wear."

When we walked toward them, they stopped to look us over.

"My man?" said one.

"Good morning, gentlemen," Akinwole said. "We are not from around here. Could you direct us to this place?"

He presented the letter with the return address. The one old guy looked at it, worked his gums, and passed it over to the other, who studied it with greater care.

"I don't got my reading glasses, so I don't look so good," said the first. "Willie here's still able."

"Oh yeah," said Willie after he saw the address, "that's in one of them hysterical neighbourhoods they're talking of fixing. They ain't come down there yet."

His friend nodded his agreement.

"Sounds bad," I said. "A hysterical neighbourhood?"

"No, no," said Willie. He returned the letter to Akinwole. "Used to be nice there, in the day. Old houses. Now, they's mostly busted or burnt. But, it's all good and it's going to get better."

"Yeah," the other one added, "they still got nice old ones there for fixing."

"He means historical," Akinwole said.

Willie nodded. "Yeah, that's what I said, all right."

Akinwole passed him the map. "Can you show us where that is from here, sir?"

Willie nodded. He knew where we needed to be. He didn't need a map to tell us. He said, "You turn left here past the church and go on down a couple of miles. After a while you're passing a bunch of A-rab stores with that funny writing on them, and there'll be a Kia dealer right there at the intersection. You'll recognize it because Mohamad's got his picture up there with the Ko-rean cars. Turn right there. And you're pretty close, I'd say. Got that?"

Akinwole nodded. "I have a good memory for details. Thank you, sir."

Willie said, "Where you come from? That's an unfamiliar accent."

"My name's Mulumba, Akinwole. I come from Africa, brother. My accent is British," Akinwole said, "because when I was a boy, I spent some time in the United Kingdom. England, that is. The accent stuck. I suppose."

"African, huh?" Willie nodded like it all made sense. "Well, that's a nice car you have, son. A '68 Firebird. She's a beauty. I recall working the line when they still made great cars in this town. Those were the glory days."

"You fellas don't be driving that around here at night," the other guy said. "You're liable to get into some situation."

Akinwole said, "Thank you for your advice, we will take that into consideration. Rest assured, we are perfectly capable of looking after ourselves."

Both old men laughed, and Willie said, "This ain't Africa, son. This place has a habit of being dangerous."

"Yes, sir," said his friend, "this here's Deetroyit. That rhymes with destroy-it. We got burning and looting and shooting. Now, it's all good and getting better."

"More than a million folks moved away from here in my lifetime," said Willie. "We been called the angriest city in America once. Before that, we used to be the proud engine of the nation. Now we're seized up. Broke and broken. Half the city don't even get running water. Nobody left over except teenage welfare mothers and old folks. No one works anymore. No one's angry anymore. We just tired."

His companion nodded. "We got a front-row seat to the Apocalypse. Take a look around, boys, this is the future."

Willie rose out of his lawn chair and shook his fist at the sky. "If America knew how we live here, at the centre of the End of Days," he said, "they'd be shitting their beds in fear at night. Because it's coming to their town. At the End of Days, the mighty Angel of the Lord, with his face shining like the sun and his legs like pillars of fire, will look upon us and roar like a lion, and the seven thunders will speak. And there will be reckoning."

Akinwole stepped back, unprepared for this outburst. He looked at me and tipped his head toward the car like he meant to bolt. Instead, Willie grabbed Akinwole by both hands and said, "Brother, you and me, we don't need to worry. We're all right. We have no fear of His judgement. We are righteous men. Paul, in his letter to the Corinthians, said, 'And the work each man does will at last be brought to light; the Day of Judgement will expose it. For that day dawns in fire, and fire will test the worth of each man's work. And if a man's building stands, he will be rewarded, and if it burns, he will have to bear the loss.' And, brother, surely those responsible for all that has fallen on our heads will have to bear this loss themselves in God's great eternity."

"Amen," intoned his friend, "that's how it's going to be."

Willie looked around the street and folded his arms across his chest. We all revelled in the glory of his speech, nodded our heads, and looked in awe at the destruction that lay around us.

"All's good and getting better," Akinwole said under his breath.

EIGHTEEN

Shirley Rose and the Dipshit Kid

SHELTERED FROM the glazing sun, we waited on the covered porch for someone to answer the bell. The modest clapboard bungalow was painted white, with red trim around the sturdy door and windows. A wall of blue morning glories poured over a trellis. Two Adirondack chairs overlooked a thick patch of well-tended grass in front of the house. Next door had been firebombed sometime earlier. Ashes and sooty timber spilled through a charred hole from an explosion where the front door and a bay window used to be. The dandelions were littered with mangled metal chairs and a brown-stained mattress. The grimy scent of smoke still clung to the afternoon breeze. The next four houses were boarded up. On the street, a dented Cadillac sat on concrete blocks, all four wheels gone. No people anywhere.

After a few moments, the inside door cracked open, and a boy of about eight peered out behind the screen door. He wore a clean white T-shirt and camo shorts. The Dipshit Kid. Like his picture: expressionless. He didn't say a word. He looked like he wasn't all there. I leaned down and smiled.

"Is your mother home? We're friends with Mr. Hornsmith from Toronto. We're here to say hello."

"Theo? Who's at the door, honey?" a woman called from somewhere in the house.

"Dunno," he hollered over his shoulder. He rubbed his nose with a finger while he looked us over. He wasn't about to let us pass.

Akinwole looked at me. Confused.

"Who's Mr. Hornsmith?" he said.

But there was no time to fill him in before she came to the door with a dishcloth in her long, elegant hands. She stood tall. Thin. Since the picture, she'd cut her hair short. The simplicity of it made her beauty breathtaking.

"Shirley Rose Holbert?" I said.

"Yes?" She stood between the kid and us.

"My name is Paul Wint," I said, "and this is my friend Akinwole Mulumba. I'm a friend of Mr. Hornsmith. May we come in?"

She must have concluded we were harmless, because she put her hand on the kid's head to gently push him out of the doorway.

"Go play in your room," she said.

A threadbare rug lay over the scarred oak floor of the darkened living room. Outside it was hot. Inside the world felt cool and orderly. She sat in an armchair across from the sofa where we balanced glasses of iced lemonade on our knees.

"Tell me about your trip," she said. "We don't see a lot of visitors passing through. I mean, who comes to Detroit, right?" Her smile seemed weak, apologetic.

"We couldn't call ahead," I said, unsure how to get into it. "We didn't have your number. Just an address. Besides, it's spontaneous."

"Everything about Albert's always been like that. Last minute." Her gentle laugh betrayed her affection. "He's been on my mind lately, like absent friends get. I was sure I saw him on the street last week. Tell me why you've come. How is he?"

An old electric fan whirled on the buffet. Akinwole rattled his ice cubes. Our eyes met. He didn't have a handle on why we'd come, either. There was no good way to say this.

"I'm sorry to say, he's had an accident," I said. "At home. He fell down the stairs."

"Oh," she said and reached for a small wooden box on the coffee table. "He always had a clumsy side."

She took the seashell-studded lid off and rummaged a finger about to extract a silver ring with a milky opal, which she started to polish on her dress.

"Will he be all right?"

"The fall broke his back," I said. "A private funeral was held last week. Attended only by his family."

She rolled the ring around in her hands, her lips pursed. She closed her eyes, her long lashes like so many delicate antennae. Akinwole let out a sigh and sat back on the couch beside me.

"If it matters," I said, "he was already sick with advanced bowel cancer. He passed quickly without suffering."

I guess I could've told her about the dope and about not feeling any pain on his way out. But, still unsure of my own complicity, I kept my role out of the story.

She wiped a tear from the corner of her eye with the back of her hand. She licked her lips like she wanted a drink.

"Albert and I hadn't spoken in almost a year. How long was he sick?"

"No one knew. He kept it to himself. It was very sudden," I said. "I'm sorry for your loss."

"He was a strange and wonderful man," she said. "I'm going to miss him."

"How did you meet?" I said. It sounded inane and was only meant to keep the silence at bay.

"I'm a nurse. He walked into emerg one night after a car accident, he said. He'd broken two ribs. That much was for sure. The next night, I saw him in a bar. When he recognized me, he bought me a drink."

She stared at the floor. Tears welled up again.

Akinwole presented a clean handkerchief from his pocket. She blew her nose.

"For years, I hoped we'd find a way that worked for both of us," she said, "until I resigned myself to the fact that it never would."

"It looks like you made it work," I said.

"No, we didn't. I knew he was married." She strangled Akinwole's handkerchief in her lap. "For the longest time I told myself he'd come to me. That we had something no one else had. It turned out different. His way wasn't good for me. He was who he was. I wanted what I wanted. I finally gave up."

Akinwole leaned forward and took her hands in his.

"Everyone has limitations, Shirley Rose. We should love each other despite them. If we truly love someone, we love without expectations. Without hope."

"Without hope." She closed her eyes and shook her head a little. After a while, she said, "There were a thousand ways we could've said or done it better. I wasn't asking for much. I loved him till it ached. And in my way, I never let him go. I could've tried a little harder. Instead, I kept my emotions in check."

"I'm so sorry," I said.

"Thanks," she said. "It wasn't all bad for me. I loved him. Albert had a special soul. I don't regret any of it."

I produced a folded envelope from my jeans pocket and straightened it out on the coffee table.

"He wanted you to have this," I said.

She tore it open and examined the money order drawn up in her name.

"No, that's not true," she said through her tears, "but I'm grateful, regardless of how you managed this."

Shirley Rose asked us to stay for supper. She had a small garage behind her house where we could lock up the Firebird. I guessed she needed us to help her mourn. For now, Hornsmith hovered around us. Between us. Unseen. Unheard. He'd never come back to her. We could postpone that inevitability for the night, at least.

Ben and Barry barked while I stashed the car. They demanded answers. Why wasn't the car farther down the road?

"I'm lost," I said. "I'm tired. I got up early. I need sleep before taking on the next part of the drive."

"Listen, fuck nuts, don't make us send someone to sort you out," they said.

"It's Detroit," I said. "Not a town to drive around in after sundown with a car like this."

"We better see you on the move bright and early," they said, "or there's a shitstorm coming your way."

Whack jobs. I'd heard enough threats for one day. Still, I didn't push back hard with them. After vowing to be on my way by dawn, I locked the garage and put the matter out of my mind.

Later, we sat at Shirley Rose's kitchen table while Theo played in his room. She produced a bottle of red wine, which we approached with relief. Then, with her permission, we smoked a joint from the pot stashed in my shaving kit. Louis Armstrong sang "Stormy Weather" in the next room.

Relaxed, Akinwole rolled his head from side to side.

"I have smoked no ganja since I was a boy," he said. "It used to grow wild in the fields near our house." He rose from the table and opened the refrigerator to take stock. "Eggs. Onions. Ketchup. Any mushrooms?"

Shirley Rose pointed and said, "There're dried ones next to the Arborio rice in the cupboard above the stove."

"Arborio? I make a good risotto," Akinwole said. "I am in the mood to cook for you."

"Knock yourself out," she said.

We drank some more wine while Akinwole marshalled ingredients from various cupboards. Louis sang the blues.

"No real Parmesan cheese," Akinwole reported from inside the fridge. "Only these dried flakes. I make no promises."

Shirley Rose watched him move about her kitchen. Tears streaked down her cheeks again.

"He used to come around unannounced," she said to me, "and we'd sit here sometimes till dawn talking about who knows what. Politics. Poetry. God. Time stood still around us. In the mornings, if he was still here, I'd call in sick and we'd sleep all day. We used to call it an upside-down day. Then, he'd be gone. I'd feel so empty and so alone after. For weeks, sometimes. I'd yearn for him to come back. Funny. I didn't want him living with me. I didn't want to cook for him or wash his underwear. Still, I needed him to be here. Which he mostly wasn't. To his credit, he made sure I wanted for nothing. Albert was attentive in his absence. Except for the one thing I so wanted."

"Are you lactose intolerant?" Akinwole held Shirley Rose in his big brown eyes while he scooped spoons of butter into his risotto.

"No." She laughed in spite of herself. "Besides, it's a bit late for that. That's enough butter for a full-on heart attack."

Akinwole waved his wooden stir spoon in our direction.

"Yes," he said in a Julia Child falsetto, "it's all about the butter."

Shirley Rose wiped a tear away and laughed. Her eyes flashed like crushed diamonds in the sun.

"Wait and see, sister," Akinwole said, "this is food for your soul."

He stirred the pot. He bobbed his head and hummed along to the jazz that floated through the house.

Theo appeared in the kitchen.

"I'm hungry. When's dinner?"

"Young man," Akinwole said, "you are about to have the best risotto of your life."

Theo shook his head. "I don't like that."

Akinwole said, "I bet you have no idea what risotto is."

"I don't care," said Theo.

Akinwole handed the kid the wooden spoon and drew him in. "Some of the finest Italian food in the world is cooked in Africa."

"It is?" Theo said.

Akinwole took the kid's hand and made him stir.

"Sure. Africa is filled with homesick Italians who spend their lives perfecting the foods of their childhood. Like risotto."

The kid stirred a while and glanced up at Akinwole from time to time before he said, "You're full of shit, mister."

Shirley Rose jolted out of her grief.

"Theo," she said, "that's no way to talk. Apologize to Mr. Mulumba."

Akinwole chuckled. "That is all right," he said. "The boy has good instincts." He tousled the kid's hair. "I am serious, Theo. Africa is full of homesick gangsters who spend a lot of time and money getting their food right."

Theo was interested now.

"You mean like *The Godfather*?"

Akinwole nodded. "Yes. Except for real."

"And that's where you learned to make this?" Theo nodded at the simmering pot.

"My first girlfriend. Her father was the Godfather in Africa. Not New York. We lived in Nairobi. Where is that, Theo? Nairobi?"

"In Africa?"

"Africa is a big place with many countries. After dinner we can find a map and I will show you where I come from." Akinwole grinned at the kid.

"You said you were from Kinshasa," I said. With two wives and a pack of kids. I stayed mute on that part because Akinwole was spreading peace.

"Yes, I lived there." He looked at Shirley Rose. "I was born in Nigeria. Grew up in Kenya. Raised in England by a British family. Moved to the Congo to seek my fortune. Shall I go on?"

If Shirley Rose was listening, she hid it well. She stared into her glass, adrift, while Akinwole chopped, stirred, and chatted. I guessed Hornsmith remained under her skin. Louis blasted his horn into the night.

We ate a simple supper: mushroom risotto and a tossed green salad. Not much was said, a true compliment to the chef. Akinwole had created magic from the meagre ingredients he could muster. The kid seemed to like the meaty mushrooms steeped in pepper and butter. At least, he didn't complain. Afterward, Shirley Rose invited us back into the living room for coffee and black sambuca.

She said, "I rarely drink it myself." She took a bottle from the cabinet where the fan still whirled. "But I always keep it on hand because he liked it. Funny, he'd usually complain of a headache the next day."

She poured us each a generous shot in small crystal glasses.

"To the Dutch in Old Amsterdam and the folks in Siam," said Akinwole. "To love."

We raised and drained our glasses.

"I'm glad you could stay," Shirley Rose said and poured again. "I'm not sure I'd have made it through the rest of this day alone."

"We're sorry we came with bad news," I said. "He was one of a kind. He'll be missed."

"And I am so sorry your boy will now be without his father," Akinwole said. "A boy needs a father. I wish there was something we could do."

"Theo will be fine," she said. "His father passed away when he was young. He'll find a way through this."

Akinwole glanced at me for help to soothe the tears that brimmed up once more. Shirley Rose smiled through her tears.

"Oh no, I see," she said. "It's not like that. Theo's father died years ago. He was a cop. Killed in a gang shootout. Theo never knew him. Albert was a family friend to him. Uncle Albert."

"We assumed," I said. Mixed kid. Single mom. Crazy Hornsmith.

"Yes, you would," she said.

The kid not being Hornsmith's changed everything. I could've kept the money. Instead, I'd connected the dots incorrectly. Seen the wrong picture. Drawn the wrong conclusion. And then I realized I was an idiot for thinking, even for a moment, that I should've done it differently. I wanted to apologize without being sure to whom or for what.

"You had some hard breaks, sister," Akinwole said, his voice soft, almost inaudible. "Third time lucky. I wish for you." He raised his glass. "Love. For all of us."

Lovers, mournful together. We drank. Circled. Reminisced. Now no longer alone. Released. We toasted Hornsmith with sambuca one last time. By the time I lay down on the couch, Akinwole was snoring in the armchair next to me. In my leaden eyes, the room spun overhead. I saw Shirley Rose spread a blanket over Akinwole and peck him on the cheek while he slept. That could've been part of my dream.

NINETEEN

The Crossing

DETROIT TO LOS ANGELES is a three-day drive if you put your back into it and your car is sound. The twins' threats were enough motivation to get it finished. To get away from these people. Get them out of my life. Get to the ocean. Start something new, something to call my own.

After an oil change in Lansing, Michigan, we committed the Firebird to charge at speed across Iowa and Nebraska into Colorado, Utah, and beyond. What the pioneers had done in months, or sometimes years, we were attempting to undertake in a matter of gas stops, along an almost-straight line of four-lane freeways southwest across the Great Plains, through fields of wheat and corn over the western mountains to the Pacific Ocean and the City of Angels. Endless miles past tractor-trailers, road gangs, and Denny's restaurants. Anonymous service stations and nameless towns came up over the hood and vanished in the rear-view mirrors. It was a tedious business and why most people fly to California.

The morning we left Detroit, Akinwole lay prostrate on the flattened passenger seat. With every bump in the road, he moaned. One arm hooked over his eyes. The other held his stomach. His big lips kissed the air with each groan. Sambuca wasn't his drink.

The day warmed up enough to take the top down. The open air helped. By noon, Akinwole was upright with a bottle of Gatorade. Cheap gas station sunglasses shielded his eyes.

"We should have stopped in Chicago," were his first words of the day. "The Windy City. Home of the blues."

"We're on a schedule," I said.

He gulped some Gatorade and said, "This country has so much to offer. I must see some of it. What about Kansas City and the crazy little women?"

"Can't," I said. "It's not on the route."

"Well, it could be." He unfolded the map. "If we travelled farther south. Stayed away from places where nothing has ever happened. Like Des Moines and Lincoln, Nebraska. Have you never wanted to go to Kansas City? See what all the fuss is about?"

"There's no fuss, Akinwole," I said.

"You are wrong," he said, "Walt Disney opened his first studio there. Charlie Parker was born there. Ernest Hemingway lived there."

"Ernest Hemingway lived everywhere."

"That interests me."

Akinwole sighed.

"If we stray," I said, "those crazy twins will let a killer off his leash to hunt us down. Hunt me down. Do you have any idea who?"

Akinwole removed the sunglasses, rubbed his brow, and made like he wanted to say something. I didn't care to hear it. He had no idea who these people were.

"It'll be someone like that psycho I saw in Kirkland Lake," I said. "A knife-wielding, coke-snorting, hot-rod-driving, tattoo-covered, stone-cold killer."

"So what?" Akinwole said. "We can leave the car in a parking garage. They will send their man to retrieve it. Who cares? We hop a Greyhound. Get lost in America. By the time they find the car we could be anywhere."

"You're a bad influence," I said. "You're going to get us killed."

"I crave an adventure," Akinwole said. "Life has been tedious for a long time."

Akinwole sulked. Akinwole wanted to live the Dream. Get his piece of the pie. Not that there was much left, by the look of it. The heartland of America was cored. A straight, empty passage lined with soulless industrial parks and utilitarian, boxy buildings that peddled plastic lawn furniture and gallon jugs of Coca-Cola to people whose idea of extravagance was to run their pickup truck through a car wash. People united under God by honky-tonk, baseball, cornflakes, guns, and cars. People who willingly give up their sons and daughters to be killed in places they can't pronounce for reasons they don't understand.

"I have something to tell you," Akinwole said after a while, his hand outside the window in the rushing air. "I have no wives or children waiting for me in Kinshasa or anywhere else. I made them up. I have no one to live for. After I graduated from the London School of Economics, I ran away from my adopted family in search of my African soul. I am alone."

I stared down the road in the grips of a trance. The straightness of the highway made it hard to stay awake. At eighty miles an hour, I was well velocitized, immune to the landscape streaking past. It took a moment to digest what he was saying.

I said, "And what did you find?"

"Malaria."

"Malaria? Mosquitoes and swamps?"

"Yes."

"Isn't gin and tonic good against that?"

"No. It turns out nothing is."

"So, no wives? No kids? No happy, poor life under the African sun left behind to find work across the sea? No self-sacrifice? No sending money home?"

"No," he said. "The immigration woman who processed me misunderstood my situation. I had some photos of my cousin's kids in my wallet. She concluded they were mine. She was supportive of my coming here to find work for my family. I didn't contradict her so as to avoid being denied. I let it be."

"What about your parents? The adoption part's true, right?"

"Yes. My birth parents are still in Nairobi. My father was a minor government clerk with no connections. My mother used to wait on the porch of their shack for him to come home after work. Sometimes he came home late. Sometimes not at all. They might still be like that. I have no idea. We never communicate."

"And your English family?"

"Thinks I died."

"From malaria."

He nodded. His confession was unexpected. At the same time, his story didn't surprise me. He'd never seemed like a family guy. For one thing, someone with that many kids would've talked about them more. Kept some photos around. This reframed image of Akinwole suited him better: another lost soul without a plan.

"So, what will you do when we get to Los Angeles?" I said.

"I am unsure," he said. "Like car lights at night, I can see twenty feet out. More is a lot to ask."

The afternoon wore on. We drove due west directly into the sun. Akinwole wore his sunglasses, while I squinted to keep sight of the road. In the glare, I didn't notice the pothole, so we hit it hard. Afterward, the car handled differently. The steering wheel vibrated in a new way. The Firebird pulled to the right. Akinwole leaned over the side for a look.

"We have a flat tire," he said when he was safely back in the car. "I hope we have a spare. We are far from anywhere now."

Indeed, when I brought the Firebird to the side of the highway, there wasn't a building in any direction. There were no cars on the road. There were no trees in the fields. There were no contours in the landscape. There was only an ocean of flat, endless, shadowy land with a sunny riot of orange and red dripping behind the horizon.

Akinwole knew his way around a jack and a tire iron. By the time I found a flashlight in the glove compartment, he'd popped the trunk, tossed the spare tire by the side of the road, jacked up the front of the car, and was busy with the lug nuts. I pointed the flashlight at the wheel.

"You're a one-man pit crew."

"Sometimes in the Congo," he said, "we changed tires two or three times a week. The roads were more like bush paths, with treacherous craters as deep as a man."

He pulled the flat tire off, and in one fluid motion, heaved the spare into its place.

"What were you doing there? Besides looking for your African soul and getting malaria?"

He twirled the tire iron in his hands like a baton.

"I went for diamonds. It was supposed to be simple. You dive them out of a river, you stick them in a sack, and you take them home."

Akinwole laughed to himself while he tightened the nuts.

He said, "I underestimated how hard everything could be."

"How long did you last?"

"Three years," he said. "I lasted three years. One year in the bush, on and off. And two years a prisoner."

"A prisoner?"

"Yes. When I got malaria, I started back to Kinshasa. It was a week's journey by river barge. I stayed with a Portuguese pineapple mogul the night I came out of the bush, looking for a ride downriver. He supplied pineapples to all of Portugal. He had his own label."

Akinwole shook the new tire. Satisfied, he worked the jack to lower the Firebird onto the asphalt.

"When the Pineapple King learned I had studied economics in London, he wanted me to stay. He needed an accountant. There were kids with AK-47s guarding the place. They were under orders to keep me. At night they locked my bedroom door from the outside."

He finished with the jack. The car was ready to roll.

"So, what happened?" I said, light still in hand.

"At first, I was bedridden. Later, once the malaria burned off, I started to co-operate because I feared for my life, and for two years I did the plantation's bookkeeping."

"And then you tunnelled out?"

"There were two Belgian nuns who came for lunch every Sunday after church. Eventually, we started exchanging notes through some of the staff, who felt sorry for me. When the nuns learned of my situation, they improvised a plan for my escape."

By now, the jack was folded back into its assigned spot. He flipped the flat tire in and had almost closed the trunk when something caught his eye. Akinwole stuck his head in.

"Pass me your torch," he said, his arm out behind him.

I handed him the flashlight.

"What do you see?"

"There is a little metal box welded into the frame of the back seat," he said. "I believe it is the tracking device."

He put the flat tire back on the roadside. Then, brandishing the tire iron in one hand and the flashlight in the other, he crawled into the trunk. After a couple of metallic smacks, he emerged with a small metal casing about the size of a pack of cigarettes.

"Got it."

"That's a terrible idea," I said. "They're going to mobilize."

"You worry too much, Paul," Akinwole said. He drew back his arm and hurled the box deep into the night. "Now they have to rely on us to tell them where we are, if we so choose. Now we are free. Better."

"Are you serious?"

"Sure. Soon, they will telephone and ask, why does it look like we are not moving? And you tell them you have no idea. Say you made a wrong turn and you are in Kansas City."

"No," I said. "We go to Los Angeles and get rid of this car."

Akinwole returned the flat tire to the trunk a second time. He paid no attention to my protestations.

"We cannot drive across America without doing something off the plan," he said. "Where is your sense of adventure?"

He slammed the trunk and wiped his hands on his trousers. Akinwole the escape artist. Akinwole the anarchist. The man was on a tear. He had me in a zugzwang. That's what Hornsmith would've called it.

"Come on," he said, "pick somewhere."

"Okay," I said, "how about Las Vegas? It's on our route. We can stop in Las Vegas. We do the casinos. We take in a show. We see the sights. Have a fancy dinner." I had to give him something, or I feared he'd get worse.

"Las Vegas is an excellent alternative to Kansas City," Akinwole said. "Even though I do not gamble, because I have no luck."

We took turns at the wheel through the night and into the next day. Dawn had the Rockies on the western horizon. We crawled through Denver with the morning rush hour and started the climb up to the Continental Divide. When he wasn't driving, Akinwole would sometimes fall asleep. His mouth gaped open. Other times he would fidget with the push buttons on the radio, hunting for songs. Mostly he found Jesus, political commentary, and tax reform editorials. America had more opinions than songs these days. God was in. Government was out.

"What about you?" Akinwole said once the radio had given out to the solitude of the mountains. "Did you never yearn to run away and catch malaria? Discover your soul?"

"I did," I said, "and I do. I've been leaving people and places most of my life. I lived with my grandparents in a small prairie town. My father was the local member of parliament, so he was never around. My mother was a hippie who spent her time trying to get in touch with her inner om. One day she left a note on the kitchen table and never came back. Later, when I left, no one noticed I was gone."

"Where did you go?"

"I hitchhiked to the city, bought a bus ticket, and went to another city."

It was the life of someone else. Long ago. So unfamiliar to me now.

"You drive a while. I'm tired," I said.

The twins barked for an update. Poor reception kept it short.

"The tracker shows you sitting on the side of the road in Nebraska for half a day," Ben or Barry said. "What the fuck's so interesting in Nebraska?"

"I don't get it," I said. "I'm moving along. Past Denver and into the mountains, heading toward Vegas."

Akinwole shook his head and waved his pink palms. No. No. Don't tell them where we are.

"I had a flat tire back there in Nebraska," I said.

"A flat tire? Those were brand new Pirellis."

"The right front blew out," I said.

"We don't like it."

The phone cut out. They never called back.

On the other side of the mountains, we were in a vast red desert haunted with monstrous rock hallucinations that soared over the road in the shape of old ladies, broken turrets, and strange insects. The afternoon wore on, and we drove the car harder and harder until somewhere inside Utah, near the junction for Moab, we were pulled over by a state trooper for speeding. Akinwole was at the wheel. The cop marvelled at the Firebird, then wrote up the ticket anyway.

Hours later, Las Vegas popped up over the horizon. We screamed into the valley on the I-15. The car strained in the desert heat. The temperature gauge had been on a slow upward creep for a while, until the car couldn't bear it any longer. The Firebird shuddered to a full steamy stop outside a nondescript motel called the Golden Suites. We were somewhere in suburban Las Vegas. End of the road.

Akinwole was keen to see the city right away. But that had to wait. The engine needed to cool. In the morning, we'd water the radiator and hope it recovered. For now, we pushed the Firebird off the road into the motel lot and locked it for the night.

The place reeked like a drag strip. Oil, gas, and exhaust fumes choked the air from the freeway next to the motel. Through the windows into the rooms, we saw shirtless tattooed men on their beds watching TV, drinking cold cans of beer. A little girl came out of the laundromat with an armful of unfolded clothes. While we looked for our room, a gangbanger in a wifebeater with heavy gold bling around his neck watched us from a doorway.

We were at the end of the corridor. The room stank of lemon disinfectant. The couch in the living room sagged. The kitchenette offered mismatched cutlery and chipped plates.

Across the street, we picked up a case of beer at Lee's Discount Liquor. Next to the cashier, photos taken from the store security camera of regular shoplifters and stickup artists were pinned on a corkboard. Underneath each snapshot, handwritten notes scrawled in marker by the management offered editorial comments on the offenders. "Does his girlfriend care he pees in public?" "Acts stoopid." "Is this your neighbor?"

Back in the room with the beers, we ordered off a delivery menu for "New York Style Chinese Cuisine." We flipped on the baseball game. The Braves were showing the Mets how it's done. It felt good to have something to watch that wasn't the road. Outside, trucks and motorcycles roared by so loud it was like they were coming through the room. An angry woman argued with someone on her cellphone right outside our window.

There was only one bed in the back room of the suite, so we tossed a quarter for it. Loser slept on the couch. Akinwole called heads and won. His luck wasn't so bad after all.

When Akinwole went to bed, I watched the end of the ball game. New York came in from behind for an unexpected victory. Afterward, the local Vegas news. The volume was set down low. The announcer droned off the day's tally of murder and mayhem. It comforted me. I liked hearing about troubles that weren't mine. Bomb attacks. Coups. Invasions. Plane crashes. Mass graves. The grislier, the better. I was almost under when the final news story drilled through my slumber.

"And finally, in other news today," the blond announcer-cum–runway model read off her teleprompter, "a leading Cirque du Soleil performer from the Bellagio here in Las Vegas has been arrested in Toronto, Canada, in connection with a recent downtown fire that destroyed one of that city's historical properties two weeks ago."

I drew closer to the screen to be sure I had it right. There he was: Yuri, in a dated publicity shot. His head all bald and shiny. His eyes close together. The last time I'd seen that freak, he was on the floor of the Pullman's toilet, clutching his throat.

They played a clip of the Cirque show, followed by the same footage of the Ellington fire that showed the two firefighters dragging me away from the flames before the building collapsed.

"Yuri Ivanhov was arrested earlier today, along with Burian and Pavel Volkov, believed to be relatives and accomplices of the accused. The men were identified by police using footage from a nearby security camera."

They hustled Yuri up some courtroom steps, along with the two thugs who'd beaten me senseless. Yuri looked sullen. Underbite had a bruise on his cheek. The Heavy Guy was trying to hide his huge head under his jacket. A guilty perp parade, to be sure.

"Police are keeping quiet about a motive, and a publication ban has been imposed by the court."

A commercial for a local Volkswagen dealership flashed across the screen, featuring a man dressed like a rabbit being chased by a hunter. "It's Rabbit season. No money down. Zero percent financing …" I thought they stopped making that car.

I switched off the TV and tried to sleep. In the dark, on the couch, events rewound in my head and played back in jittery stop motion: Bernstein, Yuri, and me snort coke. Yuri acts dangerous. Me, more dangerous. Yuri on the piss-drenched floor. Bernstein with the might-have-been drag queens. Hornsmith blackmails Courtney. Courtney hires Russian mob rejects to scare us. Russian mob rejects who turn out to be Yuri's cousins. I bash them with a frying pan. They torch the Ellington. The camera captures them. So much for the faulty wiring. The Russians had done it. Old Mr. Gupta the tailor witnessed them celebrating from his bar stool. They'd done it for Courtney. They'd done it for Yuri. They'd done it for money and revenge. The rest was happenstance.

TWENTY

Vegas

THE FOLLOWING MORNING, Akinwole laid into his Big Man Breakfast with enthusiasm. Three ketchup-bloodied eggs, sunny side up. Four buttered pancakes with syrup. Canadian bacon. Boston baked beans. Sausages. Hash browns. Peanut butter and jam on toast. With his head bent down to the plate, he shovelled food into his mouth. Every so often, he slurped black coffee from a mug. A restful sleep had given him an appetite.

"You are not eating?" he said between mouthfuls.

Ice cubes melted in my Coke while the fruit bowl in front of me offered flavourless bits of green cantaloupe and freakishly large strawberries infused with the palpable misery of migrant Mexican pickers hoping for a better tomorrow. My liver ached from an infernal coil that had wormed its way out of the couch into my side. I was weary of being worn out. All the dope was smoked. There hadn't been a drink since Detroit. This morning, self-medication was down to cola with a couple of Advil.

"They got the guys who burned down our building," I said finally. "I saw it on the news last night. It wasn't faulty wiring."

"So, who did it?" Akinwole rinsed his mouth with coffee before another load of hash browns went in.

"One was a performer from a Cirque show here in Vegas," I said. "The others were his cousins."

"That makes no sense," Akinwole said. "Why would a circus performer from Las Vegas set fire to a building in Toronto?"

It made perfect sense. Fate had tossed Yuri across my path and forced me to defend myself against him. Hornsmith had blackmailed Courtney. Courtney collected unsavoury types for dirty jobs. Yuri's criminal cousins. Unleashed, the Russians had taken to violence for cash and revenge. Undoubtedly, Trang had organized the publication ban to keep his new business investment out of the news. Events were so intertwined and connected that I couldn't formulate a reply.

"No," I said, "it makes no sense. I need the toilet."

Like a cow caught midthought, Akinwole stopped chewing to watch me slide out of the booth.

"Can I have your fruit?" he said.

In the can, I gripped both sides of the sink and took deep breaths to steady the rising bile that swirled in my guts. My fingers and arms jangled like they were permanently asleep. My back felt like a cold lizard was clamped to my spine. No appetite. Ache in the marrow. This was not the way toward a better situation. I splashed cold water on my face and examined my red eyes in the mirror.

From the locked toilet cubicle behind me, someone coughed.

"Hey, kid, I'd be obliged if you tossed me a roll of toilet paper from the other stall. I'm out here."

There was something about that voice, like an old familiar song, impossible to say from where or when. Chalk it up to my general condition. I threw over a roll from the next stall.

"Here you go."

I resumed the inspection of my sorry features in the mirror. Moments later, the toilet flushed, and the door swung open. The occupant emerged. He tucked his white shirt into a beautiful blue sharkskin suit. Yellow socks peeked out between the pants cuffs and a pair of two-tone Oxfords. It took me a second to be sure, while in the mirror Hornsmith zipped himself up. Ice filled my head. I kept my hands under the warm water, my tenuous connection to the world.

The washroom smelled of camphor. In the reflection, his marble pallor betrayed his condition — at least to me, since I knew him to be dead. His beard was groomed to razor-sharp perfection. His hands were hairless, translucent.

"What're you doing here?" My voice echoed off the white-tiled walls. "You shouldn't be here."

"I need to set matters right," he said. "I need to do something good before my release is complete."

He fumbled with the taps. He wasn't in a hurry to wash his hands. The dead don't wash. He was going through the motions to stand beside me. The deafening roar of the water made me strain to hear his words.

"It's my last chance, Latour, to get it right," Hornsmith said. "You make your plays. You lay your money down and pray you did it right. Pray you get it back in spades."

The money, I guessed. He was after his money.

"That's what you're here for?"

"My time is limited," he said. He straightened his collar in the mirror. "Soon, my train's pulling out of the station, and I must be on it. Otherwise, I'll be doomed to roam around here forever. Meanwhile, there's much to be done."

He patted around his pockets.

"I must've left my pocket watch by the toilet."

"You left your watch?"

He said, "I was playing with it. I like doing that while I think." He pushed his way back into the stall and said, "Latour, I'm going to settle my score soon. Bet on it."

I turned to face him. The cubicle door swayed back and forth, the stall empty. Hornsmith had vanished. In the silence that followed, there wasn't a residual glimmer to confirm his visitation. No sound. No smell. No trace. Nothing to reveal he'd been by.

Ghosts weren't within my experience. They didn't exist for me. We came from nothing and we returned to nothing. That much was certain. The business in between a miracle. Beyond that, the mysteries of creation eluded me.

Still, it was possible that Hornsmith's apparition signified something. If he'd come here to set something right, like he'd said, perhaps he planned to help set me right. Why else would he follow me all this way? From the ether of his limbo, he'd seen how I'd given the money to his wife and to Shirley Rose. Maybe that had inspired him. Now he was here to help me to turn the remaining money into a larger stake to start a new life. For a moment, I forgot his selfish nature. Instead, I surfed on the notion that he'd reached out from the Beyond to alter my fate. That he planned to do something good for a change. Make the world a better place. You can bet on it, he said. Bet on it. The notion blossomed into an urgent need to take the money and plonk it on a card table. I was fixed on the belief that Hornsmith would help me double it before I continued down the freeway to the coast. This was a sign. I was dead certain of it.

Back at the table, Akinwole had cleared off breakfast and was busy with a strawberry milkshake. I slid in across from him.

"I was getting worried," he said. "You were gone a while."

"I've been thinking," I said, "when we get the car working, we should start our day in the casino."

"Gambling is not something I do," Akinwole said. "Can we look around instead? Go to the Luxor and see the Sphinx? Drive by the Chapel of Love?"

"Gambling is something I have to do before we go sightseeing," I said. "I'm on fire. I have a feeling."

"Sounds like a virus."

"It won't take long. An hour, tops."

Hornsmith had said he'd settle the score. Hornsmith said to bet on it. I was prepared to go with that.

Akinwole wasn't enthusiastic.

"Betting eleven to win ten is idiotic," he said. "Statistically, the house keeps almost every cent that walks in."

"It's about profits, not percentages," I said. "The spirit is with me today. I need an hour. Let's go before something changes."

The Firebird had calmed down overnight. By morning, the radiator was content with a few beer cans full of tap water from the bathroom. With that, we headed down to the strip, where everything glistened, sleek and new. Where everything blended into a single shiny landscape of Gucci, Prada, and Louis Vuitton stores in bold, geometric structures. After the long drive across the bleakness of the American heartland, we'd arrived in a shimmering oasis.

Awestruck, we took in the mirage: The Great Pyramid of Luxor, created in reflective glass, sparkled in the sun. The Sphinx without the broken nose. The Eiffel Tower without the hassle of Parisians. The Statue of Liberty, perfectly identical to the real Mother of Exiles, only cleaner. Glacial steel towers of shiny black and green at the Aria. The red and blue wedge of the Westgate Towers blended into the sky — impossible to tell where one started and the other ended. Stunning monuments to modern design, all.

The broom-swept streets were lined with lush palms and emerald-green shrubbery trimmed to perfection. Discreet gardeners in starched camouflage outfits blended in with the foliage so we wouldn't be reminded that real people serviced the dreamscape. Audis, Range Rovers, Mercedes-Benzes, and brand-new American muscle cars like the Charger and the Camaro polished to showroom condition purred at stoplights. Sidewalks were crowded with people in fresh shades of blue, pink, and white. They sauntered hand in hand over to the MGM lion and the fountains of the Bellagio for holiday snaps. A calm silence like thick cotton muted the entire scene. Only the occasional shirtless, shit-stained, wild-eyed person wandering barefoot through the dream mottled its perfection.

When we reached the end of the strip, we entered another part of the city, where the casinos were from another era. Here the harsher, more familiar reality of this broken country nibbled away at the edges of the decadent desert paradise. The billboards were faded. Some were cracked or broken. There were fewer people on these streets. Some of them pushed grocery carts filled with empty bottles. Others carried green garbage bags over their shoulders. One crawled out of a culvert with a sleeping bag under his arm.

The various one-way streets were difficult to negotiate back to the shiny dream. Nothing ran on a grid, and no landmark helped us set our bearings. This city required an intuitive sense of direction that eluded us. After several U-turns and dead ends, we found ourselves under the el by the old Las Vegas Hilton, the first place that hinted we were back into the newer city. To my surprise, Akinwole recognized it.

"This used to be the largest resort in the world," he said. "Elvis lived up there in the penthouse. He played over eight hundred shows here. Can we look?"

"I didn't figure you for an Elvis guy."

Akinwole said, "My stepfather was here the night of Elvis's last show. I recognize the hotel from his souvenir postcards."

It was a lucky sign.

A life-sized statue of the King in all his Vegas glory greeted us by the entrance. The famous open-necked rhinestone pantsuit. The sideburns. The guitar slung over his shoulder. The microphone in one hand midsong. His other hand reaching out to the adoring throng. America's answer to Mozart.

The muted chimes of slot machines and the clickity-clack of roulette wheels filled the lobby. People threw dice at craps tables. Placed bets on cards. Cocktail waitresses in short skirts and stilettos brought free drinks on serving trays. There was no sense of place other than here. There was no sense of time except now.

My lungs expanded, invigorated by the oxygen pumped into the casino. Blood moved into places it hadn't been in a while. Air circulated so well that despite the clouds of cigarette smoke, the room was odourless and pure. The temperature was kept cool so everyone would stay awake to gamble.

Blackjack was on my mind. Hornsmith was going to toggle the inner cogs of this reality from the other side of the curtain and deal me the winning hand. The plan was to win a bag of money, continue down the road, and settle by the sea. I could almost smell the salty air, the surf lapping calm assurances in my ears. It was a great plan.

"Let's go," I said. "I've got some cards to play while luck is still with me. You buy some coins for the slot machines and see if the King will bless you."

He said, "How?"

I peeled fifty bucks from my roll and stuffed it in Akinwole's breast pocket.

"Stick in a coin and push the button," I said.

"Which machine do I pick?"

"It doesn't matter, Akinwole, there're all the same. Pick one you think has nice lights."

I pointed him toward the slot machines and promised to meet him in an hour at the bar of the Benihana, a Japanese restaurant we could see across the casino floor.

Soon, I was in line for chips. Ahead of me, someone waved a piece of paper at the teller's cage in what looked like a complicated transaction. Progress was slow, the line long. I worried that my window to win would close before I could jump out of it. It agitated me. The man and woman in line ahead of me seemed restless as well.

"We have to get back into action, baby," the man said.

"Yeah," she said, "you're hot."

He shifted his weight and adjusted his neck to displace his impatience.

To me, she said, "Last night, Graham made seven grand."

I smiled. Polite. I liked being next to winners. Their luck could rub off. This was another good omen.

"Yeah," Graham said, "I got lucky last night, for sure."

His girlfriend slurped a margarita through a bendy straw. "You did good, baby."

He shrugged. "That other guy, Ray? The one with the Prada shades? He scored."

"He made a hundred grand, I swear," she said.

Everyone seemed so pleasant here.

"That's great," I said.

"Ray travels with a bodyguard," Graham said.

"That fat guy?" She tipped the glass to one side for a better view of the icy sludge that was once her drink.

"Yeah," he said, "Rodney."

She held up her empty glass to a passing waitress, eyebrows arched.

The waitress said, "Another?"

"I might as well drink, honey."

"Anyone else?"

Alcohol would've been unwise. This was going to require a clear head. Graham shared the instinct. We both shook our heads, and the waitress departed on her mission of mercy.

"So, what's Rodney's deal?" the woman said like I wasn't there anymore.

"He gets twenty percent."

"What's he do for that?"

Graham shrugged. "He's a big bodyguard. I guess he's a good guy to get behind when the bullets start flying."

"Bodyguards?" I said. "People need bodyguards around here?"

The woman looked me up and down like she hadn't noticed me before. She forced a smile and said, "Oh no, hon, I don't think that'll be a problem for you."

Nervous, I smiled and nodded. I understood what was meant by a twenty percent guy. A twenty percent guy like Rodney might be useful when Lover Man's boys came for me. Akinwole was my friend. I didn't want to see him hurt. When the going got dangerous, a professional would be the way to go.

After my turn at the teller, I was anxious to get started. Everywhere, the mood was relaxed. It could've been midnight and it could've been sunrise. It could've been Sunday and it could've been Friday. It made no difference. We were all here for one thing. The rest of the world no longer mattered.

At the first table I came across, giddy, I stumbled over the footrest of the high chair and almost fell to the floor. The edge of the table kept me up. The dealer tossed me a glance to make sure I was sure. I nodded. I was. The dealer settled back into his game.

The crisp flick of the cards and the plastic on plastic of the chips tinkled in my ears. The cards came, the bets mounted. It was different from those days back in the greeting card company before Hornsmith, when the boredom had been so profound I'd lost the will to live. It still wasn't clear what was in store for the future, but certainly, times were more interesting nowadays.

Soon, my losses totalled four thousand dollars. It took thirty minutes. My hands were clammy and cold. My mouth dry. My jaw hurt from grinding my teeth. There was no sign of Hornsmith anywhere. Around me, people gambled away their dreams. Nothing else mattered except to find the bottom. Fast. No one looked up. No joy could be found around the room.

Numb, I wandered through the casino contemplating my next play, until two paramedics shouldered their way past me to a bank of slot machines. They lugged big black plastic cases of emergency supplies and a stretcher toward an old woman collapsed on the floor. Her cigarette still dangled from her soft camel lips. The paramedics tried lifting her onto their stretcher. The old bird fought back. She thrashed her arms about and yelled, "I got one more. I got one more. Let me play."

They paused their rescue to let the old lady insert her last coin into the slot machine. Everyone stopped to watch. The wheels spun round and round. One orange. Two oranges. A collective gasp of anticipation from the crowd. A lemon. The crowd groaned. The old lady buckled back onto the floor and the paramedics resumed their revival of another loser in the City of Sin.

That was my sign. I returned to the cashier for more chips. All or nothing, that was the way to go. Play like the old lady. Play it all to the end. An urgent message went out to the universe: Paging Mr. Hornsmith, paging Mr. Hornsmith. Mr. Hornsmith is requested to report to the gaming tables immediately.

Back on the floor, my first hundred-dollar bet on a new table summoned the king of hearts and the jack of diamonds. The dealer showed the eight of spades. An easy hundred bucks for me. The next round I bet another hundred for an ace-three combination. I took a hit for another jack. Common sense said to stand. Instead, I took a hit for a six and held on twenty points. The dealer busted and another hundred came my way. My game finally started to climb.

Heady now, caution went out with sense. A thousand-dollar bet on a double down while the dealer drew twenty-three put me up five thousand dollars. In the next hand, the dealer returned with an ace-king combination. I blindly pushed out all my remaining chips and hit a blackjack. Hornsmith was doing his thing.

Soon, I was up thirteen thousand. I did the math. I ran the numbers. I was on my way. I was going to dump the car and start a new life. Make a payment on a little place on the beach. Get a motorcycle. A Ducati. I liked the sound of it. Ducati. Like a dangerous ice cream.

Then, in a moment of sheer inspiration, I took the entire night's win and bet it all. The dealer showed the ace of diamonds. I held the ace of hearts and the jack of spades to back me up. Blackjack again. I was up over thirty thousand dollars. The money had doubled. I hadn't wanted to come to Las Vegas. Akinwole had made me do it and Hornsmith had blessed me. Across the casino, Graham and his girlfriend laughed at a craps table. He kissed her hands before she tossed the dice. They hugged and kissed some more while everyone around them applauded and cheered. They were gambling their way into their dreams. We were all on fire.

Inspired, for my last play I bet the entire wad. A hush washed over the room. One by one, the players at my table watched their own hands play out to naught. In the end, with nothing left to do, their sole source of amusement now was to see if fortune would crush me. That's how it is when you're winning, people will stick around to see you lose. A sickness comes after the drive to self-destruct has wrung out all self-respect, and the loneliness of losing seeks solace in the destruction of another. I smelled their sour disappointment without counting myself one of their miserable ranks. I would finish a winner.

For my sins, the six of spades and the nine of spades lay there like the two turds they were. The cards snapped on the table. No one cared. Only my hubris locked in combat with Lady Luck, who sent out the queen of hearts, that violent monster of mayhem. I was bust. Wiped out in one play. A satisfied grunt circled the table. The game broke up and people drifted off to other diversions. Across the crowded casino, over by the hotel lobby, I caught the back of a blue sharkskin suit going out the door.

TWENTY-ONE

A Bad Turn

THE BENIHANA was what you'd expect if some designer conjured up an antique Japanese village from plastic, paint, and foam. A fortified gate of fake timber and iron protected the entrance. Inside, past the monstrous fanged statues in Ali Baba shoes were huts and trees. A mossy brook babbled between the tables while a demure staff and a bevy of chefs performed theatrics with knives and flames by the hibachi tables. Diners gasped and clapped.

Mercifully, the lounge stood apart from the village. It vibed more conventional bar than an ancient Nipponese evening in some bogus shogun hideaway. There was nothing left to do. I'd wait here for Akinwole. The money was gone. My confidence shattered. I'd wait for him, if it meant forever. It was the only plan left.

I slumped in a lounge chair beside the walkway between the Hilton and the convention centre. Like an indoor laneway, it was lined with a few other bars and restaurants. The busy foot traffic completed the feel of an intimate little street somewhere in limbo. In Vegas, inside felt like outside, only better.

A waiter came from the village with a steamed face towel on a lacquered tray. He offered it with bamboo tongs.

"You look tired, sir," he said. "This will revive you."

The hot towel soothed my eyes. Road-weary and fed up, I felt depleted. Stuck in a rut. Unable to turn. Headed toward an uncertain end, with an ill-conceived, rootless plan. The threats from Courtney and the twins. The death and resurrection of Hornsmith. My misfortune in the casino. I was tearing at the seams. It was a miracle I didn't have a stroke. A drink was in order.

A porcelain carafe of warm sake and a glass of iced vodka Red Bull arrived. The booze soon coursed with a welcome rush over the cracked mud flats of my brain. The power grid came back online. The shock of defeat was rounded off. Sanded down. Ghosts didn't exist. I'd been moved by a delusion brought on by a general grinding of my spirit over the past months. It could've been worse. I had eight hundred dollars left. Far from the fortune that had slipped through my fingers, but if I was careful, it was enough to get me to California. That was a small consolation.

By my watch, Akinwole was twenty-five minutes late. Most likely, he'd pissed away the money and gone for a walk. Taken the elevator up to the thirtieth floor in search of the Elvis suite. Lost track of time. Gotten caught up in pursuit of the King's ghost. If he didn't come back soon, there'd have to be some new plan. Meanwhile, I was content to sit and drink. The waiter who'd been skulking in the shadows reappeared. My order for another sake and a vodka Red Bull slurred out wrong.

"A sed rull and bakay," I said. Earlier, I wouldn't have mixed that up. That was then. Now, I was a new man.

The waiter leaned in close enough for me to smell his cologne. Stale Pine Sol.

"I beg your pardon, sir?"

Somewhere a woman screamed like she'd been goosed with something cold. People laughed and cheered. I zoomed in on a group of drunks at a fake French bistro across the way. I watched while the waiter hovered. A woman poured a shot into the mouth of a man on his knees, his head tilted back, eyes closed in prayer. The others cheered her on. In the middle of the group, Akinwole laughed on a bar stool.

"Was there anything else, sir?" the waiter said.

"Bill." I groped through my pockets for some cash. "The bill."

When he saw me, Akinwole waved me over.

"Paul, you found us at last. Come and meet the Mississauga Duplicate Bridge Club," he said, "fellow countrymen on a weekend excursion."

"We were meeting at the Benihana," I said. "I've been waiting there."

"Cheer up," Akinwole said, "you sound like a pouting girlfriend. You found me, which is what matters. You look like shit. Have a drink."

He reached back and, from the bar, produced a shot glass of thick green liquid. It looked like snot. There were about thirty more shots lined up. I knocked it back. It tasted like mint with a good kick. I passed one eye over his new playmates, who laughed and shoved one another. A few of the men talked in loud, enthusiastic voices about the marvels of a new lawn tractor one of them had recently bought back home in Mississauga. The second shot went down like the first. Easy.

"What're we celebrating?"

"I struck it rich," Akinwole said. "I hit the jackpot."

"And these folks? They strike it rich, too?"

"No," he said, "I picked them up along the way and bought them some drinks."

"What happened?" I said. "How much money did you win?"

"I selected a machine, like you said. One I liked. It had a painted safari scene. Elephants in silhouette. I dropped in a coin. Pushed a button. It spun around for a while until lights went off and bells started ringing. And out popped a slip of paper."

"Which you took to the cashier?"

"I was unsure what to do with it until a gentleman who looked like Sherlock Holmes in a blue sharkskin suit stuck his head out from behind the machine and told me I was a winner. He showed me where to take the slip."

Right after I'd given up on ghosts.

"What was he doing behind the machine?"

"I suppose he was playing on the other side and heard the commotion. It attracted a small crowd."

"So, what did you win?"

"At the cashier they gave me three hundred and seventeen thousand dollars," he said. "They asked how I wanted it. I said cash. In response, they gave me a briefcase to carry it in. On the house."

He pointed to a metal briefcase on the bar next to him. Gobsmacked, I stared at Akinwole. He smiled back and counted fifty dollars from a wad in his pocket.

"Thank you for the loan," he said. "This would never have happened otherwise."

He peeled off some more bills without counting and pressed them into my hand.

"You are a good man, Paul," he said. "You need to find your way back to the light."

"Sure," I said.

"Come, have another drink with our new friends before going," Akinwole said.

"Where're we going?"

"Not we, friend — me," Akinwole said. "I have decided not to continue to Los Angeles with you."

He passed me another glass of green snot and took one for himself. With a nod, he offered up a wordless toast, swallowed, shuddered, and wiped his mouth with a paper napkin.

"I have my own plan, Paul," he said. "Now that I have some means, I intend to make a change. Do something constructive. Have some fun."

"How does that translate?"

"I plan to return to Detroit. There is a beautiful woman waiting there. I think I will give her a call. See if she will have dinner with me."

"And then?"

"And then see what happens."

"That's your plan? Have dinner with Shirley Rose and see what happens?"

"I see many opportunities in that city. A chicken place. A literacy drop-in centre. A Jiffy Lube franchise. Who knows? We will see."

"LA has so much more to offer," I said. "It's a big place with all sorts of interesting people. A person could do anything he wants in that city."

Akinwole wasn't moved. "Good needs to be done elsewhere. Besides, she is not in LA, is she?"

The Mississauga Duplicate Bridge Club had settled under an alcohol mist around their table. They murmured amongst themselves, reeking of jet lag and shooters. One woman rested her head on the table. Two of the men arm-wrestled.

"When are you planning to go?"

"I checked with the concierge. There is a plane early this evening. I would like it if you brought me to the airport."

His pronouncement left me winded. He grounded me. He gave me courage. The notion of his departure filled me with loneliness.

"Do not be upset with me," Akinwole said, as though he sensed my despair. "Something is calling, and I must go."

"And go you shall," I said. "It wasn't part of my plan to have you come along with me. Finally, I'll be rid of you."

"You're an asshole, Paul, and you're still my friend."

He grinned and put his arm around my shoulders.

"I am, and you are," I said to keep it light.

I could've dropped him off on the curb. Instead, we parked the Firebird in the airport garage and together found the counter inside for Akinwole's ticket. I needed to be sure he left without complications. I also needed to keep our connection. His departure wasn't yet complete, and already a quiet sorrow crept in on socked feet at the notion of my travelling on without him. Not that I mentioned it. Instead, I made sure he had his ticket.

Afterward, there wasn't much time, so we hustled over to security, where we said goodbye.

"You have her address," Akinwole said. "Get in touch in a few days. She will tell you how to find me."

"Sure," I said. "I'll have finished the drive by then. I might come back to Detroit."

"Yes. Do. And thank you for taking me this far," he said. "Do not become a stranger."

"See you around," I said, and with that, we parted in different directions. Despite our well-intentioned words, I didn't believe we would share the same highway anytime soon.

With a walking waking hangover and unsure of what to do next, as usual when faced with uncertainty, I moved into a bar to refuel and regroup. This time, a fake little beach bar with a plastic swordfish mounted on the wall. Little white Christmas lights over the cash. A plastic pelican perched on a plastic barrel marked *Rum* in stencilled letters. Thin reggae music piped through tinny little speakers. A soulless spot with two stand-up tables across from the car rental counters. A place people stopped for a few fast shots before they carried on with whatever had led them to the need for a drink.

The vodka Red Bull combination should've been the right mixture to keep me engaged. But this time there was no effect. Unease and anxiety lingered. I missed Akinwole already and wished he hadn't bolted. To reassure myself all wasn't lost, I played with the diminished roll of bills in my pocket. My walk-around. At least it was something.

At a car rental desk, someone tried to sort a ride. An uninterested clerk processed the reservation. The clerk shook his head. Something was wrong. The man tapped his foot. Black cowboy boots. Silver caps over the toes and heels. He wore expensive designer jeans meant to look old and faded. His hand straightened a beautiful black braid that ran down his back in contrast to his tanned buckskin jacket. A glint of silver rings flashed. He reached across the counter in what seemed like an attempt to grab the clerk. Or, he could've been reaching for a pen. Hard to say. The man looked both ways like he was checking whether anyone noticed. That was when I recognized his profile. Eagle Creek.

I seized up at the table, afraid to move lest he spotted me. I visualized myself as another plastic bamboo pillar under the bar's fake straw roof. I held my breath. Was that knife in his checked bag, or was it already tucked into his waistband? Eagle Creek peeled off his Ray-Bans. He scanned the scene. He started to look toward me when the clerk distracted him with a piece of paper. Eagle Creek turned back to address the clerk.

I stepped out of the tiki hut bar and walked back into the airport, casual. I zigzagged around to make sure he wasn't following me. I locked myself in a toilet cubicle for a while. After an hour, he still hadn't caught up to me, so I retreated to the parking garage and slouched in the front seat of the Firebird, hidden from view, hyperventilating. My hands clenched the steering wheel until my knuckles ached. Sweat rolled down my armpits. Akinwole was right: telling the twins our location had been a mistake. They'd dispatched their man to hunt me. Now he was close enough to touch.

I stared through the windshield at the hood spinning before my eyes. Overcome with nausea, I opened the car door and retched, the only sound in the garage the splash of vomit on the concrete floor.

After a while, I sat up. Wiped my mouth. Locked the doors. Another hour passed before I felt sure he wasn't near the airport anymore. Finally, I fired up the car. I knew what to do. Outrun the devil. Take the car and vanish. It wasn't part of the plan but the plan had been shape-shifting since Toronto anyway. It had only ever included some cash and a ride out of town. The rest had been an improvisation.

Going back to the hotel wasn't a choice. Eagle Creek would track me there soon enough. He'd waste a day or two staking it out once he found it. That would buy some time. I pointed the Firebird out of Vegas the way we'd come, back into the desert. He'd figure I'd left town for sure and with luck, he wouldn't consider that I'd doubled back. The I-15 northbound stood straight and long. The land vast and wide. In the fading sun, any vehicle coming up from behind would've been easy to spot. No one followed.

After a while, somewhere past Salina along the I-70, my eyes closed, and the car almost slipped off the road. Down came the windows to let the night air and the noise of the wind keep me awake. Useless. My eyes drooped again. My head bobbed down. Chin bounced on chest.

I followed an exit off the freeway onto a darkened county road to find a place to pull over and sleep awhile. Disoriented by a crossroad, I turned onto a bumpy desert road. The Firebird's high beams cut through the dark. You could've seen them from outer space. The car felt warm and safe. Silent. Except for the dull growl of the engine, content at work. Out of the night, something small flashed across the road. A rabbit. A fox. Hard to tell in the dark. I swerved hard to the left. It made no difference. There was a soft bump bump under the wheels.

To stay out of the ditch, I oversteered hard in the opposite direction. The Firebird spun sideways across the road. At this speed, the tires lost grip. They squealed in protest. Burnt rubber smoked around the windows. Out of control, the car skidded off the road into a gully and rolled over onto its side. The wail of shearing metal and the dull crunch of shattered glass mixed with the roar of the outraged engine. The roof started to tear off its posts.

The wreckage slid across rocks and brush to a halt on a gnarled stump under the stars. The motor fell silent. When quiet was restored to the prairie, a few night peepers cautiously offered up their commentary.

I crawled out of the wreck on my hands and knees. My palms were covered with blood. Otherwise, I seemed unhurt. Behind me, an orange fireball lit up the darkness. The Firebird exploded into flames.

TWENTY-TWO

Rescue Me

ORANGE FLAMES as high as the roof snaked around the wreck. Dry grass crackled and snapped in the fire. I cowered behind a boulder to shield myself from the burning debris. Burnt rubber seared my throat. A flaming wheel blazed past my leg into the desert. Overhead, fiery metal swarmed the starry heavens. The car's hood blasted out of the inferno, flying so close it grazed my forehead. In the heat, both headlights exploded, the staccato pop pop of the glass like pistol shots into the inky prairie night. The driver's door rocketed by, embers in its tail. Sparking bits of handles, panelling, and armrests showered all around.

Afraid something might drop from the sky and scorch me, I covered my head with both arms, my back protected by the rock. Before long, a burning brick-sized packet exploded in the dust within arm's reach. It was powder wrapped in plastic, wrapped in newspapers. Burning packets started to fall all around me. Red puffs of dirt billowed off the ground each time one landed. Other flying packages ripped open and caught fire midair. Soon, a cloud of flaming powder snowed over the whole scene.

The Firebird had been trapped from the start. Lover Man moved dope, like Trang said. Of course, they'd sent Eagle Creek after me. It was about the dope, not the car. They'd played me for an idiot. I was a mule. A stooge.

My throat tightened, gasping for air. My intestines dammed up tight, their base primal urge barely suppressed. I turned and hugged the rock, digging my nails into its crusty lichens. I licked its ancient surface. Its rusty taste grounded me. I closed my eyes and pictured my fingers along the small of Marla's back, around her pelvis, and down her long satin legs. My head in her lap. My arms wrapped tight around her waist. One by one, I counted the frizzy hairs around her navel. Every time I reached ten, I lost track and started over.

After what seemed like hours, the fury faded, the fire stopped by the rocky desert beyond the perimeter of burnt shrub and grass. The wreckage clanked with the cooling and contracting of twisted metal. Somewhere a coyote howled an all clear. A dispassionate crescent moon and a cold star watched overhead.

I released the rock and rolled over. Arms and legs trembled. White bone glistened through the rasped skin of my bloodied palms. To protect the open wounds, I held my clenched fists under my armpits. Futile. The effort only increased my agony.

On the road, the sound of an engine crept up from the distance. Lights appeared around the corner. For a moment,

I feared that Eagle Creek, the relentless hunter, had me. But the car didn't stop. This was someone uninterested in the troubles of a burning wreck in the night. It dissolved into the distance until silence returned. No one heard me. No one came for me.

At dawn, wisps of smoke still twisted from the razed Firebird, vaporizing in the cloudless sky. A couple of vultures rode the thermals. A mosquito drilled into my nose. I swatted it with a bloody hand and squinted at the shimmering horizon. Another car failed to stop.

In time, a pickup truck pulled over. I stayed flat behind the rock and watched a weathered tree of an old man limp his way around the boulders and shrubs toward the wreck. A tall heavy guy with jeans pulled high up over his gut. His unshaven double chin tucked into a brown-checkered shirt. He had the hands of a giant mole, shovels used to paddle the air while he walked. A tuft of white hair topped his head like an exclamation mark. At the wreck, he studied the scene, scratched his ass with one massive flipper, and spat a stream of brackish-brown tobacco juice.

It was time to move. Get away. Have my hands cleaned and bandaged. Find sanctuary. Revise my plans. So, on the chance the codger wasn't a killer, I sat up. The old man noticed me right away. He came over for a look.

"What're you doing behind that rock, son?"

"I'm hurt," I said. "I need a ride."

I raised my hands for his inspection.

"Sweet Lord, there's a fine mess." He whistled, impressed.

"I escaped the burning car," I said. "I guess it could be worse."

He reached under my armpits and lifted me to my feet, his hands like steel forklifts. The old boy still had a grip.

"Can you walk, kid?"

"Sure, I can," I said. "I need my hands fixed."

"There's first aid in the truck," he said. "Follow me."

The windowless charred frame of the Firebird was beyond recognition. Warped bits of black metal scattered the prairie. Lover Man would demand retribution. Eagle Creek's black eyes glared down from the blue. His knife slashed through the sky. At best, a painful death loomed.

The old man headed for his truck. He wasn't concerned. My trouble was unknown to him. Unsure of what came next, I followed in hopes that somehow this would turn out right. We walked along the trail the car had torn through the brush, over the rocks, and back up to the highway. Both of us hobbled, for different reasons.

The pickup truck seemed even older than its driver. What looked like a bullet hole pierced the front windshield on the passenger side about where a person's throat would be. In places, the scratched white paint revealed rusty brown stains in its dented body. In the back, a basset hound peered over the sides of the bed. Droopy eyes leaked doggy eye goop. Something reeked of carrion.

The dog barked a couple of times. *Hey, Boss, whatcha scrape off the desert floor? This guy don't look good.*

The old man flipped down the tailgate and pointed.

"Sit here," he said. "Don't mind Albert. He's harmless. Only smells bad."

From the cab, he produced a red first-aid kit and a flask.

"Drink and then we'll clean your hands with it," he said. "It works for both."

I took a long pull. It burned going down. Moonshine. It felt good. At first. Then I fought the urge to puke.

"Bet it works in the engine," I said when I could breathe again.

"I guess it could, in a pinch," the man said. "These old diesel engines will go on anything. Not like those no-lead-gas electro hybrid contraptions they got these days."

A spurt of tobacco shot from between his unshaven lips and sizzled on the road. Without further ceremony, he splashed the moonshine over my wounded hands. It felt like he'd lashed me with a strip of barbed wire.

"What happened out here?" His huge hands scraped the dirt from my palms with tiny pieces of gauze.

"Hit a rabbit, I think."

"Figures. We found one on the road over there." He nodded his head in the general direction. "That's why Albert stinks. The bugger likes to roll around in dead animals."

Albert kept a close eye on the doctoring. Slobber foamed off his leathery lips onto my shoulder.

While he wrapped my hands in bandages, the man said, "You're lucky this is all's you got. Cars can be replaced."

A rocky, jagged brown and red terrain without beginning or end surrounded us. Tufts of yellow grass and green shrubs dotted the landscape. Sun-baked boulders and buttes in harsh geometry littered the plain. Far off in the distance, where the arid earth blended with the windless sky, a couple of snowy mountain peaks shimmered like a mirage.

"Where've I landed?"

The man pointed up the road. "We're about twenty miles from Moab." His hand stroked the horizon. "Over them hills there is the valley of the Green River. Runs into the Colorado River. Across that and beyond eventually is the promised land, California," he said. "They got a good hospital in Moab. I can run you over."

My hands balled into fists. The bandages felt secure.

"I'm going to be okay," I said. "I don't need a hospital."

Eagle Creek would be sure to check there.

"Well, then," he said, "how about I take you over to the state troopers so's you can file an accident report for the insurance."

"No, no police either."

His blue eyes narrowed with new interest.

"You didn't steal that car, did you, boy?"

"No. But it's not mine, either."

"You in trouble with the law, then?"

"No," I said.

"Well," he said, "it's your own business, I guess. There's no shame in being on the wrong side of the law. Hell, fugitives been hiding in the hills around these parts since Butch Cassidy come here after robbing all them banks and such."

Albert barked at the mention of Butch Cassidy. He liked that story. More dog goober flew through the air.

"I'm not in that situation," I said, "though I'd be grateful for somewhere to rest up."

"Get in the truck," he said.

The truck was from before seat belts. A 12 gauge Winchester over-under was racked in the back of the cab. I could see the road through a rusty hole in the floor between my feet. He fired up the engine. The radio sparked to life. Mavis Staples sang, "Praise the Lord," through a cracked dashboard speaker.

He shot a squirt of tobacco juice over my feet through the hole in the floor, then rammed the truck into gear. In the back came a dull thud as Albert's body lurched against the metal sides of the truck bed. The old man wiped some brown spittle from his chin and offered me his hand.

"Name's Archie," he said.

We drove along the two-lane blacktop for about twenty minutes. Archie didn't talk. He looked at the road and steered the truck carefully with both hands on the wheel, like he was at the helm of a ship in an ice storm at night.

"Where're we going, Archie?" I said after a while.

"The man I sometimes does chores for, he's all right," Archie said. "He's okay. Not Christian but at least he's an American, like us. His place is out of the way. Most folks around here never heard of it."

It sounded good. No sense correcting him about who I was or where I came from. "Who is he?"

"He's a Boo-dist. He minds his own business. Works on his land. Walks around counting ducks. Right now, he's digging them a new pond. You can do some work around his place and rest a spell."

My bandaged hands were starting to throb. "I'm not sure what work I can do."

"Let's see what he says."

Nothing marked the turn when Archie veered the truck off the paved road into the desert toward the mountains. We rattled over a cow grate. The truck shook in all directions. In the back, Albert tossed from side to side stoically. His nails clawed the truck bed for traction. Archie spat another gob of tobacco out the window and geared down. He shut the radio off. The wind sighed through the grass. In the distance, a killdeer cried out. Prairie sage scented the air.

"It's remote," he said. "Mike built it up from nothing. Made it into a nice spread. He came in '93 and spent the first winter in a tent."

"He lives out here alone?" The land supported an occasional gnarled tree and a lot of red rock.

"Yep. He's an odd guy, Mike. He likes to walk around out here. He went away for a while. Folks believed he was killed overseas. That didn't turn out to be right."

The track dipped into a small valley surrounded on three sides by snow-capped mountains. Unlike most of the place, which looked inhospitable, this valley rolled with emerald grasslands. Lanky poplars glistened in a slow breeze. The cool morning air filled my lungs, the first good sensation in some time.

The truck stopped in front of a big log cabin with a couple of rocking chairs on the wraparound porch. Behind the house stood a barn with a red roof. A rusty horse trailer rested on concrete blocks in the tall grass. It looked like it hadn't moved in years. Next to it was a metal pen, like a cage for livestock, or maybe a trap for cougars and coyotes that came close to the house. The door stood open. An empty water bowl lay turned over on the concrete floor.

In the distance, a dust bowl gathered. A green and yellow tractor emerged from the cloud, coming straight for us at speed.

"He's a maniac on that thing," Archie said. He pulled up the handbrake. "He loves racing that John Deere. Even if he's a holy man now. They're not supposed to do things like that."

"Like what?"

Archie watched the tractor bounce over the prairie.

"He says Boo-dists ain't supposed to take pleasure from what they do."

Albert barked at the tractor, his front paws up on the truck bed.

"Shut up, Albert, it's Mike on his tractor."

Albert continued barking like we were under attack until Archie tumbled out of the cab and made a half-assed attempt to whack the dog with his open hand.

"One of these days, I swear I'm going to whoop you."

Albert growled, black lips pulled back over yellow fangs. Nevertheless, he moved out of range.

The tractor skidded to a halt beside us, swallowed by a haze of red dirt. Grit clogged my eyes and throat. Archie coughed, and Albert howled again. When the swirling dust settled, a bald man wrapped in an orange robe climbed off the tractor. He wore construction boots with the laces wrapped around his ankles. Dark welder's goggles protected his eyes. Midforties. Thin. Fit. A half woman, half bird with a sword in hand danced around a sequence of mysterious geometric patterns tattooed down the wiry muscles of his left arm.

He peeled the goggles off his head and grinned.

"Greetings," he said.

"Been digging?" Archie said.

"There's always something to clear away."

"Anyone out helping today?"

"Only the tractor. I call it a mechanical meditation so it sounds less pleasurable." He chuckled and wiped his forehead. "I doubt I'm fooling anyone. Who's this?"

Archie pointed his thumb at me. "He wrecked a car up on the service road."

I showed my bloodied bandages. "Paul Wint."

The man put his hands together in greeting.

"I'm Mike. Mike Pike." He giggled at the sound of his own name. "You're wounded."

His ruddy clean-shaven face glowed. His open smile dispelled any notion that he had misgivings about harbouring a stranger. I felt welcome.

"Archie's got me fixed," I said.

"No doubt. His combat hospital training."

I looked at Archie. He acted so of this place I couldn't picture him any other way.

"Combat hospital?"

Archie shrugged. "Orderly. Drafted. Korea. Two years."

He leaned on the hood of his truck and looked away.

"We're brothers in arms," Mike said. "Archie in Korea, me in Kuwait."

"Desert Storm," I said. "You were there? You look more like some Buddhist monk."

Mike snapped his fingers in rhythm. "They taught me how to hate and they sent me to Kuwait." He laughed. It rang pure, up from the soles of his feet. "I transformed."

Archie studied the mountains and absently worked a fresh tobacco plug under his bottom lip. Mike tugged at the tractor's spark plug covers. In the back of the truck, Albert farted and stretched out on his back in the sun. Somewhere, an eagle screeched. Its cry echoed off the distant mountains. All there was left on earth was this moment in this bewitching valley with its easy silence and its majestic views. For the first time since leaving Harmony Greeting Cards, I felt good.

Archie shattered the spell with a test shot, like he was calibrating the range of a new hunting rifle. Fresh brown tobacco juice exploded in the dust. Satisfied with the new chaw's balance in size and consistency, he grunted. "He says the car weren't his, but he didn't steal it, neither."

"Good," said Mike. "Theft is pointless."

"The kid needs a place to hole up for a spell."

Mike adjusted his robes. His knobby legs rooted immobile into the boots. I glimpsed a tiger tattoo across his chest.

"Is that all right?" I said.

I hoped not to have to explain my story in detail. It sounded implausible — or, at least, like trouble. Turned out, neither man cared to hear anything about what had brought me here.

"Everything's exactly like it should be," Mike said. He smiled again and opened his arms. "The ranch is a sanctuary to all who come in peace. We eat once a day at sunrise. No alcohol. No violence. Everyone helps with the work. Meditation at eight and three. If you don't join me, you're expected to be quiet. Lights out at nine. Archie will tend to your hands till they're better."

That settled it, for the moment.

TWENTY-THREE

Home on the Range

MIKE OPENED the screen door and pressed a pair of old, clean overalls along with some balled-up T-shirts into my hands. Archie led the way over the knoll away from the main house to a cabin in a stand of trees. A one-room hut big enough for a single bed beside a wood-burning stove. No power. No lights. In back stood an outhouse next to an outdoor solar-heated shower that fed off a wobbly water tower.

After Archie left, I gulped the pitcher of water he'd placed on the railing outside and then lingered in the shower for a good ten minutes till it ran cold. The last hours of the day were rocked away on the porch in the shadow of the Rockies that clawed at the cobalt sky. In the distance, between the hut and the mountains, a river frothed over rounded boulders along its banks on its surge to the sea.

Eagle Creek wasn't going to find me here. If he found the Firebird burnt to a shell, he'd figure my body was consumed by flames. Vaporized. And if there was a trail to the road, that was where it ended, at the spot where the truck picked me up. On asphalt. No tracks. And even if he smelled blood and went down the highway on a hunch, where would he go from there? Which direction would he venture? Nothing marked this place. Archie said that for most people, this valley didn't exist. For now, I'd vanished.

The first night, coyotes and owls serenaded me with a symphony of plaintive cries and whoops, while overhead outside my window stardust swirled across the galaxy. In the morning, a few white-tailed deer grazed near the cabin. Between the sun and the moon on opposite ends of the horizon, the grass glistened with dewy crystals under their hooves.

Hungry, I followed the path across the field and over the hill to the main cabin, where Mike meditated on the porch. He seemed unaware of my arrival. Inside, Archie banged about in the kitchen, busy with breakfast. When it was ready, Mike came in, and we ate in silence. Steel-cut Irish oatmeal, butter, and maple syrup. Best meal in weeks. My spirits lifted with every bite. Fed, clothed, and rested, for the moment nothing could harm me. Everything was going to be all right. Afterward, Archie and I cleaned up while Mike vanished without a word.

"Let them hands heal for a few days before you get to doing chores around here," Archie said when he changed my bandages. "I usually come around in the mornings to help with the cooking. Look around if you like. I'll return tomorrow."

With that, he bounced off in his truck, Albert in the back. His ears flopped to the rhythm of the road.

I took to daily hikes and soon discovered a small overgrown orchard protected by a ring of Colorado spruce. Pears, apples, and plums grew in haphazard rows amongst sunflowers and wild roses. The fruit trees were full of broken branches. Thorny weeds and tall grass choked the flowers. In the middle of the grove there was a wooden bench where I sometimes passed the entire day unaware of time.

After several visits to the place, a rake and pruning shears appeared propped up against one of the gnarled apple trees. There were no instructions pinned to them, and neither Archie nor Mike mentioned anything. It seemed like an invitation by the orchard itself to restore order. So, I passed a few hours every day with the rake and the clippers for as long as my hands could stand it. I found an unexpected satisfaction in the twang of the metal rake over the dry earth, raking little mounds of twigs and leaves that I'd periodically burn. The sweet blue smoke curled into the sky as the fire released the old, the dead, and the decomposed. My new vocation.

"Persistence and initiative get you there," said Mike, who materialized one day to watch me work. No greeting or idle chat. Just bare feet. Orange robes. I grinned at him over a small pile of rotten apples.

"More like boredom drives me to it."

"Good. You keep being bored. The orchard will transform into a better place. Negative into positive. That's how it should be."

From the satchel over his shoulder he produced a brushed aluminum Zippo embossed with an eagle holding a clutch of swords in its talons.

"Are your goals compelling now?" He lit a cigarette. "Or are they ordinary, like the ones you used to have?"

I paused to admire the liberated sunflowers craning toward the light. Mike settled on the bench, content to blow smoke rings, a vague smile on his face. Goals? My goals were to avoid getting killed by Eagle Creek. Not something I wanted to discuss with Mike.

"I never had goals," I said. "I pushed on. Blind. Went with it." Which was true once, before my goal of not getting killed eclipsed my goal of getting by.

"So, the goal of an orderly orchard is a step up for you," Mike said. He flipped ash off his lap. "You can get through anything if you set a goal. Goals are important. The army taught me that."

"What was your goal?"

"The recruiter said for twenty bucks I could get laid in the Philippines. I was an eighteen-year-old virgin. I'd have done anything for that. I was in."

"Some goal," I said.

Mike nodded. "It changed."

He fell silent, the smile fading to a blank stare at the trees. The wind whispered something to him in the leaves. After a while, he cleared his throat.

"They made us hard," he said, his voice hushed. "They abused us. Exposed us to unspeakable cruelty. Made us break our ties with the world. Fed us red meat, porn, and booze. Told us we were invincible. Then they armed us with the best weapons in the world and sent us to liberate Kuwait. Liberate. Kill or be killed. Stay alive. That was the goal. It was spectacular."

Kill or be killed. We had some common ground, after all. The fear of being killed. A diet of red meat and porn might've made me more prepared to defend myself.

"Kill or be killed?" I said. "And what was that like?"

He looked at me sidelong.

"You're not from around here, are you?"

I shrugged. Let it go. Didn't want to be the one responsible for dredging up the violence he'd sought to leave behind. Best to disengage before Buddhist turned back into rabid dog.

Mike flicked another ash and offered me a mint from a tin in his bag. "It doesn't matter. We're talking about something else now, aren't we?"

"Goals," I said through a mouthful of mint. "Mine's to prune fruit trees and liberate sunflowers."

Mike nodded, his mind at war.

"We liberated, all right. Behind enemy lines one night on recon we came across a burnt truck filled with dead Iraqi soldiers." He drew in the smoke and rolled the Zippo around in his hand. "They were a caramelized lump about the size of a dining-room table. The only way to tell they were once human was by the white teeth. Teeth don't burn so well. The next day I was granted leave to Thailand."

"Did you get laid?"

Mike didn't smile. He shook his head. "I went north. Up near Laos in the forest. Someone told me about magic temple tattoos with powers of protection. I wanted protection. I wanted to live."

"That's a good goal."

"When they learned I was a soldier, the monks blessed me with amulets. They chanted prayers and over three days, they carved spells into my flesh with smouldering hot bamboo pens. At times, I couldn't feel a thing. Other times, the pain was so great I wanted out of my skin to get away from it. I realized if I hadn't been moved by desire, I wouldn't have joined the army. And if I hadn't joined the army, I wouldn't have found myself in such danger and such pain. That's how I came to understand about desire as the root of suffering."

He rubbed a hand over his chest.

"Later, back in Bangkok, I learned my squad was killed by friendly fire. I was listed MIA. Taking advantage of this clerical error, I took the bus back up north to that temple and stayed for three years."

"Did your goals change?"

"Yes, and I'm no longer certain I'll achieve them in this lifetime," he said. "Do you believe in anything yet?"

"I believe in the all-knowing dog," I said.

He looked blank, like he didn't get jokes or light conversation because he had to concentrate on whatever he needed to accomplish out here on the fringes of the world. Transcend, or whatever these people did.

He said, "Here's what I've learned: a serious life begins when there's an element of illusion in reality and something real in our fantasies."

The warmth of the sun on my face made me glad to be alive. That much was certain. The rest was up for grabs.

"Sure," I said.

"Look around you." He waved his arms at the mountains. "It's real. It's imagined. It's potential. It's actual. Beautiful, vibrant, all in flux with us, changing and vibrating right along with it. We're all part of the grand unfolding. The eternal ebb and flow. The only meaningful question is, how do you conduct yourself through it?"

He tucked his feet up cross-legged on the bench.

"Most people are consumed by the details of finding their worth and their happiness in others. In worldly business. They don't see that happiness and meaning grow from within. From right conduct. You have to fulfill yourself. The rest comes by itself."

He pointed to the sky, where two prairie hawks flew circles around each other in what might've been an elaborate mating ritual. Or maybe they were locked in aerial combat.

"That's what most of us concern ourselves with: eating, sleeping, fucking, fighting, and surviving." He grinned and touched my hand. "Their concerns are simple, predictable, and desperate. We can do better than that."

I sure wanted to do better than that. This living business was wearing me down. I laughed out loud at how unlikely my life had become. How simple, predictable, and desperate it seemed to be these days. How lost I felt. Mike nodded and smiled like he knew.

"Okay," he said.

That evening, I sat on the porch with the mountains. A murky sky boiled out thunderbolts in a prelude to rain. A warm gust whipped up in growing violence. The trees bent and swayed like a troupe of anguished dancers. Across the field, a lone black crow fought frantically against the wind.

My recovery was steady. My hands scabbed over. At night, the bandages came off, and in time, they stayed off altogether. The rest of me healed as well. No great surprise. There wasn't any dope to smoke. No coke to snort. No J&B, no Oban, no espresso. No sugar. No hot dogs. No Doritos. Not even a generic tablet of ASA. My regular intake had been replaced with a single organic meal every morning, washed down by a cup of lemon grass tea and all the well water a person could drink.

At first, the new regime created dull pain. Not only my hands hurt. Everything hurt. Everywhere. From the detox. For days, crushed glass scratched through my veins. My head felt like someone had used a hard rubber mallet on the base of my skull. For a while, my watery calves couldn't even take the weight of my body. Sounds startled me. The patterns in the clouds made me sad. At night, I curled in a tight fetal ball. Breath uneven. Sweating till the sheets were soaked. Until, after about ten days, I finally slept through the night and I started to feel better in my skin. For the first time since my arrival, I turned to the notion of what to do next. What would drive me out? For that matter, why would I ever leave?

For now, the rain drummed me off the porch. Inside, the cabin had no lights, and there weren't any matches for the oil lamp on the bedside table. Instead, I contorted around the chair and the cold stove through darkness into bed.

Before the current of sleep slipped me away, biblical thunder exploded overhead. For a moment, the night filled with white electrical light. The outside door crashed open to batter the wall. Furious water lashed across the threshold. Lightning tore through the sky to reveal the mountains through sheets of rain.

I clambered out of bed to shut the door when a figure appeared in the entrance. More jagged lightning flared up behind him. He poured himself into the hut, a slight stagger to his movements. A waterfall flowed from his stetson when he removed it. With a free hand, he wrung the water from his beard and smiled at me. Even in the dark, Hornsmith's ghost was unmistakable.

For fear he'd bamboozle me, I held up my hands before he could say a word, and over the thunder said, "Leave me alone. Go to where you're trying to get. You have no business here."

Hornsmith clutched his hat in his hands. The storm flashed in the whites of his eyes. He said, "I can't stay out there. There's still so much to do."

In the tight quarters of the hut, he smelled of vinegar and sweet, damp lilies. If I could've caught him by surprise, I would've thrown him back into the storm, forgetting he was dead and impossible to throw out of anywhere.

I said, "I'm trying to look at life from another angle. These days, I'd be happy to make an honest wage. Cook an honest meal. Wash my own socks and stick to my own counsel. I'm not going your way."

Hornsmith coughed. He looked around. "Any water?"

"I'll pour you a glass," I said, "and put it outside on the porch for you. Then, you must go."

The lines on his face were deeper than before. His back slumped. His belly extended. His white hair stuck out in all directions. He gulped a few times like a hooked fish flopping on a dock.

"You're right, Latour," he said at last. "You should find your way, and I should find mine. I shouldn't have come."

He turned toward the door, stopped, and looked at the floor. He straightened the hat back on his head.

"Beware of your complacency," he said. "There's unfinished business, whether you like it or not. Guard yourself. Your enemies seek a resolution. Contend with them."

"Your water," I said and reached around for the pitcher. The door hammered in the wind. I was alone. He'd eluded me again.

Afterward, the rain outside rapped on the window. Sleep wouldn't come. Hornsmith troubled me out there in the netherworld, doggedly engaging me. I wasn't sure if he was a chimera out of my mind or if there was something else to it. He'd made good in Las Vegas, like he said he would. Not how I'd imagined, but it still remained a good and real result. Now, this new message resonated. It was true, in the passing weeks the feeling of danger had subsided. A sense of safety had settled in. At the ranch, it seemed no one could ever find me. In time, I expected my past would be of no consequence, perishable and at last invisible. Lying in bed that night, I was no longer so sure.

At sunrise the next morning, troubled by Hornsmith's warning and still trying to make sense of Mike's lectures, instead of going to the main house for breakfast, I followed one of the cow paths through the grasslands into the hills. The storm had passed, with only the wet field as evidence of the previous night's violence. The cold air felt crisp in my lungs. The hush of the dripping grass and the distant murmur of the river were the only sounds.

After about half an hour, the trail became so steep I needed my hands to steady myself over the rocks until things levelled on a small plateau overlooking the rocky desert plain. Winded, I rested on a boulder like some solitary Navajo warrior who might have sat on this exact spot and reported the same arid vista, unchanged in a thousand years. From this spot, the desert was without the grandeur of the mountains or the mystery of the ocean. In the desert, nothing grew. Nothing moved. Nothing shimmered or shined. Nothing was revealed. Nothing was promised. Like some flat, soulless primordial monster, the desert lay in wait to kill hope. Boulders. Buttes. Stone arches. Patches of dead grass and dirt. I surveyed this forsaken place and listened for a signal in the wind. Nothing came. The reassuring resistance of warm rock against my leg was the only certainty. My relationships out here were few and intimate, peppered with ghosts and unseen threats.

Once my breath settled, I scuttled down the other side of the hill onto the plain for a closer look. My eyes adjusted to details unseen from up high. Occasional pools of brackish red water cradled in rocky crevices sparkled white highlights under the brilliant sky. Pink cacti the size of my thumb hid amongst tufts of emerald grass that poked through unlikely bits of cracked earth. Shiny purple beetles crawled through the sand while tiny yellow butterflies flitted inches above the ground. Then, unexpectedly, I came across a bright copper rattlesnake coiled asleep in the sun. Aroused by my footsteps, it raised its head to look me over. Curious, it flicked its red tongue a couple of times and smiled. Careful not to startle it, I sat down a few paces away and smiled back.

Life in all its teeming mystery, the whole cosmological unfolding of nothing into this rambling, expanding, heart-thumping something exploded behind my eyes in a riot of pinks and reds and blues. Bugs, birds, bushes, and rock swirled. Circles of light haloed the landscape. The intoxicating smell of sage and red dust filled my head. The sun boiled sweat out of every pore from my scalp to my feet. It all was beyond my understanding. The snake's little bumpy brown head nodded as if it understood how overwhelmed I felt.

Through the silence, its thoughts drifted on the wind into my own. *Don't be alarmed*, it seemed to say. *Stop looking for meaning. In all these thousands of years, you're no closer to a resolution.*

The snake had the words to soothe the chaos. *Consider this*, it said. *The only meaning is of your own making.* With that, it flicked its tongue a couple more times and settled back to sunbathing. And I started to consider a new course. Maybe I should do like everyone always says: set goals, confront fears, create meaning, and carry on. Even if it felt a bit like a yoga class I wanted out of.

Then, after almost twenty minutes of silence, a small metallic reflection on the horizon glanced off the sun. A shadowy figure moved amongst the boulders before vanishing behind a scruff of bush.

TWENTY-FOUR

Town

A WHITE ATV with monstrous knobby tires gleamed outside the main house. I stopped to admire the beast before heading inside for breakfast. Oversized black fenders swept back like dragon wings. *Raptor 700* blazed in gold Gothic letters across the fuel tank. Its chrome exhaust the width of a cannon barrel glistened in the sun. Next to Archie's ancient pickup, the rig was otherworldly. Because we hadn't seen any visitors since my arrival, I figured Mike or Archie had a new ride, even if it was hard to picture either one of them on the thing.

In the kitchen, Archie dished up Irish stew. Mike was already into a bowl when I settled at the table.

"New Raptor outside? You guys going to ride the range with that?"

"Nope. It belongs to a birdwatcher," Mike said through a mouthful of stew. "I found him on the property. Says he's from Rochester, New York. He's hoping for a glimpse of a Fulvous Whistling-Duck."

A wide-brimmed hat with brown camo patterns lay on the table next to a pair of binoculars with some kind of compass device in the top of one of the lenses. Down the hall, the toilet flushed. A door creaked. Someone else was in the house. The extraterrestrial Raptor rider.

"What's that?" I said.

Archie handed me a bowl of stew and a spoon. "A duck that usually nests in Texas or California," he said. "They don't often come 'round here."

Mike said, "Apparently, our pond is perfect. Dense. Cattails. Marshy. Shallow water. He wants to place decoys and see what happens. How about that, Arch?"

Archie clanged the empty stewpot under the tap. He shook his head in silent awe or disbelief. Hard to say which.

"That's right," someone said from the hall, "the Fulvous Whistling-Duck has only been spotted in Utah three or four times since 1908."

In the doorway was Simon Trang, decked out in a lightweight mesh hunting vest and beige desert-camo pants. He grinned when he saw me.

"Hi," he said, "my name's Billy Chang."

He extended his hand, which, stunned, I shook. He'd shaved off the Fu Manchu and now sported heavy horn-rimmed glasses for the complete duck geek look. Trang sat down to eat like all was normal. I stayed quiet. Best to wait and see what his game was.

Archie dried his hands on a rag. "So, what's a guy from

upstate New York doing looking for ducks that almost never come here?"

"You have no idea," Trang said. His smile suggested a boyish enthusiasm. "It's been an exciting time for me. I've pursued reported sightings for weeks. Followed flight patterns. Checked landmarks. Chased small clues here and there. I'm close now."

That must've been him in the desert amongst the high rocks. I pictured Simon Trang out there on his Raptor 700, scanning the horizon with field glasses. Watching. Waiting. Certain the others wouldn't be far behind. If he'd found me, they would, too.

"See anything?" I tried to sound casual.

He shook his head. "Some signs, but nothing confirmed. I'll keep looking. I'm not worried. It's early days. This could be a real score if I'm right."

"And what makes you think you'll see anything?" said Archie.

"Call it a hunch," Trang said with the confidence of someone who doesn't rely on hunches. "I've studied this duck for a long time. Followed it right across the country. Mike's been generous, letting me stake out his pond. Now, I have a decoy situation ready in the perfect habitat."

"So, a couple of days?" I said to gauge how much time was left.

"Who knows?" said Trang. "Days. Weeks. I can wait. I'm retired. I took a room at the Apache Motel in town. I'm all set. I have all the time and money I want to travel around looking for rare birds."

"You alone?" Archie said. "Or is this something other bird people will jump on when they figure it out?"

Trang nodded. "This duck's special. There's a bit of a competition going on for who'll get him first."

"Rival duck watchers?" I flashed on Eagle Creek dressed like Elmer Fudd. Duck season. Rabbit season. "Sounds crazy."

Archie shrugged. He cleared Mike's plate. "Can't be worse than those hippies last summer looking for a portal to the parallel universe. Talk about rivalries."

Both men chuckled at a shared memory, but offered no further elaboration. Trang shook his head, too, amused. But we didn't ask to hear the details. We weren't talking about hippies now.

"If those other guys show up," Trang said, "it's going to get plenty hot around here. This is a big deal for them." He looked at me. "They play for keeps."

"For keeps?" I said.

Trang laughed. "When a birder wants to be the first to claim a rare sighting like this, there's nothing he won't do. Sugar in gas tanks. Diversionary fires. Thugs have been hired to beat people up and scare competitors off. You name it."

"Jesus wept," said Archie.

"Oh, yes," said Trang, "people have even been shot at."

Mike rose to his feet and moved toward the door.

"I had no idea birding was competitive." He bowed briefly. "I wish you all the best and hope you get what you came for. Go in peace."

Mike was out of time to talk about business that didn't bring him closer to his higher purpose. Trang stood up and bowed in return.

"Thank you," he said. "I'm grateful for your permission to wait here."

Once Mike was gone, Archie was also keen to get on with his day. He said to me, "Time's wasting. Got a grocery run. Mike says it's good for you to tag along. You ready for a trip into town?"

Without waiting for an answer, he stepped outside and called Albert to the porch.

"I see they have no idea what brought you here," said Trang when we were alone. "That's good. No sense getting these people excited about our business. Go to town. See if you can flush them out. I'm sure they're around. We can end this soon."

Before, nothing used to matter. I'd endure the untenable because everything always passed. I used to be drawn into stories that weren't good for me. Stories that weren't mine. Stories that made my life turbulent in an alien ebb and flow without commitment or responsibility. Aimless and disconnected, I'd been a sleepwalker for a long time. That dog outside in the sun was more engaged in his life. Until this moment. Now there was an urgent call to take control of my situation. The last thing that made sense was to go into town to flush out Lover Man or Eagle Creek. That reeked of suicide.

"How'd you find me?" I said.

Trang adjusted his hat over his ears. He said, "About six weeks ago, someone driving along the road saw a fire out in the desert. They called it in to the state troopers. No one was fussed, so it took a while to go out and have a look. You left some blood on a rock and some tracks on the ground. A report was filed. I picked up the scent. You should've called."

"I was sure I'd vanished."

"You did for a while." He slung the binoculars around his neck. "Lucky for you, I got here first. Now, go show the world you're alive. Once you're in the open, it won't take long. I'll handle it from there. I got your back. Soon, you'll be free from this business."

Trang, my guardian angel. I didn't feel reassured. Were his transborder warriors poised behind the mountains, ready to swoop in with my well-being top of mind? Hard to picture. More likely, I was his bait. A bleating lamb tethered to a stake to draw out the jackals. More likely, I'd get killed in the crossfire. On the other hand, there wasn't much choice. His presence was the harbinger of a much bigger problem to come. He'd found me, and they would, too.

The narrow highway lay crooked in red rock canyons, under ancient natural stone arches, past petrified pinnacles hundreds of feet above the scrub. A faded yellow centre line marked the route toward town and the snow-capped mountains beyond — the final barrier to the Pacific Ocean. Occasionally, a heavy tanker truck laden with flammable liquids bore down on us. Sometimes, an impatient car passed us at great speed. Mostly we were alone under the infinite blue sky.

This visit to Moab was nothing to look forward to. The last time out, the world had presented a dangerous gauntlet where I'd been stalked, kicked, beaten, and left for dead. I feared this time wouldn't be any different. Except in the details.

We drove in silence for a while, Archie and me. Him wrapped up in the business of driving. Me absorbed in daydreams, while the world re-emerged over the horizon. Behind my closed eyes in the warmth of the morning sun, Marla's face appeared. She'd been absent from my thoughts for weeks. With Akinwole's departure, the car wreck, Eagle Creek on my tail, and my vanishing act into the isolated world of Mike and Archie, there just hadn't been time for her. Now, as the world started to press in, I wondered how she was doing and who she was with. Not in a jealous way, like before, with her and Lover Man. More in a gentle way, like the way you'd miss someone you loved who'd died. Once we were in town, I'd decided I would call her. Tell her I was alive. Tell her I missed her. Find out if it was safe to come out of hiding. Sure, it was a bad idea. I planned to do it anyhow. Trang had my back. I'd go with that for now.

My attention drifted to our shopping list, scratched in Mike's spiral handwriting on a scrap of yellow paper. It confirmed the practical nature of our life on the ranch. An inventory of provisions needed to carry on. The longer I stared at it, the more it reminded me how far I still needed to go. How much needed to be done before I was safe on the other side. Before I could make a practical list of my own.

The first order of business was a new radiator hose for the tractor. Not that it was broken. Mike required a new hose, he said, in case. I guess he'd had some vision of his tractor with a cracked hose. Who knows? Not every premonition offers up the Apocalypse.

Fifteen pounds of galvanized nails seemed equally precautionary. Barns, houses, docks, and decks were forever coming apart and in need of hammering back together. Judging by the 149 cedar planks and the 137 pounds of cement also called for, it looked like Mike had construction plans. No low-grade material for him. He planned to build on a solid foundation with quality materials. Could be a sauna or an observation deck by his duck pond so Trang wouldn't have to lurk in the reeds.

I pictured them together on the new deck, waiting for the arrival of the elusive Fulvous Whistling-Duck, which Trang knew would never come and which he'd never recognize even if it landed on his lap. And Mike, oblivious to Trang's true purpose, blissful in dharma dreams, at one with the pond while Trang soaked up the sun till his prey showed up.

"The wife was born in Moab," said Archie, with no particular context, "and she's buried there. We never had no kids. Ruthie was a good woman."

"Funny name," I said, "Moab." The word rolled around in my mouth like a pebble, my tongue feeling out its contours.

"The bible says it's the land of sinners," Archie said. "A land of blood and sorrow. Called after the bastard son of Lot who was seduced in a cave by his daughters after they got kicked out of Sodom and Gomorrah."

"What were people thinking, calling it that?"

"There was talk of changing the name a couple of times. Never amounted to nothing."

Archie knew his Old Testament, chapter and verse. He lectured on for some time about the summit of Mount Nebo, where Moses had stood with the Lord in the land of Moab and viewed the plains. Look at the horizon, the Lord said to Moses. There it is, the promised land, on the other side of the River Jordan. What you've been searching for all this time. You'll never get there, but your people will. While Moses had accepted God's words, you can bet after forty years in the wilderness, this must've pissed him off a little. Dying in the land of whores' sons, false idols, misery, and atrocity within a stone's throw of Paradise after so many years wasn't what he'd pictured for his end.

Telephone poles flipped past the windshield. Strands of black wire rose and fell between each pole in lazy waves. The canyon walls and the desert were mute and static, as if we were driving on a moving belt made to create the illusion of motion against a vast and static landscape painting.

"Them Mormons came through here in the 1800s," Archie said. "They named everything from the bible. Zion. Jordan. Eden. Canaan. And Moab was a bad place for a while. All them outlaw fellows were here. Butch Cassidy, the Sundance Kid, the Blue Mountain Gang, Flat Nose Curry. But nowadays nothing much happens here. Tourists and hippies."

After all that talk of Moses and outlaws, Moab offered a small refuge amongst the canyons and the rocks in the middle of nowhere. More like a sleepy green patch than a wild outlaw hideaway. Main Street was a clean and orderly collection of restaurants and shops in low brick buildings. Pickup trucks and large-wheeled off-roaders roamed the streets. Old ladies gossiped with each other outside the bank.

Archie stopped the truck in front of a psychedelic sign painted in Day-Glo colours: *Mom's.* Flowers and ceramic pottery embedded with glass beads littered the front patio. The sign in the window said *Open.*

"Go in and ask for Deer," he said. "I got to do another errand. I'll be back in ten minutes and then we'll drive with her over to her place for our vegetables."

Inside, loud Asian pop music blared through four battered speakers hung from ceiling chains. An Asian girl behind the counter wiped glasses and lined them along a shelf. Long, shiny black hair framed her sharp cheekbones. Her white apron hid none of the delicate contours of her tiny body. Next to the cash register, a hand-printed sign with a little smiley face, tongue out, advertised *Cambodian Spoken Here.*

"Deer?"

"Who's asking?" the girl said. She could've been fourteen, and she could've been forty.

"I'm Paul. Archie said to tell you he'd be back in ten minutes to pick us up for the vegetable run."

She smiled. "Bet he's longer."

While we waited, she made me a real cappuccino from an Italian machine.

"Are we going to pull carrots?" I said.

She worked the steamed milk with precision.

"No," she said, "my plot is out of town but I keep the produce at home. We'll go to my place."

Her coffee was hot and full-bodied. After all this time without any dope or booze, a simple caffeine jolt felt spectacular. I sat on a stool at the counter and looked around the diner. My first time out in the world in weeks. Three shafts of yellow light refracted through a crack in the window splayed out over the floor. A row of seven mugs stood above the sink like an a cappella group humming "The Tennessee Waltz" while the dishwasher swish-washed through its rinse cycle under the counter. The world seemed a bit different since the accident.

"Where'd they find you?" she said.

"In the desert. I had an accident."

"Come to Moab to hide out?"

"Sort of. No." I needed a simple story that people wouldn't question or find too interesting. I'd have to work on that. For now, I stirred the coffee, stared at the backs of my scarred hands, and tried to recall Marla's number, the one she said to call when I got to California. Three, one, oh, something, something, seven, something, six …

Archie showed up twenty minutes late. Deer locked up and the three of us squeezed into the cab of Archie's truck. The gentle smell of sweet whisky seeped from his pores. A redness in his watery eyes further betrayed his new state. I said nothing. I didn't care. Deer smelled of Sunlight soap. Her leg bounced against mine. She wore pink rubber boots with a thick felt lining.

"Nice boots," I said.

"They're my garden boots," she said. "I hate cold feet."

Archie drove more or less straight to a small trailer park. About twenty trailers. Some better than others. A few chance trees shaded the grounds. Deer's place was plain and clean. An American flag on a pole graced the door. An old Duster was parked at her neighbours' with a handwritten *For Sale* sign in its window. Slicks. Pipes. A confederate flag airbrushed across the hood. A real rebel racer.

"Come in," she said. "This is going to take a while. I need to sort the vegetables. There might be something in the fridge if you want a drink. Help yourself."

Inside, Archie headed for the couch while I poked through her fridge for anything besides water or soy milk. A beer. A Coke. A juice. What the hell, I had a day pass. But the fridge offered nothing except a small plastic bottle of brackish goop. I held it to my nose. Something between chocolate and dog shit.

"Don't drink that," she said. "It'll take the top of your head off."

My scalp tingled.

"Shit," I said.

She emptied out a burlap bag of vegetables on the counter. They rumbled, thudded, and rolled about in happy chaos. The dusty smell of dry earth filled the air.

"No," she said, "ayahuasca. It's a hallucinogenic from Peru."

"I didn't figure you for a dope head," I said.

"I'm not. And it's not dope." She sorted potatoes, carrots, and peas into separate piles. "It's more like a magic potion. A gift from Mother Earth."

Archie snored in the next room.

"So, you're like the good witch."

She nodded. "It was a tip for delivering club sandwiches from the restaurant to some old guy in the Apache Motel last week. Vern, he said his name was. He was travelling with a dancer from Reno. He had a big cowboy hat and lots of facial surgery. Later, on TV, I saw he'd been arrested for insurance fraud. They said he faked his own death and ran off with millions. He was a nice man, Vern." She said it like she was speaking about an old lady down the road. No judgement. No comment. Unaware how odd her story sounded.

When all the vegetables were packed into cardboard boxes, she took the bottle of putrid liquid from the fridge and said we could go.

"We're taking that?"

"No," she said, "it goes to the restaurant. I'm going to sell it to some hippies who're camping out on the desert."

"How entrepreneurial."

"I should work harder," she said. "Send more money home. Unfortunately, I don't have the time."

"Sounds busy," I said, poking Archie from his siesta.

Deer continued from the kitchen. "I wish I could deal with the world on my own terms and not struggle so hard to make it work for me. I don't care if I never find a man. I only look for some peace."

She came into the room with a woollen cap pulled over her ears. "Are you ready?"

Back at the diner, she made us fried egg sandwiches. While she prepared the food, I ducked into the men's to wash my hands. A pay phone on the wall jolted Marla's number from my memory. I wondered if she'd be pleased to hear from me.

I munched the fried egg sandwich in silence. Marla's number rolled in my head like a mantra. I shouldn't call her. It would open old wounds. It would probably alert Lover Man and Eagle Creek to my whereabouts. That'd make Trang happy. And likely get me killed. But Marla was the key. Marla could tell me if the coast was clear.

Deer broke a twenty into coins after I said I needed to make a call. Archie watched, curious for a moment. I went to the back and fed the pay phone. A tinny bell rang like a slot machine for every quarter dropped. I held my breath. She still lurked under my skin. When she picked up, the world vanished. It was just the two of us again. Alone. Nothing else mattered. I'd conjured her back.

"Marla?" I pictured her lips by the phone. I shivered. "Miss me?"

"Where'd you go?" she said. "Everyone's been looking for you."

"Sorry I didn't call. I couldn't. I had an accident."

"Yes. They found the car," she said. "They said there were tracks and some blood. They think you might still be alive."

"They sent a killer after me. I got scared and ran."

"He's not allowed to come home without you."

"You put me in a bad situation, Marla. Why are they doing this?"

"They say you stole their dope."

"I didn't do anything. I had an accident. It all burned up with the car."

"Well, it's gone, and it happened with you. So, in their world, you owe them."

The connection momentarily disintegrated.

"I'm losing you," I said.

"That's LA," she said between the interference. "The reception sucks."

"What should we do?"

"Stay away. Convince them you're dead."

"And you? What happens to you?"

Marla laughed. "I'll be fine. I'm always fine."

Silence broke our connection. I cradled the phone. She hadn't asked if I was all right. Stay away, was all she'd said. I owed them, she said. Now I knew.

Back at the counter, Archie waved his massive hands through the middle of a tale. Deer listened and laughed. They'd forgotten about me. They'd returned to their world. The one from before I'd washed up on their shore. The one that seemed so fragile now.

TWENTY-FIVE

Bad Things

I SLUMPED in a booth near the cash and watched Deer read the *L.A. Times* behind the counter. She moved her forefinger along each line with concentration. Archie was gone to gas the truck with the promise that we'd hit the hardware store after. It sounded more like an excuse to slink off for another drink. I didn't care. There were other matters to concern myself with, like my violent death.

The aroma of carrot muffins in the oven wafted through the diner. Cambodian country music yowled through the battered wooden speakers. A couple of tourists muttered in German at the menu. The rest of the place was empty. No sign of Trang. If he was around, his disguise was working. I should've gone with Archie for a drink.

Deer glanced up. A strand of hair fell across her eyes while I rolled my coffee cup around in my palms. The heat felt good on my scars.

She said, "Everything okay in there?"

"I'm thinking about buying that car from your neighbour," I said. After all, my health was back, and trouble was around the corner. With Trang already on the scene and Eagle Creek surely coming soon, an escape plan needed hatching. The money from Akinwole was stashed under the floor of the cabin. A few hundred bucks for a getaway car seemed like a smart bet.

She leaned on the cash register. "I know those guys. I can get him for a special price."

"If I get it," I said, "could I leave it with you for a while?"

"I charge extra for parking." Her grin revealed a tiny gap between her front teeth.

"I'll give you anything."

"Why don't you take it to the ranch?"

"It has to be a secret," I said.

"You're buying it and not using it?"

"Not right away," I said. "I'd like to have one standing by."

"Like a getaway car?"

"Yes, like a getaway car."

"So, why do you need a getaway car, Paul?"

"I might need to get away."

She fidgeted with a gold Buddha pendant around her neck. The deep-yellow gold chain glowed off her brown skin.

"You can drive my truck," she said.

"That might not work out for you."

"I trust you," she said. "You bring it back when you're done."

"I could be gone a while. I'm unreliable that way."

"You in some kind of shit?" she said.

Outside, a polished black sedan landed a spot in front of the diner. Tinted windows. Low-profile white walls. My scarred hands went numb. I rubbed them on my jeans to return some feeling. The driver stepped out. His arm muscles strained the seams of his white T-shirt. He adjusted his embossed cowboy belt, its shiny buckle big as a rodeo. His black-opal eyes looked through the diner window right at me. Trang was right: it hadn't taken long. Eagle Creek had tracked me down.

"Yes, I'm in some kind of shit," I said.

"What?" She laughed.

I said, "See that man looking at me? He's a ferocious killer sent here by a drug dealer to kill me."

Deer laughed again. Eagle Creek pointed a finger at me like a pistol and smiled.

"He looks friendly," she said.

"They say he once sawed off someone's head," I said. "Be careful, he's not particular who he hurts."

"Don't worry." She mimed a karate chop. "He messes with me, I kick butt."

The diner door chimed. Eagle Creek stepped in. His body blocked the sun.

"Buddy, you been hiding on me?" he said.

He gave Deer a once-over.

"Hey, doll. How about some of your pie?"

She looked disinterested.

"Apple, peach, or cherry?" she said.

"Cherry. And turn down that shit. That's not music."

He tapped the counter with his forefinger. Deer offered no reaction. Deadpan, she killed the music. Eagle Creek slipped into my booth. He pointed to the car outside.

"Like that?" he said.

Clogged with fear, speech was impossible. Instead, I nodded. Sure.

"That's a Bentley Flying Spur," he said. "I decided to treat myself to a good ride."

I nodded again, like I understood.

"Any idea what that car costs to rent?"

I shook my head. No.

"Fifteen hundred dollars a day with insurance and mileage. I figured, what the hell? For a few days, why not. Business is good. I can afford it. Besides, when the locals see me in this, it gives them pause."

I nodded again. Oh.

"I could've gotten the new Porsche Panamera. That was five ninety-nine a day. It's a nice car. German. But the Bentley's another level, right? It's a quarter million dollars to buy."

I kept my eyes on the car outside. I smelled my own sweat.

"Oh, yeah?" I managed to say. It felt like a hard-boiled egg had lodged in my throat.

Eagle Creek calculated the money. "Fuck, yeah. So, that's one day in the Bentley or three days in the Porsche. Right?"

He inspected his fingernails and sighed in an apparent attempt to muster the patience to help me through a complicated philosophical argument beyond my intellectual ability.

"It's like this: I get a call from the rental company in Vegas this morning. They're wondering when I might be returning their car. I wasn't sure, I said, so they asked if I could make an installment payment for the rental so far."

"They called you?" I said. "For an installment payment?"

He nodded. "They wanted I pay them sixty thousand dollars."

His hands curled into mallets. Silver rings flashed at me.

Skulls. Vulture heads. Snakes and lightning bolts. He narrowed his eyes and spoke without moving his lips.

"I've been looking for you for forty days. Forty days since you wrecked our car and burned our dope out in the desert. That's what the car rental company says it's been. I've lost track of it."

He squeezed my leg under the table until it felt like he might pulverize my kneecap.

"What's the retail value of the Panamera?" he said through clenched teeth.

"No idea." I tried to shake my knee from his grip.

"I can buy one for a little over seventy grand."

"New?" Okay, he wasn't going to scalp me. He wanted to talk cars.

"Listen, nutsack," he said, "you miss my point. If I'd known, I'd have rented a cheaper car. I practically could've bought the fucking Porsche for what I'm paying to rent the Bentley. You eluded me longer than expected. But now I got you."

Deer put a plate of cherry pie in front of Eagle Creek. He winked at me and leered after her. He jammed a fork into the cherry pie. Red filling oozed over the plate. He doodled a finger through the mess and licked it off. The bit of cherry stuck to the corner of his mouth might've been comic, except he leaned forward and said, "We're going for a ride. You and me. I'm going to get my money's worth. My pound of flesh. We're going to party."

"That's not my first choice," I said.

Eagle Creek wiped his mouth with his hand.

"I'm going to start by cutting your feet off, so you can't run," he said.

He took some more pie. He chewed and waited for my reaction. His eyes reflected back my own dumb face. I boxed it up. Sucked it in. I couldn't outfight or outrun him. Instead, I waited. Prayed Trang would show. Prayed for a crack to open in the floor wide enough to vanish into.

From his pocket, he produced a cellphone. He pushed a number on speed-dial and spoke.

"I finally got him," he said to someone. Most likely Lover Man. "We're in Moab, Utah, in a diner called Mom's." He nodded. "Yes, I'll be back tomorrow night."

On the street, Archie's pickup truck rolled up behind the Flying Spur. Albert was in the back; his snout drooped over the side. Archie locked the truck and started over to the diner. If he knew, he would bring the shotgun. I tried a silent distress transmission. Only Albert sensed the vibe. His ears twitched around for the source. Pointless.

"Hey, Paul," Archie said, his voice mellow from the whisky he'd been into down the road. "Saddle up, son. Got to get to the hardware."

Eagle Creek put the phone away and mutilated the pie some more.

"Tell the old guy to get lost," he said, low so Archie couldn't hear.

I stared back and wished for the over-under in Archie's truck. I pictured Eagle Creek shot in the chest with both barrels. Pictured his chest like mashed cherry pie.

"Hey, Arch," I said, "we're having pie."

Archie came over to the booth. He peered at Eagle Creek from under his ancient yellow eyebrows. He extended a shovel-sized hand.

"Howdy," he said.

Eagle Creek ignored the outstretched hand. "That your truck out there?" he said through a mouthful of pie.

Archie nodded. "A '59 International Harvester. B120. Four-wheel drive. They don't make them like that anymore."

Eagle Creek said, "I've seen that truck around. Your dog always ride in the back?"

"Albert smells bad. You can't put him up front."

Eagle Creek looked out the window at Albert, who stared back at us like we were some show on TV he couldn't comprehend.

"He's an ugly old hound," Eagle Creek said.

Archie narrowed his eyes. He said, "That dog's got sense more than most."

"Coffee, Archie?" Deer said from across the counter. "Fresh pot."

"I'll take one to go," Archie said. "I got to use the head."

"How about you, mister?" Deer said to Eagle Creek. "Some coffee with that pie?"

Archie shuffled to the toilet. Eagle Creek looked around. Eagle Creek sized up the situation. Eagle Creek needed to get on with it.

He said, "I'll take one to go."

"Not for me," I said. "I'll stay here."

Eagle Creek leaned across the table. "You're not getting out of this. Give me a hard time, I'll be back for her. And then I'll go visit the old man, for laughs."

To show he meant business, he lifted his T-shirt. A silver-plated Colt was stuck in his jeans. By the counter, Deer dropped a sugar shaker on the floor. Startled by the clatter, Eagle Creek drew the weapon and then with equal speed it was back in his pants when he saw there was no danger. I looked at Deer. She looked at me. We'd both seen it. Now she knew I wasn't kidding.

"Sorry," she said. "Butterfingers."

Eagle Creek didn't react.

"How's that coffee coming?" he said.

Deer ducked her head into the fridge.

"It's coming," she said. "Milk? I'm getting Archie milk. That's how he likes it."

"Black's good," Eagle Creek said.

He rose from the booth. Grabbed my arm. Jerked me to my feet.

"Out," Eagle Creek said. "Let's go before the old man's back."

The stuffed mountain lion over the cash register watched with yellow marble eyes. That would be me soon. Dead. Resistance was futile. His threats against Deer and Archie convinced me to go along. This was no longer about me and Marla and Hornsmith and Trang and Lover Man. This had become an oil slick that threatened people who had nothing to do with us.

Eagle Creek took the Styrofoam cup that waited on the counter.

"Thanks for the coffee, sister."

He tossed a twenty on the counter.

"What's your name?"

"Deer," she said. "People call me Deer."

"Keep the change, Deer. Maybe I'll see you around."

"I guess we'll see what happens," she said.

"Tell Arch not to wait," I said. "We're going for a drive in the Flying Spur."

Eagle Creek moved toward the door.

"Let's go, kid."

We stepped into the street. Far overhead, a silent jet cut a thin white streak across the cloudless blue sky. Its vapour trail expanded and dissipated into the atmosphere without a trace. There was no other way this could have unfolded. The inevitability was comforting. I smiled to myself. Calm in the face of it.

Albert watched me get into the Flying Spur. His mouth hung open, a string of sticky drool suspended from his lips down over the side of the truck. He shook his head. *You not coming to the ranch? Come with us?* No, buddy, I told him, not this time. Numb, I got into the car.

Eagle Creek drove for a couple of blocks. The .45 lay in his lap. He sipped the coffee with one hand, elbow out the window. At the Apache Motel parking lot, he crept to a stop and backed the car into a spot in front of the last door facing the road. He fished a room key off the dash.

"We're going to get my bags," he said, "and then we're going out into the desert. We'll not be coming back here again."

He tossed the empty coffee cup out the window and spat.

"Your girl makes lousy coffee."

I stayed paralyzed in the passenger seat. He nudged me with the gun.

"Out, peckerhead."

He pushed me ahead of him into the room, where I sat frozen on the bed while Eagle Creek gathered his belongings. A zipped duffle bag. A tool box. A briefcase. When he was in the bathroom, my legs couldn't agree with my head's urge to take advantage of the moment and flee. There was nowhere to run that he wouldn't find me. And kill me. Best to delay that.

CNN was on the TV. At the Afghanistan-Pakistan border, business wasn't great, either. A lucky shot from a rocket launcher had taken out an army helicopter in some mud village. Drones now shot the place to pieces, brick by brick. Lean dogs and ragged children ran for cover.

Eagle Creek came out of the bathroom with a roll of duct tape in one hand, the Colt in the other. He looked at the TV and shook his head.

"Fuckin' towelheads," he said. "I was there. They only respect brute force. We should of set the whole place on fire. Including the Pakis. Just because those assholes have the bomb doesn't mean we should be scared of them."

He sat on the edge of the bed beside me. Sweat beaded his face. He rolled his shoulders as if to shake something off. He sighed. Then, almost casually, he pistol-whipped me across the forehead. White light seared through my eyes. I fell back. He wrapped several rounds of duct tape around my ankles in one move, like he was roping a calf. With equal speed and precision, he taped my wrists together behind my back. He slapped a piece of tape across my mouth.

"This'll make it a lot easier later," he said.

When he had me secured, he fell backwards onto the bed beside me. He rubbed his eyes.

"Something's going on here. Something's not right. Someone's calling me."

I rolled away from him and accidentally fell off the edge of the bed. The green shag muffled the sound of my fall. I lay motionless. The pain across my forehead expanded. Blood dripped across the bridge of my nose, slow and thick, into my eyes.

Eagle Creek sat up. He tore off his shirt. He tossed it across the room. He rubbed his face with both hands.

"One of these days," he said, "the council will judge me."

He carried the duffle bag out to the car. When he returned, he sat back on the bed. He held his head between his legs. He started to gasp and grunt. He rocked his body. He seemed to hyperventilate, with fast, deep breaths between little moans like a wounded animal. After a bit, he reached for the little trash can under the desk and threw up.

I stayed on the floor. Trussed up tight. A struggle might've brought him round and reminded him of my presence. That was the way to get killed. Remind him where I was. So, I didn't move, my nose pressed into the carpet. Its smell of smoke and socks offered sordid stories. Tired salesmen. Migrant workers. Hitchhikers. Lonely lovers. But not one story reeked like this one. This one was bad.

Eagle Creek sobbed. From my angle on the floor, I watched him pull at his hair. He unravelled his braid. He stood up and took off his jeans. He rolled off his underwear. He peeled off his socks. He looked at his naked reflection in the mirror.

"Yes, Grandfather," he said, "I am far away, where I do other men's bidding."

He climbed up on the desk. With a swoop of his massive arm, he sent the telephone, the lamp, and the local brochures onto the floor. Perched on his haunches, he surveyed the room.

"Those men make me do evil deeds, Grandfather," he said. "Let me come home."

He leapt from the desk to the bed, his long hair an angry ink-stained halo around his head. He took his knife from the nightstand, and with both hands high above his head, pointed it down at his chest. Invisible at his feet, I turned away, unwilling to watch. It felt like a ridge had formed across my forehead where he'd hit me with the gun. The bitter taste of the tape filled my mouth. Overhead, Eagle Creek sobbed.

"I see you, Grandfather. I see all of you waiting by the river."

Then, the knife clattered to the floor, and he stumbled off the bed toward the door.

"Tell them I'm through. If I see them coming for me, I'll kill the motherfuckers."

He snorted. Spat. And vanished.

Outside some kids laughed. A church bell chimed.

TWENTY-SIX

Visitors

BLOOD DRIPPED into my eyes. No amount of blinking or head twisting could stop it. Pressed into the floor, my face itched from the sour sock carpet. Across the room, a hushed TV voice forecast gusting winds in the morning. With some urgent twists and kicks, the tape around my ankles loosened enough that soon I worked my legs free. On my feet, my reflection in the mirror over the dresser wasn't good. That guy looked messed up. Blood on his face. Silver tape across his mouth. Hands lashed behind his back.

Fuck you, Simon Trang. Fuck you. Pop up when I don't need you. Tell me you're always in the wings. Never around when you should be. Fuck you. Fuck you. I vowed I'd never speak to him again. Useless.

The edge of the bathroom counter was sharp enough to saw my wrists free of tape. My hands broke the tape and flew apart at the same moment Archie came around the corner, shotgun ready. Deer peeked out from behind his shoulder.

"You okay?" she said.

I nodded and said, "He's lost his mind."

"No. I saw his gun in the diner and thought about what you said. So, I put the ayahuasca in his coffee. He's fucked up."

She touched the gash across my forehead. It hurt, deep and wet. Albert lurked by the door. He shook his mangy head. *You should've come with us. None of this would've happened. If you never listen, you'll never learn.* Self-righteous mutt was getting on my nerves.

"I'm sorry," I said, "this has nothing to do with you. Dump me in the desert and pretend you never saw me."

Archie grunted. "That's bullshit," he said. "You have anything else to tell us?"

"I'm in deep trouble with a bunch of drug dealers," I said. "It was their car I wrecked. It was full of their dope when it caught fire. You never asked, so I never talked about it."

Archie nodded. He knew it was true. They'd never asked. It was part of their code. Everyone free. Everyone equal. No past. No judgement. In future, they might be more interested in the stories their visitors had to tell.

"Is this the end of it?" he said.

"No," I said, "there's another one coming."

"And then?"

"It depends how that goes."

"All right," Archie said, "we'll get through it."

"You should know the duck watcher is in on it. He's been waiting for this part to start. His name's Trang. He's a narc with a secret cross-border task force."

Archie sighed and brushed the dog aside with his foot to get out of the room.

We left Deer back at the diner and headed for the ranch. Outside Moab, we passed Eagle Creek on all fours by the side of the road. Puking. Archie stopped the truck. He studied the wretch through the rear-view mirror. After a while, Archie pulled a tire iron from under the seat.

"Come with me," he said.

We approached the naked figure with caution. He was, after all, a known killer and violent freak act. Eagle Creek seemed unaware of our presence. He continued his crawl along the side of the road, oblivious to the sharp gravel that cut his hands and knees. We stepped along beside him.

"You're not doing so well," Archie said.

Eagle Creek grimaced. He grasped for a rock and clutched it like a weapon.

"I've been to war," Archie said, "where I learned some things."

Eagle Creek started to raise his arm like he wanted to strike out with the rock. Archie stepped on the man's arm with his cowboy boot and knelt down with the tire iron wedged under Eagle Creek's jaw. Old Archie: nimble and dangerous. Eagle Creek growled, immobile. Archie pushed the tire iron a bit harder, like he meant to pop Eagle Creek's head off.

"Arch," I said, "take it easy."

Archie said, "I learned you can't go around kidnapping and threatening to kill folks without retribution. I also learned I can forgive, if you let me. If you give me a reason. So, what's it going to be? Are you ready to let this go? Surrender or retribution, motherfucker?"

Eagle Creek blinked fast a couple of times. The rock slipped from his fist. He slumped to the ground, his face sideways in the gravel. Archie poked him with his foot.

"Okay, brother, I forgive you, too," Archie said and turned to walk back to the truck.

"We can't leave him here," I said.

"The hell we can't," said Archie.

Eagle Creek seemed unconscious.

"I wanted him to surrender. Say uncle. I don't care what he does now," said Archie.

The night he'd driven me in the rain, Eagle Creek had been animated and seemed concerned for my well-being. Laughing. Joking. Dangerous, sure. But also helpful. Now that he was naked and unconscious, he posed no threat. Though I'd hated and feared him, I also felt a twinge of compassion.

"Let's take him to the ranch. Give him to Mike for repair. Dry him out."

"You hear that?" Archie said to Eagle Creek. "He wants to save you. Give you sanctuary. After what you did to him."

No response. Archie turned to me. "There ain't nothing here that deserves saving. Let's go."

It felt right to save Eagle Creek, now that he was broken. Besides, as Hornsmith used to quote from Sun Tzu: keep your enemies close.

"You're wrong," I said. "Let's take him in, and if Mike says no, we'll cut him loose."

Eagle Creek shuddered and twitched. Archie chewed his lip and scratched his ass, and after a long look at the sad sack of misery Eagle Creek had been reduced to, said, "I don't like it, but I guess we could do that."

We tossed Eagle Creek's naked, puke-caked body in the back with Albert, who looked disgusted. Eagle Creek, drugged and limp, offered no resistance. We covered him with Albert's old horse blanket and resumed the drive.

Back at the ranch, we locked Eagle Creek next to the barn in the steel cage Mike used for cougars and mountain lions. He didn't kill predators around the ranch.

Here, Eagle Creek wouldn't come to any harm while he rode out the tail of his trip, and he wouldn't pose a threat to us should he still have the urge to kill when he came around. He twitched for a while between further bouts of dry heaves before curling up and falling asleep in the blanket. By then, Archie had gone home, and Mike had retreated into a deep trance. That left me alone to rock on the porch and think about this terrible day. Think about LA and Marla. Stay away, she'd said. Make them think you're dead. It was too late for that.

Dawn never came. The sky faded up from darkness to grey to brown. Sand cyclones swirled around me when I tried to reach the house for breakfast. The side door to the barn banged in the wind. A dozen or more tumbleweeds as big as rolling men hurtled past. While the storm gathered, a motorcycle came up over the ridge. Its headlight cut a yellow swath through the dust. Had the visitors been recognizable, I'd have hidden in the cattails down by the river. Instead, curiosity made me stand and watch.

Two figures struggled to dismount. The first had an aura of sand and filth, kept at bay by a pair of dark-green goggles and a full-length blue-leather coat. In one hand was a long-barrelled revolver. The second person saddled over the motorbike was Deer. Her hair swirled in the wind. With my hands up to protect my eyes from the sand, I peered through the tempest, undiscovered. Motionless in the steel cage across the yard, Eagle Creek watched the same sight, squinting to make sense of it. Through the swirling sand, Lover Man and Deer wrestled until he had her by the hair. He looked around for a moment. Then, he made his way to the main house, holding Deer in front like a shield.

Archie stepped onto the porch with his over-under at the ready. Without hesitation, Lover Man shot him. Point blank. No discussion. No mercy. Archie dropped the shotgun, sank to his knees, and slumped over sideways. Lover Man paid no further attention. He pushed Deer over the old man into the house. The door closed behind them. The house was swallowed by the sandstorm.

Considering the short work he'd made of Archie, it seemed certain we were all doomed to the same fate. Lover Man was here to clean up. We were loose ends. Including Eagle Creek, who'd failed to close the book on me. He had no way to escape should Lover Man see him in the cage. There was a chance, however, that with Eagle Creek out, we could improve our hope of survival. A desperate plan started to boil.

With the wind in my ears and dirt in my eyes, I crawled on my belly through the grass toward the cage, taking the long way around so as to remain hidden from the house. The plan was to free Eagle Creek and hopefully convince him to help me save Deer. He sat with his back to me, bars gripped in both hands, paying keen attention to Lover Man's arrival. Pressed against the cage, I tossed a pebble to catch his attention.

Startled, Eagle Creek reeled, his face obscured by his knotted hair. His mouth open, teeth bared. His muscles like hard-plated armour that protected his naked body. He looked ferocious. The cage was barely large enough for him to move from side to side or turn around.

"I'm getting you out," I said, unsure of sure what he'd do. I hoped he could be convinced that my danger was his, too. That we shared a common enemy. Best-case scenario, he'd go after Lover Man. He might also vanish in the wind. Disappear up the mountains to kill wild rabbits with his hands.

"If we don't stop him, he'll come for you," I said. "You failed him. You're no use to him now. He's going to kill us all. I'm letting you out so you can get him before he gets you."

Eagle Creek said, "I'd take him to hell with me if I could."

"Yes, that's the spirit," I said.

The bolt that locked the cage slipped open with ease.

In seconds, Eagle Creek scampered out on all fours into the tall grass. Together, we scurried to a more secure spot behind the barn. From there, we had a clear view without the risk of being shot. Archie lay on the ground between us and the house. Hard to tell what shape he was in.

We leaned against the weathered barn boards and looked at each other. His face was expressionless. He'd done this killer business for a while. He'd be fine, even if he was still tripping, I told myself. What, if anything, he made of me, was impossible to say.

"Are you ready for this?" I said.

"That devil has done me much harm. I seek a reckoning."

"Good."

Although Archie remained down in the dirt, by now he'd crawled a distance through the dust to hide behind his truck for some cover. He rolled over onto his back. His chest heaved. His arm twitched from time to time. Alive for the moment.

"How about," I said, "I go around back and throw some rocks through the windows so he's drawn to the back of the house. Meantime you go for the shotgun and come through the front door shooting." I pointed to where Archie had dropped the gun. "You're better with weapons. When I hear shooting, I'll come in through the back for the girl."

Eagle Creek nodded. My slim plan passed his tactical analysis. It was flawed, but no alternative presented itself. There was nothing else to do. Eagle Creek had to deliver his attack.

The back of the house had three windows. Two big picture windows overlooking the valley, plus a smaller frosted one in between. From my vantage in the grass, Lover Man wasn't near any of them. My mouth was dry. My throat felt tight. The rock in my hand was round and hard. It was a good distance, so it took a bit of a windup to hurl the rock. Glass exploded into the house. A second rock smashed the other window for good measure. The sound brought some clarity to events: right away, Lover Man's silhouette stood framed in jagged glass until the sound of gunfire drew him away. That was my sign. I bolted across the stretch of grass. Go, go. Go before he kills us all, I told myself.

"Deer," I called.

My legs churned through the tall grass. She appeared and waved in my direction. More gunfire came from another part of the house. Deer smashed the rest of the window with the end of a floor lamp. My hand extended to help her down. In the distance sounded the wop wop of an approaching helicopter. Simon Trang, no doubt, swooping in from the safety of his perch. His trap finally sprung.

"We have to go," I said.

She'd have none of it. "Mike's in the bedroom. We can't leave him."

Someone yelled in the house. It could've been in anger or it could've been in pain. Eagle Creek and Lover Man were in combat. Sounds of heavy objects being crashed about echoed through the halls. More shouts were exchanged. Deer didn't react. She wanted me in there to dig Mike out.

"Hurry," she said. "He's in a trance and won't budge. I can't carry him by myself."

I was going to die for Deer and Mike Pike. Pure souls and good hearts. That was the new plan when I climbed over the broken glass into the living room. Inside, there was a fire poker propped against the fireplace. I grabbed it.

I said, "I'm going down the hall."

She nodded and let me past, poker ready. Around the corner, Eagle Creek and Lover Man had their hands around each other's throats. A splintered cabinet littered the hall. The spent shotgun lay on the floor next Lover Man's pistol. Lover Man had a hole in his coat. Blood leaked from his back. Lover Man broke loose from Eagle Creek's grip, rolled across the floor, and recovered his weapon. He fired immediately. Eagle Creek darted through the house. Bullets flew overhead. The sour chemical smell of gunpowder burned the air.

There was a pause in the battle. Eagle Creek had vanished in the blue smoke that hung like a low morning mist. No target presented itself. Lover Man scanned the room for his foe. With his back turned, he hadn't noticed me. My chance. I charged him with the poker held overhead. At the last moment, he spun to face me. Not what he'd expected. He opened his mouth to say something. I brought the poker down on his forehead, which split open, soft and wet, like a pumpkin. There was no resistance. He crumpled and fell.

Afterward, my ears rang in the silence. Deer emerged and knelt beside the fallen man. Outside, through the open door, the storm had let up. A helicopter stood in front of the house.

It brought people. Most of them were armed with automatic weapons and dressed in jeans with tactical vests over T-shirts. One with a medic's kit worked on Archie. Another, Trang, surveyed the scene. He took his time. He drew his gun, casual, and approached the house. I held back, concealed behind the door. I had no use for him. We were through. I stayed hidden, unwilling to have anything further to do with Trang's business.

From this vantage, I watched Trang move around the wreckage. When he discovered Deer on the ground by Lover Man's prostrate body, he signalled with his gun for her to move away. Trang poked the body with his foot.

"Leon?"

Lover Man groaned.

"Who hit your face, Leon?"

"Fuck you, Trang."

Trang smiled, holstered his gun, and flipped a pair of handcuffs off his belt. He cuffed Lover Man's wrist to his ankle and returned outside to confer with his associates while Mike materialized down the hall. I stepped out from my hiding spot to stop him.

"It's under control, Mike," I said. "These aren't people you need to get involved with."

"Such excitement," he said, "disturbs my inner peace. Makes me mad up here." He pointed to his head. "Where's Archie?"

He pushed me aside and headed outside while Eagle Creek, wrapped in a green blanket like a cape, sprinted over the prairie into the hills, unseen by anyone but me.

Trang and the medic heaved Archie onto the rear seat of the helicopter. Two other men carried Lover Man from the house and hoisted him into a seat. The chopper fired up while

Trang shouted something in Mike's ear. He pointed at the house. Mike shook his head. No.

Trang looked around the ranch like the answer didn't satisfy him. Something bothered him. I imagined he wanted me, but Mike hadn't given me up. However, I couldn't be sure. Finally, Trang climbed into the cockpit.

Dust swirled when the helicopter lifted. Mike stood in the vortex until he vanished in the whirling dirt wind. Next to the barn, Albert howled up at the departure of his master.

TWENTY-SEVEN

Nowadays ...

I'M AN OLD HOUND who dreams by the fireplace of hunts past, weary legs uncontrollably quivering; I only bark in my sleep. Grey flecks in my muzzle. Soupy eyes. Wide, calloused paws. After Moab, I'd left behind the business of the Business for good. Since those days, I've minded my own business.

I travelled to Big Sur to live by the ocean in a little rented place. An old woman named Joycelyn put the ad in the *Monterey County Weekly*. I stepped off the Greyhound, I thumbed the local classifieds and called up. A little renovated garage between million-dollar oceanfronts.

Nowadays, a few ghostwriting gigs here and there pay the rent. Once in a while, I buy and sell a fast car to make some extra money. There are also odd jobs for Joycelyn and her millionaire friends. Mostly old ladies. Tending to the sunflowers type of thing. Nothing dangerous. Or interesting.

After Lover Man was jailed, I reckoned I might find my way back to Marla. For a while I asked myself, if I could hold her again, what would that be like? I suppose we could have done it with a little effort. And then what? It couldn't be like before, all hot and confused. So much had changed for us. I tried to picture me and Marla, new in California. Nothing seemed clear. The heat was over. Those days had faded like an old love letter at the bottom of a trunk. Sometimes I hear her songs on the radio. Sounds like she's doing fine.

I bought the Ducati. Occasionally, I tear along the Pacific Coast Highway or over the mountains for a long weekend in Moab. Eagle Creek settled there. He's Joey Two Feathers again. Mike's showing him the Middle Way. Archie healed, too. He has a new F-250 Lariat. It's a good thing Albert is dead — the way Archie licks that truck clean, he would never have let that smelly creature ride in the back. I flirt with Deer, and for now she makes me sleep at the Apache Motel. We take it slow.

Akinwole calls me now and again. He's a businessman himself these days. He did all right, Akinwole. A Cadillac dealership. Some gas stations. A kosher deli. He volunteers at a homeless shelter, too. Married with three kids of his own. He and Shirley Rose stay in touch. They talk almost every day, he says. And that's where the problem lies. They've sent the Dipshit Kid to visit me.

The Dipshit Kid. Theo. Theodore. These days he calls himself Ted. He stands on the porch with a loopy grin. He's grown into a good-looking young man who hasn't shed his dopey vibe. Awkward, he shuffles from foot to foot. I wave him in.

"I want to start something for myself," he says after pleasantries. "Something I can build up, like you and Mr. Hornsmith."

He tells me he's graduated from Queen's with a shiny new

business degree. He's only twenty. Some species of genius. What a waste.

"Why?" I say. "You can do anything you want."

"Exactly," he says. "I don't want to grind away at some insurance company or investment firm. I don't want to go for the M.B.A. or law school. I want to take control of my own destiny, build my own business. I want you to tell me how it was for you. How you and Mr. Hornsmith did it. What worked and what didn't."

"I don't know what stories you've heard, but they're all lies. We hustled. We bottom-fed. We threatened and cajoled." I say it to throw him off the scent.

"That's business." He smiles because he presumes he knows what he's talking about.

"Coffee?"

I go to the kitchen and put the kettle on.

"I've got an opportunity," he says from the other room. "I could use some help."

Gas lit and water on, I go back to sit with him. At first, I think I want to give him something to carry in his hopeful heart. Something that gives him courage to continue down his road. Something he can take out occasionally and stick in those bastards' eyes when they leave him outside looking in. Instead, I figure the best thing to do is send him on his way.

"Stay with what you know," I say. "Play the game. You don't have to fight so hard or get that lost. Stay calm. Colour between the lines."

"I don't want that. I don't want to be one of those smug assholes in a glass tower. I don't fit in."

"It's possible," I say, "that with a bit of perseverance, you might actually grow up to become one those assholes. After all, isn't that what it's all about?"

The kettle whistles from the kitchen. It's hard to say if he understands what I'm talking about.

"Don't be afraid," I say. "Stick with it. In a little while, what I'm saying will make more sense. You'll feel a lot better about yourself, and your mother will worry less. You'll see."

"I want to make my own way, like you and Mr. Hornsmith," he says from the other room while I fix the coffee. "Only better."

I dig around under the sink, between the detergent and the garbage bags. Somewhere there's a bottle of rum down there. Emergency rations. Give the genius a shot of Dutch courage in his coffee and try to move him on to something else. I take a shot, too, for old times' sake.

When I hand him the hot cup, the poor bastard looks so earnest and hopeful. He's certain he's going to glean some nugget of truth from me.

"I put some rum in your coffee," I say. "Careful, it's hot."

The Dipshit Kid. Ted. He takes a tentative sip. He came for answers. He wants to hear how we grabbed the world by the tail. How we brought the rain. How we did the Business. He hopes to get some insight into Hornsmith's slippery ways. Hornsmith, the mysterious hero from his childhood. The father he never had.

"Listen," I say, "it's hard manoeuvring through the bullshit without getting skinned. You don't realize what you're asking to get into."

"I want it all," he says, "for one low price." He grins again, like he gets it, while he doesn't.

"Ever heard of Jim Rohn?" he says after a while. Now he has something important to tell me. I shake my head, no. I don't care. "He's a businessman. He mentored Tony Robbins." The rum was a bad idea. Now he's going to talk like he knows things. "Jim Rohn said something like, if you don't have your own plan, you'll fall into someone else's. And you know what they have planned for you?"

I recognize it's rhetorical. But I can't help myself. He doesn't know that I sold these sorts of predictable platitudes once upon a time.

I say, "Nothing?"

The kid nods, pleased I understand.

"You can't take life too seriously," I say. "You won't get out alive." He looks at me, blank. Like the first day he stood behind his mother's screen door, his finger in his nose. It's my turn to smile. I say, "People attribute that to the great philosopher Bugs Bunny."

The Dipshit Kid squirms, uneasy in his chair. This isn't what he came for.

"Actually, I'm pretty sure he stole that from Elbert Hubbard," I say. "Look, we did it because we were outcasts. Not because we wanted to. It was a vortex of chaos and daily uncertainty. Business is a fundamentally soulless endeavour, so get yourself a steady situation that won't grind you too much. Settle in. Get a hobby if you're looking for some fun."

"I have a real shot," he says, petulant. "I can do it."

"Doing it is the easy part." I start to feel for the misguided runt. "You can persuade anyone they can become number one. Inspiration by aspiration. That's what you're selling. That's what it takes. The actual shot makes no difference. The hard part is you need to want it. 'It,' with a capital *I*. You understand? It."

The Dipshit Kid seems at sea. I've talked to brighter dogs. It would be so easy to rope him into a plan. Hornsmith would've eaten this sad sack alive. The perfect shill. Listening to my rum talk, I fancy I could get back into it if I had the urge. No, let's banish that, for now.

"You don't even look the part," I say. "The first thing is you need to look the part."

I get up and open the drawer in my desk where I keep a cash stash for the just-in-case moments. I peel off a couple hundred, so the kid doesn't leave empty handed. He watches from his chair, uncertain what's transpiring. Or is he?

I give him the money.

"Now, fuck off," I say, friendly like. "Go find yourself some decent shoes. Those sneakers don't cut it."

"Shoes?"

"They say a lot about a man."

For a moment I'm curious: What's his shot look like? Does it have legs? No. It's undoubtedly idiotic. That's it. I'm not telling him another thing for now. Let's see what he does with this.

"Let me know how that goes."

The kid sits for a moment. Sighs. Shifts his ass on the chair. Stretches his neck and scratches the back of his crewcut head.

"Okay," he says and takes the money. "Okay. Thanks."

When he stands, the sound of the chair on the blond hardwood floor rings off the bare white walls. His squeaky rubber footsteps echo across the room. He closes the door behind him without looking back.

After he's left, I stand by the open bay windows above the Pacific Ocean. The cloudless steel-blue morning feels thin and raw. A briny draft creeps up the jagged cliffs. In the distance stands a gnarled cypress bent against the wind and rock. Down below, past the undulating green dune grass and the glistening yellow sand, silent alabaster waves churn on the open sea. Gulls screech and swoop lazy circles under the sun while a lone dog plays happily in the relentless surf. Life: it goes on.

Pretty sure I stole that from Robert Frost.

ACKNOWLEDGEMENTS

With thanks to Alexandra Leggat, David Adams Richards, and Russell Smith for your help along the way.